An Unbridled Passion

"Ah, Clarinda. . . ." She could feel his uneven breathing on her cheek as his arms went around her. "Beautiful Clarinda."

She tried to pull back. "Sir, I am in mourning for another, and I really don't think—"

"Then don't think," he answered roughly. His lips came down on hers. At first his kiss was slow, thoughtful, gentle. But then he smothered her lips with demanding mastery. She found herself responding, slipping her arms around his neck, returning his kiss with reckless abandon. Blood pounded as he rocked her in his arms so tight she felt every hard inch of him. Then, just when she began to wonder if she had lost total control, he pulled his lips from hers.

He stepped away and looked down at her. Hoarsely he murmured, "Say you didn't like that, Clarinda. . . ."

The Rebellious Twin

Shirley Kennedy

A SIGNET BOOK

SIGNET
Published by New American Library, a division of
Penguin Putnam Inc., 375 Hudson Street,
New York, New York 10014, U.S.A.
Penguin Books Ltd, 27 Wrights Lane,
London W8 5TZ, England
Penguin Books Australia Ltd, Ringwood,
Victoria, Australia
Penguin Books Canada Ltd, 10 Alcorn Avenue,
Toronto, Ontario, Canada M4V 3B2
Penguin Books (N.Z.) Ltd, 182–190 Wairau Road,
Auckland 10, New Zealand

Penguin Books Ltd, Registered Offices:
Harmondsworth, Middlesex, England

First published by Signet, an imprint of New American Library,
a division of Penguin Putnam Inc.

First Printing, February 2000
10 9 8 7 6 5 4 3 2 1

 REGISTERED TRADEMARK—MARCA REGISTRADA

Printed in the United States of America

*Dedicated with love and gratitude to
Julie Gettys and Sally Keenan Sanders.
Dear friends . . . best E-mail buddies . . .
excellent writers and critiquers*

Chapter 1

1806

Seated at his massive mahogany desk, stern-faced John, Lord Capelle, Earl of Carstairs, heaved a frustrated sigh as he gazed up at his daughter with hardened eyes.

"You are a severe disappointment to us, Clarinda. Refusing to dress like your twin, and now this latest—refusing even to consider Lord Sufton. I shall no longer tolerate such conduct."

"Nor shall I," echoed Lady Edwina Capelle, who stood beside her husband, thin as a stick and ramrod straight. Her hand, firmly gripping his shoulder, was a clear indication of her support. She regarded her daughter with unmitigated disgust. "I do not appreciate being called away from London, missing Lady Ponsonby's ball, by the way, and all because of you. Your conduct has gone from bad to worse." She bobbed her sharp chin for emphasis.

The willowy blond young woman who stood before her parents felt like an accused prisoner in the docks. Tears brimmed in her cornflower blue eyes, but she fought them back. Her rosy cheeks had paled. Her full red mouth, which ordinarily was curved into a pleasant smile, was tight and grim. Beneath her muddied riding gown, her knees were shaking. She had been in trouble many a time, but never had her parents displayed such wrath.

Silently she gazed about the spacious library, ordinarily her favorite room. In happier moments, it provided a cozy retreat, with its dark paneled walls, ormolu and rock crystal chandeliers, and recessed velvet window seat where she spent many an enjoyable hour curled up with a good book. Occasionally she would pause to rest her eyes, never failing to find pleasure in gazing through the arched Venetian window at the beautiful gardens of Graystone Hall that stretched beyond.

It was no cozy retreat today. Clarinda drew a deep breath and squared her shoulders. "Papa, Mama, I am truly sorry if I displeased you. It's just that I am twenty now, and I want—"

"Want? Ha!" Papa, sniffed his arched, aristocratic nose in disdain. "I do not care if you are twenty or a hundred-and-twenty, you are under my roof, you will do as I say."

Mama's always humorless eyes narrowed. "It is time you put aside your rebellious thoughts. In truth, you have given us grief from the day you were born, so unlike Clarissa. Well, I am sick of it. You *will* dress like your twin. You *will* give your most serious consideration to Lord Sufton as your suitor." She addressed her husband. "The perfect match, m'lord. Twins marrying twins. What could be more suitable? Lawrence shall wed Rissa, and Larimore"—her eyes bored into Clarinda's—"shall marry you, my dear, whether it suits your selfish pleasure or not."

"Selfish pleasure, indeed," echoed Papa. "How many of your Seasons did I pay for, and all for naught? You rejected suitors right and left, for reasons I cannot begin to fathom. Well, this is the end. It is time you were married, and soon."

How it twisted her heart that she could never please Papa! "But in London they were all fops and dandies. So frivolous and self-centered. I—"

"Think of the wealth those two possess," interrupted Mama, not about to be distracted from the fortune of the Sufton twins. You would live in Bolton Hall, which, as you very well know, is one of the finest estates in all England."

Clarinda could not contain herself. "But they are both such prigs. You could fit their brains into a thimble. They spend most of their time in London where all they care about is how their cravat is tied and which snuffbox to carry." She made a face, wrinkling her nose. "Larimore agrees with everything I say. So utterly boring."

Mama took an outraged breath, her chest expanding beneath her fashionable green muslin tea gown. "Your personal opinion is of no import. Oh, why cannot you be more like your sister?"

"She's not married, either, Mama."

Her mother looked as if she was about to burst. In a voice trembling with anger, she said, "You know full well your dear sister would be married now, had not Jeffrey died at Trafalgar."

Jeffrey. The very mention of his name brought a pang to Clarinda's heart. But no one must ever know her sorrow the day she heard that Jeffrey, Lord Lansdale, captain in the Royal Navy, had died of his wounds on the very deck where Lord Nelson had perished. ". . . and any *good* daughter," Mama was saying, "would be delighted she and her sister could marry into wealth, thus helping her poor, impoverished family."

"Impoverished?" Clarinda asked, surprised. "Us?"

Papa replied, "Certain debts have been incurred which must be paid." He flicked a sharp glance at his wife. "That's all you need know."

Mama's been gambling again, thought Clarinda. How galling that must be for Papa, who, rich as he was, hated to part with as much as a farthing.

Mama wasn't through. "Look at the bright side, Clarinda, if you and Rissa marry the Suftons, you could live together at Bolton Hall the rest of your lives. Twins should always be together."

If you only knew, thought Clarinda, her stomach wrenching at the thought. "If Rissa wants to marry Lawrence, that's fine, but I could not endure spending a lifetime with that foppish fool, Larimore."

"Enough! You are too impudent by half." His face reddening, Papa arose swiftly from his chair, reminding Clarinda of a volcano about to erupt. With a disdainful wave he indicated her less-than-impeccable appearance. "Mud on your skirt—your hair disheveled—you've been riding recklessly again, haven't you?"

Clarinda reached for her hair, which she knew had been tousled from her recent gallop on Donegal. She started to speak, but Mama interjected, "And from what I hear, *not* upon your sidesaddle."

Caught. Desperately Clarinda sought excuses to defend herself, but mercifully, Papa ignored the comment and continued on. ". . . all totally unacceptable. In the future, you will dress like your sister. You will wear your hair like your sister. You will attend the same social events." He looked toward his wife. "Anything else?"

"She must get rid of that disreputable riding dress she's wearing now. In future, if she wants to go riding she can wear the riding habit I had made for her." Mama slanted a glance at Papa. "It's black and green, m'lord, ornamented down the front, embroidered at the cuffs *á la militaire*. I cannot understand why she won't wear a handsome habit that is the absolute height of fashion."

Ugh! thought Clarinda.

"Anything else?" Papa asked.

"I do not want her spending time at Hollyridge Manor."

"Old Lord Westerlynn's estate?" Papa asked. "What the devil does she do there?"

"She rides Donegal over there nearly every day and meets with that unsuitable girl, Sara Sophia. They can usually be found in Lord Westerlynn's stables. From what I hear, they wash and brush the horses and clean the stalls." Mama sniffed contemptuously. "Chores more suited to the stable boys than a lady of leisure."

Lord Capelle glared at his daughter. "Is this true?"

"Yes, Papa." Clarinda raised her chin defiantly. "You know Lord Westerlynn now lives in London most of the time, yet he still keeps a considerable number of horses."

"Indeed, I have been to many of his fox hunts," said Papa. "He had ten hunters, I believe, at last count, and a few Arabians. Beautiful mounts, all of them. And then, of course, there are the carriage horses."

Clarinda nodded in a agreement. "But there's hardly anyone to care for them anymore, except Sara Sophia and me."

"That's strange," mused Papa. "Westerlynn is so rich he could employ an army of grooms and stable boys."

"But he doesn't, perhaps because he's getting so old and senile he doesn't realize. Have you seen Hollyridge Manor lately? It's getting all run-down. There are hardly enough servants to care for the house anymore, let alone the horses." Clarinda gazed at her father imploringly. "So that's the reason Sara Sophia and I—"

"There you have it, m'lord," interrupted Lady Capelle. "Do you see how your very own daughter chooses to run with a little squab of a female? *On-dit* has it she's merry-begotten, and by old Westerlynn himself, so the story goes. Sara Sophia has no social standing whatsoever. In my opinion, Clarinda should not be allowed to even speak to her."

Clarinda was hard put to control her flare of anger. "Sara Sophia Clarmonte is a saint. She's the sweetest, the smartest, the most—"

"Enough," said Lord Capelle, not loudly, but in his low, ominous voice, the one that signaled deep anger. "Suffice to say, you will obey."

Clarinda clenched her fists. "And if I do not?"

"Donegal," said Mama, the one word rolling with ease from her lips, almost as if she had planned it and could hardly wait to say it.

At mention of her beloved horse, fear struck Clarinda's heart. "Donegal? You wouldn't—"

"In an instant," declared Papa. He looked toward his wife again, as if making sure he was following her wishes.

Please, Papa, stand up for me, Clarinda silently cried. In the past, Papa, stern as he was, had often sided with her, and stood in the way of Mama's harshest punishments. But apparently not this time.

"Either you obey," he said, "or I shall sell Donegal."

Mama declared, "And while we are on the subject of your obeying, you must never forget you are a twin. What you don't seem to realize, Clarinda, is that if ever there was an example of female perfection, it's Rissa, who is the very soul of sweetness and refinement. Try to emulate your twin at all times. You'll be a better person for it." She eyed Papa. "Am I not right, m'lord?"

"Indeed. Now let this be an end to it." Papa appeared to be increasingly impatient to finish this unpleasant task.

Clarinda had to fight the urge to rush from the room. She could not stand much more of this. "So if I don't marry Lord Sufton you will take Donegal away from me?" she asked over a huge lump in her throat.

"Well, as for your marrying Sufton . . ." Papa hesitated.

"Yes!" said Mama, quickly jumping in. "You shall marry Lord Sufton."

Papa cast a dubious glance at Mama. "Let's not be hasty, Edwina, we cannot force the girl." Clarinda was surprised. She knew if Papa alone were in charge of discipline, he would be more lenient, but, alas, in matters of the family he always deferred to her mother.

His expression slightly softened, Papa went on, "Suffice to say, Clarinda, you will give Lord Sufton your most serious consideration."

Mama added, "Not only that, if your poor behavior persists, I promise you, you will be sent to live with your grandfather."

Ah, the old warning again. It seemed as if Clarinda had spent her entire childhood under the threat of being sent to Grandfather Montague's cold, drafty castle located in the farthest, loneliest corner of North Wales. The thought had always frightened her, often curbing her tendency toward wild behavior.

"Well?" demanded Mama, "is it agreed that in future you will model yourself after your twin?"

Clarinda briefly closed her eyes, trying to shut out the dismaying spectacle of her fashionable mother, who usually remained so aloof, raising her voice, her face all twisted, ugly with anger. Clarinda stretched out her palms. "Can you not understand how tired I am of being a twin?"

"But you *are* a twin." Mama cast an outraged glance at her husband. "There's gratitude for you. To what lengths have I not gone to dress the girls exactly alike? To ensure their hair is fixed the same? That they curtsy the same? That they—"

"But that's the point," cried Clarinda. "I am tired of feeling only one half of a whole."

"Half of a whole? I am shocked!" Mama struck her hand to her bosom in amazement. "Why, I have sacrificed my life to you and Rissa. How could you show such ingratitude after all I have done?"

Clarissa bit her tongue, trying to quell her growing resentment. *Clarinda and Clarissa*, she thought with irony, Mama's darling, adorable twins. Same names, same gowns, same hair, same everything. Even Donegal and Dublin, their chestnut Irish Hunters, looked exactly the same. Only two people in the whole world could tell Clarinda and Clarissa apart: Alexander, their little brother, and Estelle, their lady's maid. Surely not Mama and Papa, who had spent much of their time in London when she and Rissa were growing up, allowing them to be raised by a series of nannies and governesses. Clarinda longed to say, *We are the same in appearance, Mama, but oh how different we are inside!* Such a protest would get her nowhere, though, and only increase her mother's enmity. "It appears I have no choice."

"Indeed not," confirmed Papa.

"Then . . . I shall consider Lord Sufton."

"I have already invited both Lord Suftons to our ball next Friday," said Mama. Triumphantly she addressed Papa. "I can see it now, m'lord, a double wedding with identical brides, identical grooms, identical gowns, identical bridal bouquets, identical rings, identical—"

"I think I shall go see how Alexander is doing," cried Clarinda. Despairing, she hurried from the room.

After her frantic escape from the library, Clarinda fled upstairs to her little brother's bedchamber. She was worried. Alexander had been ill a week now. He had always been a sickly child, and now, at age seven, still suffered from constant bouts of asthma, flu, and fever. "So how is the heir apparent to Graystone Hall doing?" she asked brightly as she entered the room.

"I'm fine but Mama won't let me up," Alexander replied sullenly from his sickbed.

"That's because you're still sick."

"It's not fair!"

Clarinda sat on Alexander's bed and placed her cool hand on her brother's flushed forehead. What a handsome child he was, she thought, with his fair skin, blue eyes, and hair as golden as hers and Rissa's.

"By the way, Captain's fine," she said, referring to Alexander's Shetland pony. "We shall go out riding soon, you, I, Donegal, and Captain, just as soon as you're better."

Alexander pouted. "It had better be soon."

I hope so, Clarinda thought later as she left Alexander's room. He was such a fine little boy—bright, cheerful, and content, when he wasn't sick. Mama and Papa doted on their one and only son. What a tragedy it would be if . . . no, she wouldn't even consider such a horrible thought.

Soon Clarinda was headed down the path to the stone-walled stables. Troubled though she was, she never failed to appreciate the breathtaking view of Graystone Hall's formal gardens, and the lush, rolling green lawns that grew from the rise of the stately manor house to the wooded banks of the upper Thames.

"Back again, Miss Clarinda?" inquired Morris, the chief groom, who was rubbing down Jupiter, her father's prized coal black stallion. "Why, you was just here less than an hour ago."

"I wanted to check on Donegal."

"Shall I get your saddle?"

"No, I'll pick up his bridle. I shall walk him down the river path a little."

"Yes, mum." The faint smile that flitted across Morris's face told her she hadn't fooled him.

She stepped inside the stable, took down a bridle from its peg on the wall, and in the dim light found Donegal's stall. The gelding softly whinnied as Clarinda slipped her arms around his neck and buried her head in the sleek chestnut mane. "Ah, Donegal," she whispered, "do you know what trouble we're in? Do you know I shall be forced to marry Lord Sufton, and all because of you? But you're worth it," she added as she slipped the bit into her gelding's mouth. From the next stall came a soft whinny. "We'll go for a ride tomorrow, Dublin," she called. Poor Dublin. He was Rissa's, and Rissa hated horses and never rode him. If it weren't for Clarinda and the stable boys, he would get no exercise at all.

Clarinda led Donegal outside and away from the stables, along the riding path that led to the river. When they reached the heavy growth of tall trees that shielded her from the house, she gripped the horse's back and easily sprang on. Legs astride, tucking in her full riding skirt, she nudged Donegal into a trot, then canter, then full gallop.

"Faster, Donegal!"

The horse plunged forward and fairly flew along the tree-lined path that bordered the river. Clarinda leaned far forward, her head not far from resting between the animal's ears, hair flying in the wind. Her painful thoughts vanished as they skimmed the trail at a furious pace, she responding to the gelding's rippling muscles as he galloped, entirely attuned to the rhythmic shift from side to side. Soon the vast estate of Hollyridge Manor came into view. Clarinda slowed Donegal to a trot, enjoying, as she always did, that first glimpse of the ancient, largely Elizabethan manor built of irregular ragstone, brick, and timber, all of varying ages, molded by years. It was a rambling sort of mansion, essentially romantic, with Tudor windows and countless chimneys of diverse designs. It lay in its own secluded hollow amidst tall trees, close to the river, only a mile from the much more modern Graystone Hall.

Her sad thoughts returned. *Foolish girl,* she thought. No matter how fast the pace, she could never leave the distressing events of the day behind.

Marry Lord Sufton—no! Be like Rissa—no!

Approaching the cobblestone courtyard in front of the stables and coach house, Clarinda was happy to see Sara Sophia was there, brushing Sham, a magnificent Arabian stallion. She and Sara Sophia had been friends since as far back as she could remember, despite Mama's carping. "We are members of the *ton,*" Mama loved to say, "whereas Sara Sophia . . . well, nobody knows now, do they?"

Sara Sophia was neither fish nor fowl. Though not of the nobility, she was well-educated, mainly because Lord Westerlynn had seen to it that she had a tutor when she was growing up. She was never invited to the countryside's more prestigious social events, yet neither was she treated like a servant. She took her meals in the dining room and had a bedchamber on the family floor, not the servants' quarters.

Nothing was known of where she came from, other than that she and her mother, Louise, had arrived at Hollyridge Manor under mysterious circumstances when Sara Sophia was but three or four years old. Louise never ventured out. When she died of some unknown illness only months after their arrival, she was buried quietly, with none but Lord Westerlynn and a few servants in attendance. Clarinda wondered if Mama was right about the *on-dit* concerning Lord Westerlynn being Sara Sophia's father. No one would put such a scandal beyond the old rascal, but if he was responsible, he kept it to himself.

"Good morning, Sara Sophia." Clarinda slid easily from her horse and announced, "I am in deep trouble."

"Again?" Sara Sophia smiled, seeming not the least surprised. She stopped brushing Sham and straightened up.

Seeing the anxiety on Clarinda's face, she immediately grew serious. "You look terrible. What's wrong?"

Clarinda related the events of her day. ". . . so if I am to keep Donegal I must seriously consider marrying Larimore. Mama says, 'whether it suits your selfish pleasure or not,' which means I'll live to regret it if I don't. Not only that, I must make myself be more like my dear twin Rissa, who, as we all know, is the epitome of perfection, whereas I"— a wry smile played at the corners of her mouth—"am the disgrace of the family."

Sara Sophia smiled. "Indeed, you are, you naughty girl. Everyone knows you are difficult, wild, rebellious, and—"

"And I don't ride sidesaddle," Clarinda interjected. "That's from Mama. She must have found out."

"Uh-oh." Sara Sophia quickly sobered. "That is serious, Clarinda. If they catch you riding astride you're done for."

"That's not all."

"There's more?"

This was going to be painful. Clarinda hated to hurt her friend, but she wasn't one to waffle. Besides, Sara Sophia might be delicate, but she was tough underneath. It would be by far the best approach to just tell her the blunt truth. "I am not supposed to see you anymore."

If Sara Sophia was wounded, she showed no signs of it, and instead laughed. "I was expecting it. In fact, I'm surprised your parents didn't take action long before now."

"They probably would have if they'd noticed."

"And not stayed in London so much of the time." In deep thought, Sara Sophia began to brush the horse again. "They're right, you know. You should have nothing to do with me. We are in two different worlds, you and I, and nothing alike."

In looks, that was so true, thought Clarinda. She was tall for a girl, and well filled-out, whereas Sara Sophia was so small she looked as if a spring breeze could whisk her away. She had blue eyes and blond curls, whereas Sara Sophia's hair was brown and her eyes were large, brown, and luminous, lending a subtle beauty to her otherwise plain face. And whereas she was ordinarily happy and outgoing, except for days like today, Sara Sophia possessed a solemn serenity and quiet humor, which was always well contained.

As for living in two different worlds, Clarinda could not

argue with the truth. What they did share was a love of horses. Sara Sophia practically lived at the stables. Despite her slight form, she busied herself rubbing down the horses, feeding—washing—brushing them, cleaning out the stalls—all work a lady must never do, Clarinda had been informed by her disapproving mother.

Up to now, Clarinda had ignored Mama. Sara Sophia was her dearest friend, and she didn't care what people thought. In fact, she herself had helped Sara Sophia with the horses many a time. It was her great pleasure to do so. Thoughtfully, Clarinda took up a brush and started working Sham's other flank. "I've never asked, but I'm wondering. Lord Westerlynn is getting up in years. If you don't marry, what will happen to you when he dies?"

"Nothing good I'm afraid," Sara Sophia replied.

"But surely Lord Westerlynn has arranged for your care in his will?"

Sara Sophia shook her head. "I doubt it. Contrary to opinion, I doubt he's my father. I wasn't born here, nor, I suspect, anywhere in England. I have this vague memory of my mother crying a lot, and us being on some kind of ship when I was very little."

"But who inherits Hollyridge Manor?"

"There's a nephew. I doubt he'd allow me to stay, not that I'd want to. I was thinking, when the time comes, I shall leave here and find a position as a governess."

"God's blood!" cried Clarinda, then swiftly looked around. She was not beyond using an oath now and then, but only out of earshot of her parents or those who might tattle. "How could you give up the horses?"

"It would kill me, but what choice would I have?"

How unfair! Horses were as much Sara Sophia's life as they were hers. Practically from dawn to dusk Sara Sophia could be found in the stables, or out riding Sham, her favorite horse, even though it really wasn't hers.

Clarinda asked, "Do you think the nephew will keep all the horses?"

"Probably not."

"Then surely he would sell them to good homes."

"The thoroughbreds he would, and of course Sham."

"But what about old Bottom, and Nicker?" Clarinda shook her head in dismay, thinking of the two retired carriage horses. They had seen better days, but that didn't matter. She and Sara Sophia loved them just the same as the others. "Would they just be sold for slaughter, do you suppose?"

"I fear they would."

Clarinda threw the brush down. Putting her hands on her hips, she stared up at the sky and declared, "Life is so deucedly unfair."

"Are you just finding that out?" asked Sara Sophia. "The worst of it is, since we're only women, we would have nothing to say about it. It's men who rule the world. Even you, rich and titled though you are, must do what some man tells you. And not just now, all your life. First your father, then your husband. As for me"—her gentle smile was tinged with sadness—"I shall never marry."

"But of course you will," Clarinda began, but Sara Sophia firmly shook her head.

"What man would have me? I have no dowry. Worse, I have no standing. You know what the purveyors of gossip whisper about my parentage." She set her chin in a stubborn line. "But that's all right. I expect nothing from this world. I should be grateful just to be alive."

"I wish I were a man so I could set things straight."

"Well, you're not a man, and you never will be, so make the best of it." Sara Sophia laughed ironically. "Face it, everything you'll ever want in this world must be obtained from a man, mostly using your womanly wiles."

"I suppose I should act just like Rissa," said Clarinda in disgust.

Sara Sophia nodded her agreement. "You're too rebellious. You would get much further in this world fluttering your eyelids and playing coy behind your fan."

"And I should marry Lord Sufton," Clarinda added bitterly. "But how could I stand it? What could be more boring than a man who agrees with everything you say?"

"This is not a perfect world."

"But why can't I do what I want to do?" Clarinda cried.

Sara Sophia stopped brushing. Across the stallion's back she looked directly into her friend's eyes. "So tell me, if you could plan the rest of your life—have it just the way you wanted—what would it be?"

Without hesitation Clarinda declared, "I wish we could

run off, just you, I, and Alexander. We would bring Donegal for me, Sham for you, Captain for Alexander, and Dublin for extra because Rissa doesn't ride him anyway. We would buy a farm somewhere far from here with lots of green fields for the horses. We would have loads of friends from all classes, not just the *ton*, and breed horses the rest of our lives." She paused, intent on brushing Sham so furiously the horse turned its head and gave her the eye. With a wry little laugh, she continued, "Oh, I know how childish that sounds. In real life, one cannot run off, can one?" Her voice a rising crescendo of frustration, she continued, "One has to do what her parents tell her to do and be miserable!"

Sara Sophia ignored Clarinda's despair and remarked, "You said 'just you and I and Alexander.' But surely someday you will fall in love and marry and have children."

"No! I shall never love again. You're the only one who knows how my heart was broken."

"But Jeffrey's dead, and you're young, and . . . and . . ." At a loss for words, Sara Sophia stumbled and stopped.

Clarinda's laugh was hollow. "I know what you're going to say—that Jeffrey wasn't mine, he was Rissa's. And you'd be right, only"—a flash of despair ripped through her—"we can't help whom we fall in love with. I shall love my dreamy-eyed poet until the day I die. In my heart, no one can replace Jeffrey."

Impulsively Sara Sophia came around Sham and hugged Clarinda. In her sweet, serene voice, she said, "You can never know for certain what the future holds."

"I have a fairly good idea," Clarinda replied grimly. "I have a twin who's so perfect I must strive to be just like her. I have parents who want me to marry the most boring man in the world. You think I have a chance for happiness? I think not."

"Ah, Clarinda, you just haven't met the right man yet. But you will, I promise you. He's going to be tall—"

"Since you're dreaming, you may as well make him rich, and exceedingly handsome."

"Well, of course that, but more important, he will be his own man—"

"Whom I won't be able to twist around my little finger, like I can Larimore?"

"Exactly." Counting on her fingers, Sara Sophia continued, "He will honor his parents, be kind to animals, and, of course, adore horses. But most of all he will be so utterly masterful that you, my wild, independent Clarinda, will not be able to push him around."

Clarinda took over. "And yet, he will respect me for the bright woman I am and not be bossy, and he will allow me to have whatever I want and to do whatever I want."

"The perfect husband," declared Sara Sophia.

Clarinda slanted a skeptical glance at her friend. "Such a man does not exist."

Sara Sophia sighed. "I fear not. So you may as well marry that jellyfish, Lord Sufton, and make the best of it."

Wisps of late night London fog swirled around the entrance to White's Gambling Club as Robert, Lord Stormont, Earl of Marsett, stepped outside, followed by his good friend, Lucius, Lord Wentridge. Robert, a tall man with a purposeful stride, stepped to the curb and signaled his coachman. A frown crossed the handsome features of his thin, darkly tanned face as he turned to Lucius and said, "I've half a notion to give it back."

"Are you daft?" Lucius, a fair-haired, slender young man of medium stature, dropped his usual cynical demeanor and regarded his friend aghast. "You won Hollyridge Manor fair and square, did you not? Lord Westerlynn knew what he was doing, did he not? I'd wager he's been playing whist since long before you were born."

"The old man's close to eighty, if not eighty-five. What if he's not of sound mind?"

"Preposterous," scoffed Lucius. "It's not like you to question yourself. As I recall, you attempted more than once to dissuade Westerlynn from risking his estate, but the old reprobate would have none of it."

"True . . ." Robert sunk into deep thought. Lucius was right, he should be ecstatic, winning such a huge estate, but somehow he felt less than joyful. Still deep in thought, Robert climbed into his coach, along with Lucius, and settled his lean, powerful body against the squabs. He leaned to signal his coachman, asking Lucius, "Where to? Shall we call it a night?"

"No late visit to Selina?"

"I saw her last night."

"Don't want to spoil her, eh?"

Robert's deep, booming laughter filled the carriage. In truth, he was most pleased with his latest *fille de joie*, who excited him no end. Still, he had no need to see her every night. "She's a lovely girl, Lucius, but I'll soon be on to the next."

"My word, you're fickle."

Robert sighed. "No long-term attachments, that's my rule. Of course, when the time comes, I'll see she has a sufficiency of trinkets to assuage her feelings."

Lucius sniffed his disgust.

"But how often do I come to London?" asked Robert, trying to explain. "It's not fair to tie any woman exclusively to me."

"There are times I don't understand you," Lucius said, sighing in chagrin. "Here you are, a first son—rich, titled, not bad-looking by half—have I left anything out? Yet you choose to bury yourself in the dreary depths of the country-side with naught but your horses for company. Astounding!" Lucius rolled his eyes. "How could you deliberately choose to live away from London? I shall never understand how you could miss all the fetes, routs, glittering balls—let alone all those twittering young chits throwing themselves at your feet in hopes you'll marry them. Yet you won't move back, and you even refuse any serious attachment to any of your ladybirds."

"Don't fret, Lucius," Robert answered. "Strange as it may seem to you, my life is thoroughly comfortable without the joys of London. Rest assured I'm totally content to visit but occasionally."

"Incredible," Lucius muttered.

Robert remained silent. Lucius would never understand how content he was to spend his time at Oakley House, his estate in Kent, where he satisfied his passion for breeding horses—many said some of England's finest. After his father died, and he received his title, he had played the popular London bachelor for a time. But he had soon grown weary of the marriageable misses and their eager mamas. Now, as far as he was concerned, the best part of coming to London was gambling at the city's leading clubs, visiting his current ladybird, and above all, examining the fine horseflesh at Tattersall's. After such visits, he returned to

Oakley House happy and content, delighted to be back with his cherished thoroughbreds.

"My rakehell days are over," he remarked to Lucius. "I must be getting old."

"At twenty-eight?" Lucius chuckled. "It's more likely the time has come to settle down. You need a wife."

"I detest the thought." Robert shrugged. "My father warned me not to marry until I was at least forty, and that, my good fellow, is excellent advice. My parents bickered constantly when I was growing up. I hesitate to subject my own children to the same misery."

"But surely you want sons."

Robert shook his head adamantly. "It's not worth the price, at least not for now."

"But not all women—"

"Every woman I meet is flighty, full of artifice, with not a brain in her head."

Lucius chuckled. "You want a woman who would simply be herself? Not likely! Not here in London with these silly, husband-hunting chits."

"Well, then, don't tell me I need a wife." Robert was silent a moment. "Sorry. Didn't mean to sound so disagreeable. I hate to admit it, but you're right. Long ago I found the London Seasons excruciatingly superficial and insipid. Still, I know the day will come when I shall be compelled to grit my teeth, plunge into the marriage mart, and choose a bride."

"Dare I mention that if you marry, it might be for love?"

"Love? Ha! Love is an illusion. I shall never fall in love." In the dimness of the gas-lit street, Robert cocked his head and regarded his friend skeptically. "You're as old as I, Lucius. I don't see you heading for the altar."

"At least you don't have parents breathing down your neck," Lucius replied. "My parents grow ever more impatient—like you, the price I pay for being a first son. I must marry soon, but unlike you, I won't worry one whit. After all, a man of sense only trifles with women—humors them—plays with them as he would a child. So it's most certainly not required I love her, only that she possess a title and suitable dowry. After I marry, I shall take the time to beget an heir, then continue my fine life in London, just as before."

"I am so relieved," Robert answered sarcastically. "If ever there was a man who adores the bachelor life, it is you."

"Exactly," answered Lucius, nodding his head vigorously. "It's the only solution. I love all the girls and would have the devil of a time settling on just one."

"Well said," Robert answered offhandedly. "As for me, at the moment, my life suits me well enough. Someday I'll get around to looking for a wife. I don't expect her to be beautiful, and have no notion I could ever be in love with her. I would be content if I could find a woman with half a brain in her head who would just be herself. That will be many years from now, however."

They rode in silence for a while, Robert allowing his thoughts to drift back to old Lord Westerlynn and the game of whist that had ruined him.

Not fair . . .

Not right, taking advantage of an old man . . .

He could not do it!

Without warning, Robert poked his head out the window and yelled, "Stop, Jeffers! Turn around. Go back."

"What the deuce?" exclaimed Lucius.

"We're returning to White's," Robert said firmly. "I've decided to deed Hollyridge Manor back to Lord Westerlynn."

"You have lost your mind."

"Perhaps, but I cannot in all good conscience take advantage of a senile old man."

"Lord Westerlynn has left, sir," said the uniformed attendant at White's. "Climbed in his carriage a while ago— looked quite dreadful, if I may say so. I heard him tell his coachman to take him to his lodgings on Thayer Street."

"Ah, well," said Robert, "we shall catch him in the morning."

The next morning, Robert, accompanied by Lucius, presented himself at Lord Westerlynn's doorstep.

"You are too late, sir," said the butler. "His lordship has left for Hollyridge Manor, quite hastily, I might add. Said he planned to return in a few days."

"Damme!" said Robert. "Most likely he's gone to retrieve his personal possessions."

"Well, that's that," said a relieved Lucius as they climbed back into Robert's carriage. "You've made your best effort. Obviously Westerlynn has resigned himself to the loss of his estate, so why not keep it?"

Robert clamped his jaw. "I have made up my mind. When he returns, Westerlynn will get the surprise of his life. Most definitely, I am giving him his deed back."

Lucius opened his mouth to protest but quickly closed it again. He knew from experience that once Robert made up his mind, nothing on God's green earth could make him change it.

Chapter 2

Fool, fool, fool!

Miserably uncomfortable from the rocking and jolting of his ancient oak coach, Arthur, Lord Westerlynn, felt short of breath as he leaned back against the musty seat and loosened his cravat. *Hollyridge Manor lost.* What idiocy had possessed him to gamble away the estate that had been in his family since James the Second?

Fool!

But it wasn't so much the loss of Hollyridge that troubled him. These past years he had spent most of his time at his comfortable lodgings in London. Despite huge gambling losses, he still had enough blunt to keep him content the rest of his life, which, judging from those recent, nagging pains in his chest, might not be too lengthy a period or time.

But how could he have done such a dreadful thing to Sara Sophia?

It was of the greatest importance he return, at the utmost possible speed, to the girl who had lived at Hollyridge from the age of four. He must tell her the truth—give her the papers that would change her life. How negligent he had been! It was Louise's dying wish that he tell all to Sara Sophia on her eighteenth birthday. Nearly a year ago! But he, snug in his cozy London lodgings, had put off the tiring trip, thinking he had plenty of time.

If I thought of it at all.

From his pocket, Lord Westerlynn withdrew the two ancient iron keys that he had retrieved earlier from the depths of his jewelry chest. No harm done, he decided as he examined them. He might have lost Hollyridge Manor, but when he gave Sara Sophia these keys—told her who she really was and what wealth she possessed—all would be well. He had a great affection for the girl. In many ways she had been like a daughter to him. She was not, of course, but still . . .

Damme! But it was getting hot in here. He brushed beads of perspiration from his forehead, loosened his cravat. The coach was halfway to Hollyridge, rolling through a small hamlet, when he noticed his left arm was somewhat numb. A few miles later, a stab of pain hit his chest.

Instantly Lord Westerlynn knew. Pounding his cane on the ceiling of the coach, he yelled at his coachman to hurry. He must reach Hollyridge—that was all that mattered now. But another pain struck, and another, and he knew he would never make it home.

But perhaps . . . Garnering his strength, he pounded on the ceiling again, and when the coachman yelled down, "What now, m'lord?" he ordered the man to take him to Graystone Hall, the nearest estate to Hollyridge, and closer. He must hang on. Clutching his chest, he slumped back on the seat and prayed his young friend, Clarinda, would be at home, or Lord Capelle, or even Lady Capelle, who had a heart of stone but could at least be trusted.

The minutes seemed endless. Lord Westerlynn lay back on the seat, fighting the pain, until finally the coach turned into the long, circular driveway of Graystone Hall. As it rolled toward the marble pillared entrance, a pain far worse than the others slammed into chest. He didn't have long. *Please, dear God*, he prayed, *let Clarinda be at home*.

In her spacious, pink wall-papered bedchamber, Lady Clarissa Capelle stood back to view herself in her tall gilt mirror. Frowning, she plucked at one of the delicate golden curls that ringed her forehead. "This hangs down farther than the others, Estelle," she said to her middle-aged, French lady's maid who hovered nearby. "Do it better."

"Sorry, m'lady." Estelle fussed with the curl until, impatient, Rissa elbowed her aside and viewed herself again. Nodding favorably, she lovingly drew her hands down the sides of her blue silk visiting gown, trimmed at the hem and high waist with ribbon and embroidery. "Help me with my bonnet," she ordered and was soon admiring the delicate features of her face, set off by the adorable silk-covered bonnet of matching blue with a saucy ostrich plume and a ribbon that Estelle tied into a big bow, tilted beneath her chin. Rissa raised her skirt a few inches and pointed the left toe of her blue printed kid shoes. How dainty her foot looked! How darling the silk blue ribbon loops and ties around her ankle.

Estelle helped her slip on her long gloves of matching blue, then handed her the huge matching silk muff, banded with strips of fur and decorated with silk tassels.

Rissa smiled with satisfaction at her reflection. Lightly she touched the gold chain around her neck with its gold filigree "R" pendant. "Does it go?" she asked. "Or should I tuck it in?"

"Eet looks fine, m'lady," assured Estelle. "You look *séduisant*."

I do, thought Rissa, turning this way and that in front of the mirror. How she loved clothes and jewels and fancy coiffeurs! That her twin did not have the same fascination was beyond her.

"I had best see how Lady Clarinda ees doing," said Estelle, turning to leave.

"If you must." Rissa could not keep resentment from her voice. She hated having to share a lady's maid. Mama and Papa were such misers. At least Clarinda made far less use of Estelle than she did, but that was small consolation. She deserved her very own lady's maid.

A minute later, Estelle returned shaking her head. "She ees just out of the bath so eet will be a few minutes."

"Is she putting on the blue?"

Estelle's usually guarded expression dropped away for a moment, and her mouth quirked with humor. "*Oui,* though not without a protest."

Good! thought Rissa. It was time they dressed exactly the same again. Clarinda's brief rebellion had been squelched, thank goodness. In fact, yesterday in the library, Mama and Papa had done a fine job of dealing with all Clarinda's transgressions. Rissa knew they had because she'd been standing outside, listening to every word. With great satisfaction, too, especially when they threatened to sell Donegal. How *that* must have hurt. Now Clarinda would not be seeing that awful Sara Sophia anymore. That would hurt, too, but it was also for the best, and Clarinda deserved it.

Tucking her hands in her muff, Rissa announced, "I shall wait at the front portico, Estelle. Tell Mama and my sister to hurry." Rissa took a final glimpse of herself in the mirror. No question, she was dressed in the height of fashion, and beautiful besides. No one at Lady Constance Lynbury's tea this afternoon would look half as nice, except Clarinda, of course, and she didn't count. They would create their usual sensation. Rissa would never tire of how everybody oohed and aahed at the sight of identical twins dressed exactly alike.

When she stepped outside, onto the wide marbled portico, Rissa was surprised to see a coach and six rolling at breakneck speed up the curved driveway. Only when it came to a quick, dust-billowing halt did she realize it belonged to that dreadful old Lord Westerlynn who lived on the adjoining estate.

"Help us, mum," cried the coachman from above. "His lordship has taken ill."

"Indeed?" she called. How annoying! This had better not interfere with her plans for the day. She had best fetch the butler. She started to turn, but before she could, a feeble, trembling voice called, "Clarinda! Thank God you're home."

Rissa looked toward the coach again. There, his withered old hands gripping the door, was old Lord Westerlynn. He was breathing hard, face deadly white, with a stricken look in his eye. "Come here, girl," he gasped, "hurry!"

Well, really! She had no desire to go anywhere near the disgusting old man, but she supposed she hardly had a choice. And besides, she was curious to know why he was here, and so desperately anxious to talk to Clarinda. Holding her muff close, as if to shield herself, she stepped daintily down the marble steps and over to the coach. The coachman, who had climbed down from his perch, opened the door, revealing Lord Westerlynn half sitting, half lying on the seat, obviously in great pain, his hand clutching his chest. "Are you ill?" she inquired, using her extra sweet voice.

"Ill? Damme, I am dying!" Lord Westerlynn replied. "Off with you!" he cried, waving off the coachman. "I must talk to Clarinda alone."

"Sir, I am not—" Rissa began, and then thought better

of it. She hardly knew the man, and no wonder. Mama had often pointed out how vulgar and uncouth their neighbor was, so she had gladly avoided him. Not so Clarinda, who had no taste in friends and visited Hollyridge Manor all the time.

What did he want to tell Clarinda? In truth, she would love to know. Perhaps, if she said nothing . . . yes, it was safe enough. When they were children she had pretended she was Clarinda many a time, for fun mostly, and no one ever found out. Besides, he already thought she was Clarinda, so she wouldn't even have to tell a lie. "What is it, sir?" she asked, putting as much concern in her voice as she knew how.

The old man reached out a shaky, wrinkled, brown-spotted hand and clasped her wrist. How revolting. Her impulse was to grab her hand back, but she forced herself not to pull away. "What is it you wish to say?"

"Listen carefully," Westerlynn gasped, "you must give these to Sara Sophia." Calling on what must have been the last of his strength, the old man pressed two rusted keys into her palm. "It is urgent. These keys will change her life—give her wealth—give her the future she deserves."

"But what are the keys to?"

"A fortune awaits Sara Sophia. Look for the room in . . ."

The old man let out one last desperate, agonizing gasp. His head fell back and his wide-open eyes stared, unseeing, at the ceiling of the coach.

He was dead! Rissa let out one small horrified screech. How inconsiderate! Why did he have to die here? How unfair that she, so delicate, so protected all her life, should be forced to witness such a shocking sight. She turned to flee, and saw that Mama, Papa, and Clarinda were hurrying down the steps. She stopped short, suddenly realizing the drama of the scene and how she mustn't ruin it by running off. Everyone must know that she, fragile but brave Rissa, had unselfishly rushed to the aid of the dying old man, had heard his last words while selflessly putting her own feelings aside, even though she had never in her life seen anyone dead. Everyone would admire her. She would be the center of attention, not Clarinda.

"Rissa, dear, what is it?" Mama cried.

Rissa forced a tear from her eye. Hand to her heart, she backed off from the coach, managing a slight stagger. "Oh, Mama! I was trying to help dear Lord Westerlynn as best I could, but I fear he is dead."

"You poor child," cried Mama, "come away."

"Stand back, everyone," ordered Papa.

Clarinda, her stomach knotted with dread, stood on the last step and watched as Papa went to the coach and checked the old man's pulse. "He's gone," Papa finally said. "His heart, I should wager. What a pity. Old scoundrel though he was, I liked the man."

"He was up in years," Mama remarked, none too sympathetically, "eighty if he was a day." She put her arm around Rissa. "Why did he have to die here? Poor Rissa has been subjected to the most horrible experience imaginable. We must get her inside so she can lie down."

Clarinda, standing ignored on the step, felt such sorrow she could not speak. Lord Westerlynn had always shown her the utmost kindness, and shared her love of horses. She wondered if he'd said any last words. Rissa, in a half faint, supported by Mama on one side, Papa on the other, was being led gently up the steps.

"Rissa, did Lord Westerlynn say anything before he died?"

Rissa paused and heaved a dramatic sigh. "Only that he knew he was dying," she said. "Then he just gasped a little, and then he was dead."

What was that in her hand? Clarinda wondered. She watched as Rissa slipped whatever it was into her muff. But Clarinda had learned long ago that Rissa did what was best for Rissa. It would be useless even to ask.

It was late in the day before Clarinda had a chance to ride Donegal to Hollyridge Manor. A sad-faced Sara Sophia greeted her outside the stable, where she was watering some horses when Clarinda rode up. Slipping off Donegal, Clarinda declared, "You must be devastated. Lord Westerlynn was like a father to you."

Sara Sophia bowed her head. "And I loved him like a daughter."

"What will happen now?" Clarinda gestured across the

formal garden toward the sprawling, four-story mansion. "I suppose the nephew inherits?"

"All goes to the nephew. I met him only once." Sara Sophia managed a wry smile. "He wasn't very nice. I cannot imagine he would let me stay."

"That's so unfair," Clarinda cried. "Where will you go? What will you do?"

"Does it matter?" Sara Sophia's large, luminous brown eyes focused on the stables. "The horses—that's what I care about. But what will the nephew care? He won't give a fig where they go."

Clarinda wished she could assure her friend otherwise, but she, too, was sick with worry. "We shall just have to see, I suppose. And what about you?"

"Without Lord Westerlynn's support I am penniless. Poor old dear, I suspect he thought he'd live forever. I doubt he thought ahead enough to remember me in his will, nor would I have expected him to." Sara Sophia proudly raised her chin. "I shall be a governess. After all, I am well-versed in French, the minuet, embroidery, watercolors"—an ironic smile played on her lips—"all the things that count for women in this world."

Clarinda marveled at how calm her friend remained. But then, she had never heard Sara Sophia raise her voice—had never seen her angry or distressed. She was always gentle, always serene. What impressed her most was Sara Sophia's broad vision of their world that went far beyond what was in plain sight. Impulsively she said, "I wish you could come live with me."

Sara Sophia regarded her sadly. "That would be nice, but I suspect your parents might have a word or two to say about that."

Doubtless, she was right. How unfair life was! How utterly tragic that a girl like Sara Sophia, who came closer to being a saint than anyone Clarinda had ever known, should be doomed to the dreary life of a governess.

How I envy Clarinda's passion for life, Sara Sophia thought after her friend had gone. Clarinda was bold, brave, impetuous—everything she was not.

Clarinda was so very bright, too, except where Jeffrey was concerned. Love is blind, they say, and in Clarinda's case that was certainly true. Too bad he had to die on the deck of *HMS Victory,* for more reasons than one. Sara Sophia had learned, from Lord Westerlynn's letters to her, that Clarinda's dreamy-eyed poet was a wastrel and a fool—perfect for Rissa, not for herself. Had Jeffrey lived, Clarinda would surely have seen him for what he was, but alas, now he was frozen in time as a hero and would forever remain so in Clarinda's eyes. So unjust! From the grave, Jeffrey was preventing Clarinda from finding happiness.

But would her dear friend ever find happiness? Sara Sophia shook her head in chagrin. That might be difficult, considering Clarinda had a twin like Rissa, who was vain—selfish—shallow, and, from all Sara Sophia had perceived, exceedingly jealous of her twin and would do anything, even hurt Clarinda, to get her own way.

Two days later, in the main salon of Graystone Hall, Lady Edwina Capelle was conducting one of her rare Thursday afternoon "at homes." Considering she spent much of her time in London, it was an event exceedingly popular with the ladies of the countryside who could take the opportunity to catch up on the latest London *on-dit.* Clarinda, who in the past had been adept at avoiding these tedious affairs, was seated on a striped floral settee, wondering how soon she could make a graceful exit. Mama's at-homes were a giant bore. Clarinda hated sitting stiff and ladylike, sipping tea, watching every word she said. Worse, she must listen to endless gossip in which she had no interest. It was obvious, though, she was not going to avoid it today. Several prattling ladies had already arrived and were sipping their tea when that queen of gossip, Lady Constance Lynbury, swept in, accompanied by Agatha, her new, sharp-nosed daughter-in-law, who had just arrived from her previous home in London.

White-haired Lady Lynbury was an expert at collecting gossip as well as dispensing it. Today, doubtless, she would dig out every little detail concerning Lord Westerlynn's sad demise. Not only that, Lady Lynbury, her stout figure clad in unbecoming black, appeared to be bursting to impart some juicy tidbit. Her sharp eyes glittered, her many chins quivered, as if she could hardly contain herself.

Clarinda gave an inward sigh. She would much rather be

on Donegal's back, racing with the wind, than to have to listen to silly chatter.

After Lady Lynbury introduced her new daughter-in-law, she exclaimed, "How brave of you to receive us today, Lady Capelle. I daresay, if I'd had a man die at my very doorstep, I should be quite distraught."

Mama put on her somber face. "Indeed, you are right, Lady Lynbury. It was a dreadful shock. Poor Lord Westerlynn! What a dear soul he was. How we grieve at his loss."

"I understand Rissa was with him when he died?" prompted Lady Lynbury.

"Most unfortunately, yes." Mama gave an appropriate sigh. "Dear Rissa conducted herself with the utmost bravery, despite the shocking circumstances. I am afraid she won't be joining us today. She has not been the same since it happened and is upstairs lying down. Still in a dreadful state of shock, I might add."

"A terrible, terrible shame," stated Lady Lynbury, grimly shaking her head. "Such irony that he died the very day after he—well, you know." The stout matron took a sudden interest in stirring her tea.

What is she talking about? thought Clarinda, curious despite herself.

The whole room went suddenly silent. "I know *what*?" asked Mama, a bit too sharply, but perhaps no one noticed.

"My dears, you will simply never believe what I just heard." Lady Constance paused, making sure all eyes were upon her. "I have it on good authority from my nephew, who was in London at the time, that Lord Westerlynn had squandered most of his fortune, and the day before he died—you are not going to believe this!"

An impatient chorus of "Tell us!" filled the room.

"He gambled away Hollyridge Manor in a game of whist."

"What?" sounded astonished voices.

"Tossed it all," reiterated Lady Lynbury, hardly concealing her delight at the sensation she had created.

Clarinda sat shocked and horrified. What had possessed Lord Westerlynn to risk his precious family estate? And what man was greedy enough—heartless enough—to take it away from him? "Who was the villain who stole Lord Westerlynn's estate?" she asked.

"Why, it was Robert, Lord Stormont, the Earl of Marsett," replied Lady Lynbury. Having set the whole room into shocked confusion, she sat back content. "But you mustn't say 'steal,' my dear, he won it honestly enough."

"Who is Lord Stormont?" Clarinda demanded, feeling a rising anger. "I never heard of him."

"Of course not," said Mama. "He was once quite the rake, but now remains much of the time at his estate in Kent. Breeds horses, I believe. These past years, he has eschewed London society like the plague."

"I have seen him. He is quite handsome," chirped Agatha in a birdlike voice.

"So have I," Mama remarked, "many times at the balls and soirees in London, though not recently. He's rather blunt—what you would call a man's man. Never been married, either, although I can assure you, half the marriageable girls in London were after him at one time or another."

Agatha said, "He is one of those men all the ladies notice when he walks into a room." She lowered her voice as if to impart a delicious confidence. "Who knows how many high-ranking ladies he's charmed into his bed?"

"Agatha!" Lady Lynbury was so jolted her tea splashed into her saucer.

But Agatha evinced no shame. "It is true! The man positively radiates masculinity, if you know what I mean."

Clarinda couldn't resist. "No, do tell us what you mean, Agatha."

"Clarinda!" Mama gave her a warning look.

Uh-oh. Watch out, Clarinda told herself. *Think of Donegal next time you open your mouth.*

At that moment a pale, wan Rissa appeared in the doorway, dressed exactly like Clarinda in a white lawn tea gown with short scallop-shaped sleeves edged in ruffled lace, and a lace-trimmed scalloped edging at the hemline. The gown had a lavender sash that matched the rose at her bosom and her satin scarf, draped artfully over her shoulders.

The ladies burst into warm greetings as Rissa, affecting a martyred expression, crossed the room, and collapsed artistically next to Clarinda on the striped floral settee. "Do forgive me, I've had such a frightful headache," she said in her sweet, tinkling voice, "but I could not resist coming down to see you."

Lady Lynbury said, "We were sorry to hear of your recent . . . er . . . horrifying experience. How upsetting for you."

"You are too kind, Lady Lynbury," murmured Rissa, placing a hand over her heart. "I was not thinking of myself, but only how I might help poor Lord Westerlynn. Such a sad, regrettable, terrible loss."

From across, Agatha, who had been staring, declared, "Why you're twins! And as alike as two peas in a pod!"

Clarinda gritted her teeth.

Rissa blithely replied, "Yes we are, aren't we? When we were little, even Mama could not tell us apart. She still can't."

"Except for your necklaces," Mama agreed. "Show us your necklaces, girls. Do you see? On Rissa's there's an "R" intertwined among the gold filigree of the pendant. Clarinda owns the same necklace, only with a filigreed "C." They have worn their necklaces constantly since they were little, so that people could tell them apart." She flashed an annoyed glance at Clarinda. "Where is your necklace?"

Two peas in a pod again. How she hated this! Clarinda's first impulse was to refuse to say, but she thought of Donegal, and how she might lose him. She pulled out the gold chain she'd tucked beneath her dress. "Mine has a 'C' on it," she said affably, running her finger over the delicate filigree.

"It must be marvelous fun, being a twin," said Agatha. "You must be inseparable."

Radiating affection, Rissa took Clarinda's hand, covering it with her own. "My dear twin and I cannot bear to be parted."

"But what happens when you marry?" asked Agatha.

"How perceptive you are!" Rissa chimed. "But we have the perfect solution. Have you ever heard of twins marrying twins?"

"You don't mean"—Agatha's eyes went wide—"the Sufton twins?"

"Yes," crowed Rissa triumphantly. "The Sufton twins, who as you know, bring ten thousand pounds a year, if they bring one, and live at Bolton Hall when they're not in London. It's not official yet, but don't be surprised if I marry Lawrence, whereas Clarinda shall marry Larimore." Her mouth twisted into a satisfied grin. "Then we shall all live blissfully at Bolton Hall the rest of our lives."

Mama beamed approval. "The Lords Sufton are coming from London for our ball next Friday night, and to stay the weekend. Don't be surprised what announcements may come of it." She slanted a meaningful glance at Clarinda. "Isn't that right, Clarinda?"

Clarinda's heart sank. How she hated to be reminded. What was left of her freedom might be coming to an end sooner than she thought.

Chapter 3

Robert and Lucius were dining at White's when the venerable Sir Godfrey Wynne, leaning heavily on his cane, stopped by their table.

"Have you heard about old Westerlynn? The poor fellow popped off yesterday. Heard his heart gave out." Sir Godfrey cocked his head. "I say, Stormont, wasn't it you who won Westerlynn's estate the other night? Good timing, eh?"

Never one to reveal his emotions, Robert concealed his shock as he lay down his fork and quietly said, "It was I, Sir Godfrey. Where did it happen?"

"They say he was on his way to his estate, but never made it. Breathed his last breath in that old oak coach of his on Lord Capelle's doorstep." Sir Godfrey mumbled, "More's the pity," as he hobbled away.

"Sorry," Lucius ventured.

"So am I," Robert replied. "Westerlynn had his eccentricities, but he wasn't a bad sort." *Damme! I should never have let myself be talked into that game of whist.*

"It was not your fault."

Lucius possessed an uncanny knack for reading his mind—sometimes too uncanny. Robert heaved a sigh and briefly shut his eyes. He didn't feel like talking.

"Damnation, Robert, the man was at least eighty."

Robert slowly shook his head from side to side. "Give up, Lucius. It damn well was my fault."

"But he badgered you, remember? Insisted that you play. You're wrong to feel guilty."

"Never fear, Lucius, guilt's a useless emotion. I feel responsible, though."

"Look at the bright side. Hollyridge Manor is yours now."

"I suppose it is, but I don't take any pleasure in it."
Robert abruptly stood, throwing down his napkin. "What's
done is done. Now it appears I have a huge estate on my
hands."

"You had best go see it for yourself. Then you can dispose of it, or whatever you wish to do."

"I suppose I must go see the place. Where is it?"

"On the upper Thames, near Maidenhead in Berkshire.
Did you know it borders Capelle's estate?" When Robert
looked puzzled, Lucius explained, "Lord Capelle, the one
with the beautiful blond twins. One of them was betrothed
to Jeffrey, Lord Lansdale. Surely you remember." Lucius
raised an eyebrow when Robert shook his head. "You see
what you miss when you bury yourself in the country?"

"It is a miracle I survive that far from London," Robert
answered with a grin. "But I do recall Lord Lansdale.
Weak-spined, as I recall. Writes abominable poetry. In the
navy, is he not?"

"Good going, Robert. Your weak-spined Lord Lansdale
died a hero at Trafalgar, practically at Nelson's feet."

Robert grimaced. "I feel like a dolt."

"No harm done. Actually you're right. Only a noble
death could have changed Jeffrey from a tiresome fool into
a hero." Mercifully Lucius changed the subject. "Old Westerlynn was famous for his stables. As I recall, upwards to
twenty horses at last count."

Robert brightened. "Horses?"

"Prime horseflesh for the most part, judging from what
I've heard."

"I shall immediately make arrangements to travel to
Hollyridge Manor. Shall you come along?"

Lucius's eyes brightened. "But of course. The London
romps have become quite boring. I should like to try my
luck with some of those rosy-cheeked country girls."

Suddenly Robert's head was full of plans. He would
quickly dispose of Hollyridge Manor, and then . . .

How difficult would it be to transport a number of horses
from Hollyridge Manor to Oakley House? He would soon
find out.

"Rissa, we have to talk."

It was the day after Mama's "at home" and Clarinda had

just settled herself on the chaise in Rissa's bedchamber. Knowing Rissa's penchant for avoiding serious discourse, Clarinda was determined that for once her sister would hear her out, not cleverly change the subject as she usually did when the topic took on any depth.

Rissa was seated at her dressing table, twining her hair atop her head in a new coiffeur. "What do you think?" she asked, twisting around, "should I pull my hair back or cover my ears? Should I—?"

"You can cut it all off for all I care," answered Clarinda. That should get her attention.

"Why, sister!" Rissa's lower lip protruded in a pout. "My, my, aren't we testy today!"

"I have something to say to you, Rissa, and you are going to hear me out."

Rissa turned to gaze at herself in her mirror again and took up her comb. "Go ahead if you must," she said lightly. "I am all ears."

"Do you remember how close we were when we were little children?"

"Of course. I can remember looking in the mirror and thinking I was you."

Clarinda nodded agreeably. "I used to wake up in the morning and when I saw you in your bed I would wonder, how do I know I am me?"

"I loved being a twin," Rissa said brightly, "and I still do. I love dressing alike, and all the attention we receive. Do you remember all those pranks we played when we were little? Me pretending to be you, and you pretending to be me?" She giggled. "No one could tell us apart and they still can't, except for Estelle and Alexander."

"I am sick of it," Clarinda said, not joining in her sister's laughter.

"Whatever do you mean?" Rissa put down her comb. Puzzled, she turned in her chair and asked, "Are we not still inseparable?"

"That's what I came to talk to you about." Clarinda paused. She and Rissa had truly been as one when they were children. Yet, her relationship with her twin had not been all that wonderful. She could remember how Rissa invariably grew angry when she didn't receive attention first, and how everything had to be exactly equal. If it wasn't, Rissa would throw herself on the floor and kick and scream. When they were older, Rissa still managed nearly always to get her way. She had discovered that a tear or two rolling from her big blue eyes could work wonders, accompanied, of course, by a feigned sweetness, which Clarinda never saw through. Nor could anyone else. Mama—Papa—nanny—the governess—praised Rissa for her sweet disposition. Whereas she, Clarinda, was the obstinate, rebellious twin who was always getting into trouble. "What I'm trying to say is that I don't want for us to be inseparable anymore. I want to be my own person. I don't want to dress like you or act like you."

Rissa's eyes grew wide. "Why, sister, I am astounded. Don't you love me anymore? How could you be so cruel?"

"I do love you," Clarinda earnestly declared. "How could I not? You are my twin, my other self. But it's just that"—this would be so hard to explain, but she would have to try—"we're twenty now, not children anymore, and I want to lead my own life and not feel half of a whole."

"But are we not going to marry the Suftons?" Rissa's brows drew together in a frown. "Aren't we going to live together in Bolton Hall for the rest of our lives?"

"Not if I can help it."

Rissa's mouth dropped open. "Oh, how hurtful! Surely you can't mean what you're saying."

Until recently, Clarinda would have succumbed to Rissa's supposed distress and backed down. Now, perhaps because she had matured, Clarinda saw her sister through new eyes, and though she loved her sister still, she was wise to Rissa's tricks and devious ways. They no longer affected her. They shouldn't have before, except she was too young and trusting to understand such duplicity. Now she could see that over the years her twin had manipulated and controlled her in many ways. Maybe Mama and Papa were still fooled, *but not me anymore.*

"Listen carefully, Rissa. Mama and Papa may insist that I marry Larimore, but I don't want you talking about it anymore, do you understand? And I don't want you saying how we're going to spend the rest of our lives together because it is my fervent hope that we do not."

Not to Clarinda's surprise, Rissa's pout disappeared, replaced by an expression of indignation. Fists clenched, she stood abruptly and declared, "Mama shall hear of this."

"Fine. Tattle if you must. As things stand now, I shall probably be forced to capitulate and marry Larimore. I'm only telling you—*begging* you, please don't help his cause. And *please,* stop telling Mama we must dress alike."

"You never knew what was best for you," Rissa declared. Her voice had lowered. She didn't sound sweet anymore. "You don't fool me. I know why you're saying these terrible things."

"Why?" asked Clarinda, guessing she already knew.

"It's Jeffrey, isn't it? That's why you're doing this—you're jealous."

"Jealous of what?" asked Clarinda. This was just like Rissa—never taking criticism, always attacking back.

"Admit it! You loved Jeffrey and it killed you when he decided he loved me."

"Jeffrey is dead. Don't you think your accusation is a touch beside the point?" What was the use? Clarinda wondered. Arguing with her twin was like trying to capture the wind. "Whether I loved Jeffrey or not doesn't matter. All I want is to be left alone."

"It is absolutely ridiculous that you don't want to be a twin anymore." Rissa's demeanor had turned hostile.

How frustrating! Why did her sister always twist what she said? "Rissa, I don't want to fight. I want things to be good between us."

"Admit you loved Jeffrey!"

As usual, Rissa would hear only what she wanted to hear. *So why should I hide the truth?* "All right, Rissa, if you must hear it—I did love Jeffrey. I loved him for the poetry he wrote, and his gentleness, and the dreamy look in his eye. I shall love him until the day I die, but he was yours, not mine, and I would never have—" Clarinda stopped abruptly. She had been about to say that she would never have thought twice about Jeffrey if he hadn't first paid attention to her, not Rissa. Later, for reasons unknown, he had dropped her and began courting Rissa. How hurt she had been! But nothing would be gained from voicing that particular recollection. "Rissa, You must know that I did not, in any way, even consider stealing Jeffrey from you. When he died, I was grateful I hadn't tried. My conscience was clear, thank goodness. I so admired your courage. You hardly cried, and I was so proud of you, knowing the deep grief you must have felt inside."

"I suppose I was brave, wasn't I?" Rissa turned sweet again and smiled. "Come to your senses, Clarinda. We are twins, never to be parted no matter what you say."

"You will never understand." Clarinda wondered why she had even bothered. She got up off the bed to leave.

"Before you go"—Rissa cocked her head to one side— "I have a question about Sara Sophia."

What now? Rissa had never evinced the slightest interest in Sara Sophia. "What question?"

"What do you know about her? Her background, I mean, like where she comes from."

"No one knows where she comes from. Her mother's name was Louise, I know that much. She died of some illness when Sara Sophia was four or five, but where she came from, or how she happened to be under the care of Lord Westerlynn, I have no idea. Why do you ask?"

"Just curious." Rissa gave an elaborate shrug. "I was just thinking how hard Lord Westerlynn's death must be on Sara Sophia. Will she stay on at Hollyridge, do you think?"

"Probably not. She's talking of obtaining a position as a governess." Amazing, this sudden concern for the orphaned girl who had no standing. What was Rissa up to? Something devious, Clarinda would wager, since the total of Rissa's sympathy and compassion would fit into a thimble, with room left over.

Back in her bedchamber, Clarinda fell on her bed, totally disheartened. She had tried to declare her independence, but Rissa would never understand—didn't want to understand. A thought occurred to her. Perhaps, if she promised to find a husband, Mama and Papa would allow her to go to London for another Season. She could easily find a suitor, one who would marry her and take her far away from Graystone Hall. A man who, though she may not love, she might at least respect.

But the very thought wrenched her heart. She had no desire to leave the only home she'd ever known, and Alexander, Sara Sophia, her beloved Donegal, Sham, and all the beautiful horses at Hollyridge Manor. They were her life. She had no desire to marry. No man on this earth could ever take the place of her dreamy-eyed poet. Blinded by tears, Clarinda reached to her bed table for a small, worn book of poetry by Robert Burns. Jeffrey had given her this book, back before he'd spurned her for Rissa. The book fell open to a page wherein lay a withered rose. The poem on the page was the one he had read her that day in the garden when he'd kissed her and given her the rose. Her heart aching, Clarinda read "Ae Fond Kiss" once more, for at least the hundredth—the thousandth? time.

> ". . . Had we never lov'd sae kindly,
> Had we never lov'd sae blindly!
> Never met—or never parted,
> We had ne'er been broken-hearted . . ."

Oh, Jeffrey! Each night before she went to sleep she closed her eyes and pictured Jeffrey in his naval uniform, so splendidly handsome in his blue coat, white waistcoat and breeches, cross belt and sword. She would love him always, and mourn him until the day she died.

She could not even imagine falling in love with someone else.

"Good grief!" declared Lucius, nodding toward the less-than-immaculate floor in the main salon, "are there no servants in this place?"

Robert nodded his head in disbelief. They had arrived at Hollyridge Manor less than an hour ago. After he had convinced Jennings, the butler, he was indeed the new owner, and seen that the horses and Jasper, his favorite hunting dog, were watered and fed, he had Jennings take them on a tour of the manor.

"Hollyridge was built around the middle of the sixteenth century," Jennings explained as they started to look around the several floors of the huge mansion. "It was built over the ruins of a medieval castle, of which nothing remains except a gatehouse that stands in a remote corner."

Despite himself, Robert was impressed. This was indeed a magnificent estate, twice the size of his own Oakley House. "How many servants are employed?"

"At the moment only eleven, sir. Myself, the housekeeper, the cook, two footmen, two housemaids, and two scullery maids, plus the groom and one stable boy."

"Not nearly enough," Robert commented. "Maintaining an estate like this should properly require a staff of fifty servants at the very least."

"We once employed nearly sixty servants," the butler replied. "Mind you, that was back in the good old days when the house was filled with guests every week. They came in droves, mainly for the fox hunts."

Lucius shook his head. "Westerlynn must have been in his dotage to allow Hollyridge to fall into a state of neglect like this."

"A pity," answered Jennings. "Actually there's one more person living here, a girl of eighteen named Sara Sophia."

"Is she a servant?" Robert asked.

"Er . . . no, m'lord, not exactly. She is neither fish nor fowl, so to speak. Her mother died shortly after they arrived. The girl was around three or four then. As far as I know, she is not his lordship's kin, yet she always ate in the dining room and was accorded all the privileges of a guest, not a servant."

"What's to become of her?" Lucius asked. "Is she aware she cannot stay?"

"Indeed, she is, sir. I believe the young lady has plans to become a governess."

"There's a blessing," Robert commented, pleased a potential problem was so quickly resolved. "Where are the stables?" Forget the house, he had been looking forward with keen anticipation to seeing Westerlynn's horses.

A dark-haired young woman of diminutive stature was calming a skittish Arabian stallion when Robert and Lucius arrived at the stone-walled, moss-covered coach house and stables. She was probably one of the servants, Robert surmised, noting her plain gray dress, white apron, and sturdy, mud-covered half boots.

"What a beautiful horse," he called.

The horse reared upward, pawing the air wildly with its hooves. "Steady," said the girl in a calm, soothing voice. It was clear, from her firm grip on the reins, she had no fear of horses.

"Yes, he is beautiful," she called, "his name is Sham."

They moved closer. "Sham?" asked Lucius. "What kind of name is that?"

"It's Arabic for the sun." The girl regarded them with large, luminous brown eyes. "And who might you be?"

Robert introduced himself and Lucius, and informed her he was the new owner. ". . . so I have come to see the stables."

The girl stood stunned. "So Hollyridge Manor doesn't go to the nephew? It belongs to you now?" He nodded. "And the horses, too," she said softly, almost as if to herself.

"Yes, the horses. I breed horses myself and will most likely have them all removed to my own estate in Kent, at least the good ones." Robert looked toward the field next to the stable where a dozen or so horses were grazing. "They're all out there?"

"Most, m'lord." Her voice quivered. She appeared stricken.

"What is it?" Lucius asked. Robert noticed he'd been gazing at the girl steadily.

"It's just . . . nothing." The girl bit her lip, then took a deep breath, as if forcing herself to be in control. "It will be good that they have a new home. Of late they've been neglected."

"Is this part of your duties?" Lucius asked. Robert was surprised at the gentleness in his voice.

"My duties?" the girl asked, puzzled.

Lucius replied, "I would surmise you're one of the parlor maids, and because you love horses, you're here, helping out at the stables. Am I not right?"

The girl looked down at her servant's garb, then at Lucius. "Sir, judging by my appearance I cannot fault you for thinking I'm a parlor maid." She raised her chin high. "But I am not."

"Then who—?" Lucius began, then halted. "Ah yes, you must be Sara Sophia. The butler mentioned you."

"And no doubt mentioned I am neither fish nor fowl," she said wryly.

"No, er, yes, perhaps he mentioned it."

Robert noticed Lucius appeared discomfited—most unusual for a man whose easy way with women was well known in London. He started toward the field. "Want to check the horses with me, Lucius?"

"No, you go ahead. I shall join you shortly."

Robert laughed to himself as he climbed over the wooden fence that surrounded the pasture. Lucius was well on his way to making his first country conquest.

Wonderful horses! Marvelous horses! Thoroughbreds for the most part, the Arabian, and a couple of Cleveland Bays. Also two old hacks he would have to dispose of.

When Robert returned to the stables, Sara Sophia had gone. He clapped Lucius on his shoulder and joshingly remarked, "Looks as though you'll have someone to warm your bed tonight."

Before he answered, Lucius gazed reflectively at the sky. "I don't think so," he finally replied in a strangely quiet voice. "Sara Sophia is a mere dab of a girl, and yet she's . . . there's something about her I don't know how to describe."

"Beware, Lucius. She has no money, no title."

"Yes, I know," Lucius answered hastily. "And yet . . . did you see those eyes? Did you hear her soft voice? Not that I would allow myself to be smitten, but she's one of the most beautiful women I have ever met."

"Oh, come, Lucius." Robert eyed his friend with incredulity. "Perhaps you should not have left London. I fear this country air is affecting your brain."

Chapter 4

The next morning, Clarinda awoke early, as she always did, eager for her before-breakfast ride. She was searching through her walnut armoire for her old gray riding gown when Estelle entered.

"If you are looking for your riding gown, eet ees gone, m'lady. Her ladyship ordered that I give eet to the gardener to be burned."

"And did you?"

Estelle allowed herself a subtle smile. "Not really. But you had best be careful about wearing it again. Meanwhile . . ." Estelle hastened to the armoire and pulled out the fancy riding ensemble Mama had ordered made for her a good two years ago. Clarinda had stuffed it into the far back corner, where it had remained, unworn.

"Her ladyship says you must wear thees."

Damnation! But if I want to keep Donegal, I have no choice. "Oh, very well." With Estelle's assistance, Clarinda donned the riding habit, matching hat, and boots.

"You look marvelous, m'lady."

"I absolutely loathe it." Clarinda scowled at her image in her full-length mirror. The habit was of plain black, ornamented entirely across the bosom with a thick roll of rich green silk braiding. The riding hat that perched atop her blond curls was of black beaver, fancifully adorned with gold *cordon* and tassels. "How ridiculous," she declared, tweaking the long, green ostrich feather that stuck up in the front. Black half boots, laced and fringed with green, completed the ensemble, which, she thought with disgust, was totally unsuitable for her kind of hard riding. "I look like an idiot in matching black and green," she remarked with a grimace at herself as she pulled on York tanned gloves.

"But m'lady ees at the height of fashion."

"The sun has hardly risen, Estelle. The riding path will hardly be swarming with people I can impress."

Soon Clarinda was leading Donegal from the stables to the seclusion of the river path. *At least the skirt is full,* she thought, as, with a strong spring, she boosted herself onto the horse's back, and after the usual furtive look around, rearranged her skirt and swung her leg across. *I shall visit Sara Sophia, I don't care what Mama says.* With the spurt of joy she always felt at the start of a ride, she snapped the reins and urged Donegal into a brisk trot. She mustn't ride too long, she thought. The ball was tonight. Soon, the seamstress would arrive to put the finishing touches on hers and Rissa's ball gowns. Identical, of course. *I won't need a mirror to see myself, I shall just look at Rissa.*

Clarinda's joy faded. Would Mama ever tire of gloating about the major triumph of her life—producing twins? Already Clarinda could hear the tired old remarks tonight.

Why, Lady Capelle, your twins are alike as two peas in a pod . . .

However can you tell them apart . . . ?

How adorable they look in their matching ball gowns . . .

Mama never heard the other remarks, like, *they look like freaks!*

They—they—they, never *she.* Sometimes Clarinda thought she would die from the longing to be just herself, but she would have to grit her teeth and endure the ball tonight. It would not be easy. The Lords Sufton would both be in attendance. She was not at all sure she could endure Larimore, plus whatever other tortures her parents had in store for her. But she had better face the fact that Larimore, Lord Sufton, might well become her husband. Perhaps he wouldn't be so bad, she tried to convince herself. Larimore would never oppose her in anything she did. He was rich! He was titled! *But he's dull as dishwater.*

Time for a gallop. Nothing like racing with the wind on her beloved horse to chase problems away. Clarinda nudged Donegal, loving the feel of his sleek, warm coat between her knees. Both knees. How a woman could enjoy riding sidesaddle was beyond her. She could not abide having to give prompts with one leg, and for the offside rely on carrying a cane. "Let us be off, Donegal!"

The willing mount leaped forward and raced at lightning speed along the path by the river that led to Hollyridge Manor.

As was his custom, Robert awoke early. His first thought was of his newly acquired horses, most particularly, Sham. Arabians were a superb breed. What luck to find a marvelous Arabian stallion like Sham, beautiful with his fine arched neck, flowing mane, and tail. Arabians were intelligent, too, noted for their endurance. Robert would ride him this morning and test him out. With high anticipation, he quickly washed and dressed in plain riding clothes. "Come, Jasper," he called to his hunter, and hastened to the stables.

Old Pitney, the groom, was there when he arrived. "Could you get Sham's saddle for me?" Robert requested. "I'll saddle him myself." The old man hesitated, only for the merest trace of a moment, but long enough for Robert to notice, and comprehend. "Yes, I know, Sara Sophia rides Sham, doesn't she?" The old man nodded, eyeing him resentfully. "Keep in mind the horses are mine now, Pitney. Go on, there's a good fellow, get the saddle."

Soon, with Jasper running alongside, Robert left the stables and guided Sham to a heavily wooded path that ran alongside the river. He put Sham to a trot. Quickly discovering the horse's smooth, floating gait, he congratulated himself on being right about his magnificent new stallion. What a beautiful path this was, he thought as he rode along, catching glimpses of a blue ribbon of river through the heavy growth of ancient alder, willow, and ash trees. Oakley House had no river, he mused, no riding path with a breathtaking view like this one. It was smaller, too, not half the size of Hollyridge, nor half as elegant. Perhaps, Robert thought, he should not sell this huge estate after all. But that was madness. Hollyridge must go. He put Sham to a brisk gallop. The horse performed magnificently, further adding to Robert's fine mood.

At last they came to an open meadow. Robert reined in Sham and swung off. With Jasper by his side, he found a fallen log, and sat, allowing himself to relax and take in the beauty of the verdant green meadow, tall trees, and the river beyond.

He heard the sound of pounding hoofs. Swinging his gaze

to the opposite direction from whence he'd come, he saw a galloping chestnut horse—Irish hunter, he should imagine—burst from the wooded path into the meadow. Atop him sat a young woman, blond, in a black-and-green riding habit, riding astride. *Most unusual* was his first thought. In fact, he could not recall when he had ever seen a woman . . .

"Jasper, come back!"

The dog, ordinarily obedient, had left his side and was streaking across the meadow, bent, it appeared, on nipping at the horse's heels.

"Jasper! Jasper!"

Too late. The horse spied the approaching dog and its eyes went wide with fright. In a twinkling, the horse shied one way and the rider flew another—a blur of black and green, hurtling off the horse's back, striking the ground hard, rolling over—over—over.

"Dear God," Robert exclaimed, as he ran toward the small, still figure. She could be badly injured. She could be dead.

When he got close, he heard her gasping. The grunting, heaving noises sounded awful, but hearing them, he rejoiced. She was alive! He willed his heart to stop its hammering and the invisible shaking in his limbs to go away as he knelt beside her and asked, "Are you all right?"

In the bottomless, black whirlpool that had enveloped her, Clarinda could hear lung-deep, desperate gasping, punctuated by pitiful, inhuman wails. What weird sounds! Then she heard a deep, masculine voice asking someone if they were all right. As the voice kept repeating the question, the distressing noises faded away. Gradually, she became aware she was lying on soft grass, that her eyes were closed, the sun was warming her face, and her entire insides felt shaken. She tried to open her eyes, but nothing happened. She tried again, willing them to open, and they did.

A strange man knelt over her, holding both her hands. In the bright, early morning sunlight, she could see his face—quite handsome, she noted, but drawn with concern. With an effort she asked, "What were those awful noises?"

"*You* were making them. You had the breath jolted out of you."

"I did? Where am I?"

"You're lying in the middle of a meadow." Robert briefly looked around, relieved to see that her horse was standing nearby, peacefully grazing, as if nothing unusual had occurred. "You fell from your horse."

"I did?" She looked surprised and slightly indignant. "But I never fall."

He hastened to repair her wounded pride. "You are not in any way to blame. The horse shied. Because of my hunter, I regret to say. For some reason, Jasper decided to chase after your gelding. Most unusual. He doesn't usually . . ." This was no time to make excuses for his dog. "Tell me, are you all right?"

"I . . . I don't know."

"Then shall we find out?" He helped the girl to a sitting position. Her beaver hat had fallen off. "Allow me," he said, and brushed away twigs and pieces of dried grass entwined in her hair. There was a slight cut on her forehead. He reached for his handkerchief. "You've a cut," he said.

"Is it bad?" Her voice was unsteady.

"Not really." While he daubed the bleeding area gently, he could not escape a keen awareness that he was but inches away from a beautiful young woman whose hair tumbled down her back in a mass of soft gold; who had skin of soft ivory and eyes of angelic blue. There were dimples at the corners of a mouth so rosy, so temptingly curved, it begged to be kissed. She was like a Dresden doll, he thought.

A waft of her light perfume, jasmine he'd wager, reached his nostrils. From out of nowhere he felt a wrench of desire deep within himself. *Bloody hell, where did that come from? Control yourself, Stormont!* With an effort, he put away his lustful thought, but when he accidentally touched her hair, and felt how smooth and silky it was, again something intense flared deep within. *What am I thinking of?* Chagrined with himself, he quickly told her, "Move your arms—your legs. Does anything hurt?"

She did as he requested with no winces of pain. "Really, I am fine, although I feel as if somebody kicked me in the stomach with their Wellingtons on."

He felt a vast relief. "What luck you landed on soft, grass-covered ground. Except for that small cut, and getting the breath knocked out of you, you don't appear to be hurt."

She looked down at herself, discovering that her skirt had ridden up over her riding boots, revealing a long, rather extensive, stretch of her slender legs. Unconcerned, she pulled her skirt down, remarking with a faint grin, "It appears I have lost my dignity along with my breath."

"Who are you?" he asked.

"I am Clarinda Capelle, from Graystone Hall."

"Ah, one of the twins."

Instantly she stiffened. A gleam of annoyance flashed through her eyes. Puzzled, he asked, "Have I said something to offend you?"

"You would not possibly understand," she answered, though not unkindly. "Would you help me up?"

"You're sure you feel all right?" he asked, just as Jasper, wagging his tail, bounded up to the girl and gave her a friendly lick on her cheek.

"Jasper, stop that!" he commanded. *Cursed animal. If he expects his extra treat tonight* . . .

She stared at the dog, then burst into laughter. "Now he wants to be my friend." She wrapped her arms around the dog and hugged him tight. "That's all right, Jasper, you didn't mean it, did you, boy?" She turned her magnetic blue eyes up at Robert. "Don't be mad at him."

"I . . . no, of course not." His heart had recommenced its pounding, but this time for a reason that had nothing to do with alarm. Now he was the one who was breathless. It was as if this beautiful young creature had cast some sort of spell over him. *Dammit, man, pull yourself together.*

She extended her hand. "Help me up?"

When she was on her feet again, he could not fail to notice that concealed beneath her prim black riding habit were a tiny waist, finely curved hips, and firm, full breasts. She was taller than most, although because of his own great height, the top of her head came only a touch above his chin.

She bent, busying herself brushing bits of grass from her skirt. When she raised up, she asked, "And who are you?"

"I am Robert Stormont."

"Lord Stormont?" The friendliness in her eyes vanished.

"The one who stole Hollyridge Manor from Lord Wester-lynn?"

"The very same," he said, ardently wishing he could deny the fact. "But see here, I didn't steal Hollyridge, I won it. There's a difference."

"Not to me." She looked at him as if she'd just discovered him slithering out from under a rock. She backed a step away, an unconscious response, he supposed, yet a clear indication of her hostility. Coolly she said, "I had planned to visit Sara Sophia this morning. I must be on my way."

"Very well." He watched as she retrieved her hat from beneath a bush and set it firmly atop her head. She walked to her horse, which stood quietly and made no fuss when she gathered up the reins, then patted him on the nose and whispered something no doubt soothing into his ear.

"May I help you up?" he inquired pleasantly. Not for the world would he let her know he had taken note of her incivility.

She hesitated. He knew exactly what was going through her mind. It was clear she did not want him to help her, but if she didn't, he, a complete stranger, would be witness to what would have to be, at best, a most unladylike leap. He hid a chuckle. Surely her parents were not aware she rode astride.

So what is to be, Lady Clarinda? Will you leap, skirts flying, onto your horse, as you would like to do, and usually do, or will you . . . ?

"If you wouldn't mind," she said, her pert little nose high in the air, "I should like a boost."

"My pleasure," he said, and walked to the horse where she stood, ready to mount.

"When I first saw you, you were riding astride," he said. "Is that how—?"

"You are mistaken, sir," she replied without mirth. "A lady always rides sidesaddle."

"Really?" He took a long, leisurely look at the Irish hunter's bare back. "Then if you are riding sidesaddle, would it not be a good idea to put a sidesaddle on the horse?"

A frown line appeared between her golden brows. "Could you kindly put your hands together?" she tartly requested. "No doubt you are as anxious as I to be on your way."

"Quite so." If she expected him to form a loop with his hands that she could step into, she was sadly mistaken. "Bend your knee."

Startled, she asked, "What are you—?"

"Bend your knee," he commanded again in his no-nonsense voice, the one reserved for the occasional bull-headed servant. Without another word, she did so. He bent down, placed his large hands beneath her skirt, and firmly grasped her ankle, directly above her boot.

"Up you go!" With consummate ease he gave her a boost. She, instantly cooperating, lifted herself up, perching atop the horse in a movement both fluid and graceful. For an extra long moment, his hands refused to let go, and their contact with the smooth skin of her slender ankle caused that sudden heat within him to flare again. Finally he let go, though sorely tempted not to. She looked down, gravely regarding him. Their eyes locked. He could swear she knew what he was thinking. He backed off a step, keeping his face inscrutable, observing how she was sitting, both legs dangling on one side. "Well?" he inquired. "Surely you're not planning to ride sidesaddle without the saddle."

She was silent a moment, as if gravely considering the question he had posed. "No, I am not," she said, and with a short kick and a whirl of skirts, slung a leg to the other side. Triumphantly she looked down upon him. With a perfectly straight face she said, "In case you were not aware, sir, there are times when even a lady does not keep her legs together."

Why, the little minx! It was all he could do to keep from bursting into laughter, but he kept his face a blank. "But if she does not keep her legs together, then perhaps she is no lady."

She regarded him solemnly, although he would swear he caught a slight gleam of amusement in her eye. "I do believe we have exhausted that topic, m'lord. Good day."

Before he could say a word, the chestnut gelding began a skittish dance. With an expert nudge of her knees, and with a firm hold on the reins, the girl whispered, "Let us be off, Donegal."

Robert watched as the horse sprang away. At full gallop,

he and his beautiful rider fair flew across the meadow and disappeared into the trees toward Hollyridge Manor.

Lady Clarinda Capelle. An unwelcome surge of excitement ran through him as he stared after horse and rider. *But this will not do.* If there was anything he did not need right now it was an attachment. His life was complete, unshakably so. What more could he want than his thoroughbred hunters, an occasional trip to London to gamble, and, of course, an occasional visit with his current ladybird?

And yet . . . there was something different about this girl. She did not appear to be the simpering, bubble-headed belle he was accustomed to in London. Clearly she was no Dresden doll. This girl loved horses, that was clear . . .

Robert laughed to himself, remembering her saucy, most unladylike remark about ladies and their legs. He also remembered her hostile pose when she discovered he was the villain who had stolen Hollyridge from old Lord Westerlynn.

That girl does not like me, Robert mused. But all things considered, that was for the best, and hardly worth worrying about. In a few days he would be leaving, soon as he'd stripped Hollyridge of what he most wanted—those magnificent horses—and arranged for the sale of the estate. Never would he return.

So why even bother to think about her? Chances were he would never see her again.

Clarinda held Donegal to a gallop until she was sure she was well into the trees, out of Stormont's sight. Relieved, she slowed Donegal to a walk. Although she'd been loath to admit it, the fall had jarred her considerably. She was sure no bones were broken, but various parts of her body already ached, and would probably get worse.

She patted Donegal. "It was not your fault," she said aloud.

When she reached the stables at Hollyridge, she was relieved to see Sara Sophia in the courtyard, saddling one of the thoroughbreds. "I can't have Sham this morning," she called wistfully. "Lord Stormont has taken a liking to him."

"Who wouldn't?" Clarinda said as she slid from her horse. "Wait till you hear what happened . . ."

She related every detail of her early morning encounter with Lord Stormont, from the attack of his dog to that extra long moment when Stormont had boldly gripped her ankle while helping her back onto her horse.

"You're not hurt?" Sara Sophia asked after Clarinda had finished her tale.

"Only my pride. What do you think of him?"

"He seems quite civil."

"You wouldn't think badly of anyone," Clarinda said thoughtfully. "You know as well as I, he practically stole Hollyridge. The man's a villain."

"But a very handsome villain."

"True, he's not bad-looking by half," Clarinda grudgingly admitted.

"By half? The man is devilishly handsome. He must spend much of his time out-of-doors in order to have acquired that tanned skin."

Clarinda wrinkled up her nose. "It's not the least fashionable."

Sara Sophia laughed. "That sounds like something Rissa would say. Admit it. The man is most attractive."

Especially when he smiles that rakish smile, thought Clarinda, *and shows those straight, strikingly white teeth contrasted against his dark skin.* "It was extremely brazen of him to grab my ankle as he did. He held it extra long, and was not a gentleman. Papa would throw a fit if he found out."

"There's a conundrum!" Sara Sophia exclaimed. "You might wish to tell your father, but if you do, he'll doubtless discover you were riding without a saddle."

A new thought struck Clarinda. "Do you suppose Stormont was aware of that?"

"Probably. I find him exceedingly bright, and quite perceptive." Sara Sophia's eyes twinkled. "And I suspect he has a bit of the devil in him, too."

"Now that I think of it, of course he knew. No doubt he felt quite safe in allowing his hands to linger that extra moment on my ankle." Strange, how she did not feel the least bit indignant. She supposed she should express her disapproval, though. "That rogue!" How limp that sounded. No doubt Sara Sophia would see right through her pitiful attempt at indignation.

"I can see your anger knows no bounds," commented her wise friend with a slight raise of her eyebrow.

I was right. "Well, I can't fool you, can I? I suppose I

found him somewhat attractive. In fact"—she hesitated to make such an intimate confession, but Sara Sophia was never shocked by much of anything—"if you must know, I can still feel the warm spot where he clasped me. And I remember, too, there was a fleeting moment when I was lying there on the ground, and he was bending over me, only inches away, and . . ." Where were the words to explain such a sensual experience?

"Do go on," Sara Sophia said gently. "What good is a friend if you can't confide in her?"

"I was suddenly aware of him as a man. He was holding me in his arms. For a moment, all I could think was—now don't be shocked—I wanted him to kiss me."

Sara Sophia's expression grew tender. "I'm not shocked in the least. I think it's wonderful, and I wish that someday I might feel that way."

Clarinda continued, "Yesterday at Mama's tea that silly Agatha was describing him. She said, 'He positively radiates his masculinity . . . if you know what I mean.' Well, Agatha knew whereof she spoke. Now I know exactly what she meant."

"Then you like him."

"I do, and then I don't. When all is said and done, he is a dreadful man."

Sara Sophia looked puzzled. "Why so harsh? I have found him to be most courteous and kind, although"—she heaved a sigh—"I would have wished he hadn't ridden off on Sham today."

"Don't you see that's part of it?" Clarinda's expression clouded with anger. "What incredible greed, to take advantage of a defenseless old man well into his dotage. Stormont is no better than a thief, and we had better remember that. At least he has not been invited to the—" She stopped abruptly, but too late.

"To the ball tonight?" softly asked Sara Sophia. "Why do you blush? How could you think I didn't know there's a ball at Graystone Hall tonight when it's the talk of the countryside?"

"It's not fair. I did everything in the world to get Mama to invite you, but she simply would not."

"Say no more." Sara Sophia regarded her with those clear, observant eyes. "You needn't fear I'll be upset, or hurt, because I am not. Long ago, I learned my station in life. Rest assured, I am content.''

Clarinda regarded her skeptically. ''You're just saying that.''

''No, I'm not. Don't you understand? I am not the least impressed with your leisure world. It bothers me not one whit that I don't belong. Oh, of course, I love a good time, but I'm certainly not hurt, nor do I care that I'm ignored and not invited.''

''Still, it's deucedly unfair,'' said Clarinda, her cheeks flushed with anger.

''I'm only happy I have a friend like you, and I have Sham to ride—at least I did, and I've been able to live at this beautiful estate, run-down though it may be.'' Sara Sophia clasped Clarinda's hand. ''I so admire you, Clarinda—your high spirits—your passion for living. I'm so grateful you're my friend. I find it a true miracle that for some reason you want to spend more time with me than with your twin.''

''My twin,'' Clarinda repeated with a disdainful toss of her head. ''You wonder why I don't spend more time with Rissa?''

''I can guess, but you've never said.''

''I stay away from Rissa because she's selfish. No, beyond selfish. Because Rissa always gets her way.''

''But you're so strong-willed and independent. Why can't you stand up to her?''

''It's simple. According to my parents, Rissa is the good twin and I'm the bad.''

''But we know that's not true!''

Clarinda set her chin in a stubborn line. ''Let them think what they wish. I gave up trying to change their minds long ago.''

Riding home, Clarinda kept seeing Lord Stormont's anxious face as he bent over her. But enough! she told herself. She would put him out of her mind—think of the ball tonight.

Larimore. Her heart sank at the thought. She wished she didn't have to see him. Why didn't she break her skull when she fell off Donegal? Or an arm, or leg, or at the very least, sprained an ankle? Then she wouldn't have to attend the ball tonight.

Alas, she hadn't been that lucky.

*　*　*

When Clarinda arrived home, she found Mama and the seamstress in Rissa's bedchamber. They were putting final touches on Rissa's ball gown as she stood admiring herself before her full-length gilt mirror.

"Where have you been, Clarinda?" asked Lady Capelle.

Mama knew full well where she'd been. "Out riding, Mama, as I do every morning."

Mama glanced at her suspiciously. "I trust you didn't visit Sara Sophia."

Before she could answer, Rissa inadvertently saved her. "Oh, Clarinda! You've a scratch on your forehead, up near your hairline."

Damnation, I forgot. She should have checked herself in the mirror first. "It is nothing. I just had a little tumble from my horse."

Mama scowled, a not uncommon reaction at any mention of Clarinda's passion for riding. "Did Donegal stumble?"

"Donegal never stumbles. It was Lord Stormont's hunter who ran across the meadow and—"

"Lord Stormont!" Mama's eyes instantly lit with interest. "Do you mean to say he's here?"

"He's come to inspect his new property. Such a horrid man. I cannot abide the way he stole Hollyridge from Lord Westerlynn."

"Horrid?" Mama stared at her aghast. "No man is horrid who's unmarried, titled, and has an income in excess of twenty thousand pounds per year."

Rissa, who had been intent on regarding herself in the mirror, clasped her hands. "How exciting! We must invite him to the ball."

Mama nodded. "Indeed, we shall. Stormont has twice the fortune of the Suftons."

Estelle spoke up. "He's brought a friend along, m'lady. Lucius, Lord Wentridge."

"Uncanny, how the servants know everything first," Lady Capelle observed acidly. "Then we shall invite Lord Wentridge too."

Clarinda was disgusted with herself. Why did she have to mention Lord Stormont? Now he was invited to the ball. That made two men, each in his own way detestable, that she must deal with tonight.

Chapter 5

"You look splendid, Robert. The ladies will swoon at the sight of you."

"Let us hope not, Lucius," Robert answered fervently. The invitation to the ball at Graystone Hall had arrived. It was fortunate his valet had seen fit to bring along his dress clothes. In the entry hall of Hollyridge Manor, Robert pulled on buff kid gloves and offhandedly remarked, "Stay as late as you like, but I expect I'll be bored by ten o'clock and shall slip out early."

"Such enthusiasm," remarked Lucius, equally resplendent in a blue coat decorated with flat gilt buttons and black velvet collar. "Rustic, these country balls, yet they can be quite amusing."

"Lady Capelle's invitation was hardly one I could refuse," answered Robert, "but I lost my enthusiasm for balls long ago, whether city, country, or otherwise."

Robert expected his contentious friend to continue their sparring, but it appeared Lucius had another subject on his mind. Looking perplexed, he remarked, "I cannot understand why Sara Sophia was not invited."

Robert shrugged. "That's easy, she's not one of the *ton*."

Lucius let out a snort. "Those stiff-rumps in London won't settle for less than society's finest. But here? The guest lists at these country balls are not nearly as rigid."

"Hmm . . . I do believe you've taken a liking to the little wren."

Lucius immediately bristled. "Don't be absurd. I hardly know the girl, although we did engage in a pleasant chat this afternoon."

"A chat?" Robert asked skeptically. "You spent almost the entire day with her, and don't tell me otherwise."

Lucius seemed about to deny the accusation, then

thought better of it. "Though she may look it, Sara Sophia is not an insignificant little wren," he replied with feeling. "Never have I met a more perceptive, intelligent woman. Her interests know no bounds. Not only that, she has a sense of herself and her place in this universe. I'd wager she's smarter by half than most of these country bumpkins."

Robert gave him a look. "All London knows your penchant for intelligent women, Lucius. Flirtatious eyes and creamy white bosoms mean nothing to a high-minded gentleman like you."

"Laugh if you wish, Robert, I—" Lucius suddenly bit his lip and looked away, a muscle twitching in his jaw.

Robert was surprised to see his cynical friend, a master at covering his feelings, reveal such deep concern over anything besides his own well-being. "I see it's not a laughing matter. But you know as well as I, someone like Sara Sophia could not possibly—"

"Be good enough for me?" Lucius heaved what came close to a despairing sigh. "I know that. I accept that." A touch of bitterness echoed in his voice as he continued, "I have no idea why I should bother even speaking to a creature so low-born."

Robert started to protest, but Lucius wasn't through. "You're the smart one. Who would ever catch you being so impractical as to fall in love?"

"Quite so," agreed Robert. "I have much better sense, as do you, Lucius, if you'll take the time to reflect on how utterly impossible it would be for you to fall in love with a common girl with no money and no standing. Shall we go? I've ordered Sham and one of the thoroughbreds saddled."

"Very well," Lucius said, resigned. "At least we'll see the twins. There's a spectacle for you. I have never seen two human beings so exactly alike. Clarissa and Clarinda," he repeated with amusement, "even their parents can't tell them apart."

On their way out the door, the image of a slender young girl streaking across the field on her strong Irish hunter flashed, once again, through Robert's mind. The image had haunted him all day. Try as he might, he could not get rid of it. So she was a twin, not to be distinguished from her

sister? *I think not,* thought Robert as he swung upon Sham
and steadied the eager animal. There was only one Lady
Clarinda Capelle. He would always know who she was.

"Just look at us, Clarinda! No one will be as fashionable
as us tonight. We shall be the envy of the countryside."

Rissa, who had just dragged Clarinda in front of her mirror, stood next to her, gazing at herself in delight. "Don't
we look darling?"

"Darling is hardly the word," Clarinda glumly responded, although she had to admit they did not look half
bad in identical high-waisted gowns of soft white crepe,
ornamented with silver, elegantly embroidered around the
slashed sleeves and the hem with a rich border of gold
and silver.

Rissa plucked at the ringlets on her forehead. "Estelle,
you must pull these down a mite farther, just like Clarinda's
since she must cover up her scratch. Tonight we must look
exactly alike."

Clarinda was tempted to voice her disgust, but refrained.
The dress was lovely, she had to admit, and Estelle had
done a marvelous job dressing their hair in the antique
Roman style, bringing their longer tresses together and con-
fined at the back of their heads, terminating in ringlets held
by a clasp of pearls. They carried fans of mother-of-pearl
and wore pearl necklaces—no gold "C" tonight—pearl ear-
rings to match, white kid shoes and white gloves.

If I were alone, I should enjoy looking like this, Clarinda
thought. But she was not alone, she was only a duplicate.

Mama, dressed in elegant amber crepe over white sarce-
net, popped in, took a long, critical look, and nodded approval. "You'll do. Estelle, you have done an excellent job
of making them look as alike as . . ."

"Don't say it, Mama," Clarinda warned. If she heard two
peas in a pod again . . .

"Don't be a goose, Clarinda." Mama's usually down-
curved mouth actually turned up into a smile. "The Lords
Sufton have already arrived, as has half the countryside,
and that includes Lord Stormont and his friend, Lord Wentridge. It's nearly time for your grand entrance. Now be
sure to walk in unison as you go down the stairs. Hold
your fans the same. Try to smile the same, you'll create a

sensation. Lady Constance Lynbury has arrived. Be nice. You know the spiteful *on-dit* she could spread if your deportment is less than totally correct. Lord Cranmer is here. Mind you don't find yourself in a dark corner with him—you know what they say. Remember, Rissa, you are to devote your attention to Lawrence, whereas, Clarinda it is your duty to pay special attention to Larimore. Give him all your dances, unless, of course, Lord Stormont shows an interest, which, bearing in mind that Lord Stormont has twice the income of the Lords Sufton, then you must . . ."

Tired, tired, tired—I am so very tired of this. Clarinda had ceased to listen. This was going to be a horrible night. In the past, she hadn't minded the London Seasons. True, she had to dress like Rissa, but at least she could pick and choose the men she wished to dance with. Those days were over. Chances were she would betroth herself tonight to a man she didn't, and could never, love. *Think of Donegal,* she told herself, *and all the beautiful horses in the world.* That was the only way she could keep her sanity and get through this debacle.

Soon, abiding by her mother's request, Clarinda dutifully began a graceful sweep down the main staircase in synchronized step with her sister, their fans held at precisely the same angle. As for the smiles, Mama should be grateful she could manage a tiny upward curve of her lips, let alone match Rissa's dazzling effort. Below, she could see arriving guests milling about the main entry hall, most of them looking upward to watch The Grand Entrance of the Twins. *I shall be so glad when this is over.* She was halfway down the stairs when one particular pair of dark brown, nearly black eyes caught her attention—the eyes of Robert, Lord Stormont.

He was standing in a casual stance looking up at her in a manner both sharp and assessing. He briefly nodded and half smiled. She started to nod back, but then wondered whom was he nodding at—her or Rissa? In fact, how did he know which twin he was smiling at? And further, was his nod one of recognition or was he simply smiling at the freakish, ridiculous spectacle of two adult human beings striving to look exactly alike? She decided not to grant him a smile after all, but instead, turned her attention to the Lords Sufton, who stood at the bottom of the staircase looking up at them. Both were identically attired in dark, double-breasted frock coats and breeches. She was continually astounded they always dressed alike, even though they weren't compelled to. Good grief, even their cravats were tied exactly the same!

Rissa nudged her. "Which is which?" she whispered from behind her fan.

Clarinda raised her own fan. "That's Lawrence to the left, Larimore to the right."

"How can you tell?"

"Easy. Larimore's the balder of the two." Both twins had rapidly receding hairlines.

They reached the grand hallway, spectacular with its vaulted ceiling and high fanned windows. Rissa greeted Lawrence while Clarinda, turning on determined charm, murmured, "Good evening, Lord Sufton, how dashing you look tonight." What a lie. Both Lawrence and Larimore looked as bland as potato pudding with their small eyes of a nondescript color, undistinguished noses, and weak chins.

Larimore awarded her a deep bow. "You look dashing yourself, Lady uh, uh . . ."

"Clarinda."

"Ah, yes, Clarinda! I declare, you two are alike as—"

"And how was your journey from London, Lord Sufton?" This, indeed, was going to be a terrible night.

"Splendid weather," he answered, "It was a sunny day."

"Do tell. I had heard it might rain."

"Might rain? Oh, yes, yes, come to think of it, there were a few rain clouds in sight."

"Well, happily it did not rain, sir." How could she marry this milksop? She would be doomed to boredom the rest of her life.

The orchestra struck up a tune. "Might we dance, Lady Clarinda?" asked Larimore, regarding her with puppy dog eyes. "I hope I can have many of your dances. I hope . . . well, uh, uh, I might have something important to ask you before the night is over."

"Do tell, Lord Sufton." Ah, no, no, no! The end of the world was coming. How could she possibly say yes? But if she didn't . . .

What a pity Donegal would never appreciate the sacrifice she was about to make.

*   *   *

Well into the evening, Clarinda took a respite from her dancing and came to stand with Rissa and Mama.

"Well, has he asked yet?" inquired Mama.

"No."

"Hinted?"

"Perhaps. He—"

"Good evening, Lady Clarinda."

Lord Stormont. His tall presence had loomed in front of her so unexpectedly that for a moment she was speechless. "Good evening, sir," she said, recovering quickly. Remembering her manners, she performed introductions. Stormont had met both her parents in London on more than one occasion, but never Rissa, to whom he bowed briefly. Rissa, appearing instantly taken with him, started prattling her usual inanities, but he soon turned back to Clarinda. "Would you care to dance?"

Despite her aversion to the man, Clarinda could not think of a reason why not. She allowed herself to be led onto the dance floor. When they started dancing, she could not help but compare Larimore's limp clasp to the commanding manner in which Stormont's hand grasped her own. It was a firm hand, quite hard, not girl-soft, like Larimore's. *And only this morning it was brazenly clasped around my ankle.*

"You must have guessed which twin I was," said Clarinda as they began to swirl around the floor.

"It was not a guess."

"Then how did you—? Oh, I know, you saw the scratch on my forehead."

"It doesn't show."

"Then how?"

He pulled back and regarded her strangely. "Of course I know who you are. How could you think I would not?"

"But . . ." she began, faltered, and fell into silence. Could he really tell her apart from Rissa? Hardly anyone could, but then . . .

What a delightful possibility! Brightening, she looked him up and down. How magnificently tall he was, and how handsome with those snapping dark eyes and those dimples in his cheeks that magically appeared when he smiled. And how impeccably dressed, too. Perhaps he was not quite the villain she had thought he was. After all, Lord Westerlynn had been old but of sound mind. If he was fool enough to risk his estate in a ridiculous game, why blame Stormont?

"I trust you have recovered from your fall," said Lord Stormont.

"Completely." No sense mentioning her various aches and pains. They continued talking, mostly about horses, which she discovered he knew a great deal about.

"So shall you be living at Hollyridge Manor?" she inquired as the dance came to an end.

"No."

Startled, she asked, "Then what do you intend?"

"I plan to sell it."

She was almost afraid to ask. "And the horses?"

"Excellent stock, most of them," he said matter-of-factly. "I'll see they're transported to my estate in Kent."

"Including Sham?" she asked in a small voice. *Poor Sara Sophia.*

"Of course, Sham. A marvelous animal. I shall transport him, the Cleveland bays, and all the thoroughbreds. That's the lot, except for those two old pipers." He shrugged indifferently. "I'll have to get rid of them."

She had listened with rising dismay, and now a pain squeezed her heart as she realized Hollyridge's beautiful horses would soon be gone, all except poor Bottom and Nicker. Broken and winded as they were, they would not spend the rest of their days grazing peacefully in a meadow as they deserved, but would undoubtedly be quickly dispensed with.

The dance ended. She had to get away. "If you'll excuse me, m'lord."

He asked, "Would you care to dance another?"

She had half turned away before she wondered, why not tell him the truth? Stormont deserved to know what she thought of him, and why. She turned back and said with quiet firmness, "I am deeply disturbed at what you're planning for the horses. Sara Sophia will be utterly devastated at the loss of Sham, and the rest of the horses, as shall I."

He had been smiling, but now his face might have been carved in marble. "I plan to sell them, not slaughter them."

"Oh, really? Who would want Bottom and Nicker? You might as well sell them straight to the slaughterhouse."

His face took on a tolerant, but firm expression. "Lady Clarinda, you must understand that Hollyridge Manor is mine now. I have the right to dispose of the horses however I wish."

She favored him with a frosty smile. "Of course it is your *right,* sir," she said, edging the word with loathing, "and I can do nothing about it. But it is my *right* to say thank you for the dance, and no thank you, I do not wish to dance with you again." That said it all, she decided, and with a quick turn, she left the dance floor, making sure she had a pleasant expression on her face in case that gleeful purveyor of gossip, Lady Constance Lynbury, might be watching.

Nonplussed, Robert watched after her. He had no idea the girl would be so upset over a pair of worthless horses. *Women and their soft hearts.* Still, he admired her compassion. Perhaps he could find a home for Bottom and Nicker, or even keep them. Against his better judgment, of course, but he'd had no idea . . . Yes, he'd keep them.

He started through the crowd after her, but at the edge of the dance floor the other twin approached. *Damme.* Anxious though he was to find Clarinda, he was compelled to stop.

With a simpering smile on her face, the twin tapped him with her fan.

"You're frowning, Lord Stormont. What has my dear sister done?"

"Nothing, Lady . . . uh . . ." Blast! He was good at names, but this twin had made little impression on him.

"I am Rissa," she told him in a bubbly voice. "Short for Clarissa, which we don't use because the names are so alike. But I'm curious. What did Clarinda do to put such a frown on your face?"

Too late. Clarinda had been swallowed up in the crowd, so for the moment he might as well talk to her amazingly identical sister. They were not all that identical, though. Clarinda seemed surprised he knew who she was, but in truth, he'd had no problem. The way she walked was much more graceful. The way she looked at him, with that tiny gleam of devilment in her eye, was quite unlike this twin whose eyes contained a rather bland expression. Even the way Clarinda held her head when she was talking was different. She was more alert, an indication she was much more interested in the world about her than her twin. All those traits were so identifiably Clarinda's, there'd been no question in his mind when he first saw the twins together.

Stormont smiled wryly. "It would appear your sister is upset because I plan to move some of the Hollyridge horses to my own estate. Only the best ones, of course. The rest I shall sell, or at least I'd planned to. Your sister was not overly pleased with that."

Rissa burst into a peal of laughter so loud and long-lasting it had to be forced. "I know just what you mean," she said, making a great display of fluttering her fan. "I must confess, there are times when my parents and I are greatly embarrassed by Clarinda's abounding love for all animals, especially horses. But you must excuse her. She has a kind heart, despite being misguided. Did you know I also have a horse? Dublin, an exact match to Donegal, but I never ride him. I have no use for a horse that isn't hitched to a carriage, taking me where I wish to go. But Clarinda?" Rissa heaved a highly questionable sigh of concern. "You should see how she makes a fool of herself with Donegal. Sometimes I wonder if she doesn't love her horse more than she does her family. It's quite amusing, though how she can purport to love a mere animal is simply beyond me."

How can I get away from her? thought Robert.

The music started. "A quadrille," exclaimed Rissa, smiling brightly. "I do *adore* dancing a quadrille."

Trapped. Robert bent gallantly and offered his arm. "Would you care to dance, Lady Rissa?"

Later in the evening, Clarinda was still upset when Larimore, as expected, claimed her for supper. Also as expected, when they finished their dessert, Larimore led her to an isolated bench on the balcony where he ardently proposed. "I want to marry you, Lady Clarinda. Your beauty has captured my heart. I find your skin is like rose petals, your hair soft as the finest silk, your eyes—"

"Yes, yes, yes," she interrupted. She would leap up and flee if she heard one more honeyed word. *Blast it all! I must give him his answer*. She opened her mouth to say yes, but nothing came out. She tried again, but her vocal chords refused to cooperate. Finally she managed, "Dear Lord Sufton, I am mindful of the great honor you have bestowed upon me."

With a cry, Larimore took up her hand in his limp, sickeningly white one. "Picture it! You, I, Lawrence, and Rissa—just the four of us, living in wedded bliss at Bolton Hall for the rest of our days." His pale, vapid eyes actually lit with a spark of excitement. "Just think! Even our children might look exactly alike. Exciting to contemplate, is it not?"

Lord, deliver me. I cannot do this tonight. Maybe tomorrow. Yes, tomorrow she would accept. But tonight? If her life depended on it, the word 'yes' was stuck in her throat and would not come out. "May I give you my answer tomorrow? I cannot make such an important decision without thinking about it overnight. You do understand?"

"But of course," he answered eagerly. "If I must wait, I must wait, although I can guess what your answer will be." He gave her an insufferably indulgent smile. "You ladies will play your little games, won't you?"

"It's hardly a game," she responded, not totally hiding her annoyance.

Larimore hastened to say, "Oh, no, not a game—surely not a game. What I meant was, it is not beneficial for ladies to think too much. You're too delicate. Your brains are smaller."

"I shall keep that in mind," she answered, trying to conceal her disgust. How unjust that even a ninny like Larimore could talk down to her, and all because he was a man and she a mere woman. It was hard to keep the smile on her face, but she did, mindful she must keep a pleasant demeanor.

At the first possible moment, Clarinda excused herself and slipped into the empty library. Perhaps she could hide here until the ball was over and no one would come in. But no such luck. The door opened. To her chagrin, the odious Lord Cranmer entered and shut the door carefully behind him.

Cranmer was a tall man with classical good looks, in his early forties. Clarinda had seen him in London many a time, but had sought to avoid him, unlike Rissa who had seemed fascinated by him. A bachelor, and rich, he was a fixture at Almack's and all the swank balls. The young girls had been warned about him. She was not exactly sure why, except he had a reputation for "taking advantage" of innocent young women and doing things said to be "unspeakable."

"Rissa!" exclaimed Lord Cranmer. His eager eyes raked over her boldly. "I've been desperate to get you alone all evening."

"I am not—" Clarinda began, but before she could get the rest of her words out, Cranmer had swiftly crossed the room, seized her, and bent her back over one arm.

With his face only inches from hers, his hot breath coming hard, he whispered, "My darling, I've been out of my head since you left London. Rissa, my sweet, sweet girl." His hand explored the hollow of her back while he pulled her to him and crushed his lips to hers.

Paralyzed, in a state of utter shock, Clarinda had not at first offered resistance, but the feel of his wet lips, followed by—ugh!—the tip of his tongue pressing for entrance, galvanized her to action. Unable to speak, she conveyed her fury with desperate little deep-throated mmm's while whacking his back with her fan. When finally he lifted his lips, she cried, "Let me go, you villain!"

"Why you little tiger," he murmured huskily and covered her mouth hungrily again. His hand slid up her side. Stunned, she felt probing fingers slip beneath the bodice of her dress. Desperately she struggled, trying to wrench herself away. But she was helpless in his strong, sure clasp and there was nothing she could do.

Over the sound of her muffled protests she was faintly aware of a door opening. There was a moment of silence, and then a horrified, "I am shocked!"

Lord Cranmer stood back so abruptly he nearly dropped her. With an effort, she regained her balance, thinking, *it cannot be.*

But it was. Not only was Lady Lynbury staring at her with shocked surprise, but an avidly curious Agatha peered from behind her. "Lady Lynbury," Clarinda exclaimed as she looked down at herself and straightened her dress. "I can explain . . ."

"Don't bother." Lady Constance Lynbury's more than ample bosom quivered with righteous indignation. Her thin lips, set in a line of haughty incredulity, parted barely enough to utter, "Shame, Clarinda."

"How can you be so sure which twin I am?" gasped Clarinda.

"Who else could you be?" the older woman retorted. "Dear Rissa would never do anything as brazen. Well, your parents shall hear of this. Come, Agatha, this is not a sight for innocent eyes."

With a final, scathing glance, Lady Lynbury stalked from the room, followed by her snickering daughter-in-law.

Lord Cranmer had the grace to look confused. "Clarinda?" he asked. "You are not—?"

"No!" Clarinda was breathless with rage and stood taking deep gasps of breath, trying to control her anger. "I am not Rissa," she finally managed to whisper in a trembling voice. "But even if I were, how dare you!"

Lord Cranmer offered a slight bow. "First, my apologies—Clarinda, is it? My, my, so alike. Ah, well, how was I to know? But as to your question, how dare I?" He sniggered and disdainfully raised a brow. "Best ask your twin that, m'lady. I, being a gentleman, cannot say."

She was calmer now, though her heart was still pounding. "Sir, you are no gentleman, but a complete knave."

"Ask Rissa how much she prefers a gentleman," Cranmer replied. He cast an anxious glance at the door. "Now if you will excuse me, I had best depart."

"And hasten back to London before Papa hears," Clarinda retorted.

"Yes, there is that, isn't there?" He frowned in puzzlement. "But before I go, tell me, why would Lady Lynbury assume it was you and not your twin?"

Clarinda felt herself go crimson with resentment and anger. "Because I am the bad twin," she said, spitting the words out bitterly. "Who would believe my dear sister would do anything as crass as this?"

"Pity." Cranmer clucked his tongue sympathetically. He bowed again. "Good-bye, my dear. Again, my apologies. It would appear I've gotten you into a spot of trouble."

Clarinda watched as Cranmer swiftly took his leave from the library. Galling, how he had not in the least lost his equanimity. His last words spun through her head. *A spot of trouble.* Her heart sank. *Oh, yes.*

*   *   *

Throughout the evening, Robert, despite himself, had not been able to take his eyes off the slender, lithe young woman who glided with great zest and grace around the dance floor. *Clarinda.* Even her name rolled melodiously from his tongue. Her ready smile and infectious laughter were enchanting. Even the way she held herself—so straight and proud—was a delight to behold. He cursed himself for doing it, but he had surreptitiously watched when she took supper with that oaf, Sufton. Not an easy task, considering her insufferable sister had cornered him for supper. That self-centered twin must think the whole world revolved around herself. He could hardly move his eyes away, so intent was she on monopolizing his full attention. Still, he was aware when the oaf led Clarinda to that secluded bench on the balcony, where he no doubt proposed. How had she answered? He would give his best saddle to know.

Later, when he saw her go into the library, he wanted to follow. Not a good idea, though. The lovely Clarinda most definitely did not care for him. He had best remember that, and go about his business.

At the end of the evening, when he and Lucius were riding home from the ball, he inquired, "Well, Lucius, did you have an enjoyable evening?"

"I was engulfed in utter boredom," came his friend's terse reply.

"But you can't still be thinking of Sara Sophia."

The long pause that followed told Robert all he needed to know.

For a time they rode to the sounds of crickets and muted hoof thuds before Lucius finally spoke again. "Did you hear about the scandal?"

"What scandal?"

Lucius perked up, as he usually did when passing on a piece of juicy gossip. "You would never guess whom Lady Lynbury caught dallying in the library."

"I have no idea and don't want to know." Robert had little tolerance for gossip of this sort.

Undaunted, Lucius continued, "One of the miscreants was that rakehell, Lord Cranmer, which comes as no surprise. But the other! Did you not notice how tongues were wagging when we left?"

"Just tell me," Robert wearily replied.

"It was Lady Clarinda, the host's own daughter—you know, one of the twins." With a deep chuckle, Lucius continued, "Cranmer's fleeing to London as we speak. Capelle must be furious. She's the bad twin, judging from what they say, but whichever she is, I should hate to be in that young lady's shoes right now."

Chapter 6

The ball was over. The guests had either departed or gone to bed. For the second time in a week, Clarinda stood before her father's desk in the library. Papa was seated, wordlessly staring at her in stunned surprise. Mama stood next to him, nose pinched with outrage. Clarinda had thought the other day was bad, but this was a hundred times worse.

"We are disgraced," Mama's curt voice lashed at her. Fists clenched, she gazed toward some hidden deity above and inquired, "Why did you send me such a child?" She asked Papa, "What did I do wrong? Is this God's punishment?"

"Nothing wrong with you, my dear," Papa answered in conciliatory fashion, and turned his attention to Clarinda. "Have you any explanation?"

Clarinda felt her heart pounding in her chest as she stood silent, trying to think of what to say. This was her chance to set things straight, but she was well aware a simple recitation of the facts would sound like a lie. They would never believe her. Desperately she cast about for words that would ring true and sound convincing. "The truth is, I went to the library to be alone."

"Why alone?" Mama demanded, her eyes hard and filled with animosity.

"I just wanted to be alone. Then Lord Cranmer came in, and before I could say a word he grabbed me, bent me over his arm, and kissed me, and then he started taking other liberties. I was pinned in his arms. There was nothing I could do."

How limp that sounded! It wasn't believable, even to her own ears.

"Ha! You expect us to believe that?" Mama pointed a

trembling finger. "Admit it, you had an assignation in the library with Lord Cranmer. Had not Lady Lynbury walked in, Lord knows how far it might have gone." Mama squeezed her eyes shut, as if to avoid picturing the worst. "I cannot bear to think of it." She gazed at her husband and beseeched, "Why did I have twins? Why could I not have had just Rissa?"

"God works in mysterious ways," answered Papa, looking distinctly uncomfortable. It was an answer that side-stepped Mama's question, but still, again he had not stood up for her.

They never wanted me. Clarinda felt a sob rise in her throat. She flung out her hands and cried, "But I did nothing wrong. Things are not . . . not what they seem."

"Then tell us, how are *things,*" demanded Mama, voice full of contempt.

"I . . ." She wanted to tell them that Lord Cranmer had mistaken her for Rissa, but what was the use? In her parents' eyes, Rissa was the sweet, pure, loveable twin who could do no wrong, whereas she was the rebellious twin who could do no right. If she told the truth, they would never believe her. Worse, putting the blame on Rissa would further dishonor her in her parents' eyes. If that was possible, she thought with bitter irony.

"I cannot explain," Clarinda replied in a low, tormented voice, "other than to swear to you I was not at fault."

Mama stared at her with an unrelenting gaze. "I want you out of my sight, but first—"

"Yes, I know." Clarinda's mind was bursting with unspoken protests and explanations, but she knew none would help. "You're going to take Donegal from me, aren't you?"

"Have we a choice?" asked Papa. He paused in deep thought. "The other day I gave you a choice, remember?"

"How could I forget? I would consider marrying Lord Sufton or lose Donegal."

Papa nodded. "You have no choice now. There's no 'consider.' You *will* marry Sufton or you lose Donegal *and* get packed off to North Wales."

Mama added, "Where you will spend the next ten years of your life, at the very least, if I have anything to say about it." In an aside to her husband she remarked, "If she agrees to marry Sufton, fine, but will he still have her?

Tongues are wagging already. By tomorrow even London will have heard of Clarinda's disgrace. Sufton must have heard by now. Who knows what he's thinking after this debacle?"

"He'll come round." Papa did not look concerned. "I can always increase her dowry."

I cannot endure this, thought Clarinda. Over a huge lump in her throat she asked, "You would pay Sufton a huge sum to marry me?"

"You are damaged goods," answered Mama with a sneer. "How else can we marry you off?"

Clarinda felt such a swell of pain and humiliation that she didn't think she could bear it. *You shall not subject yourself to this degradation,* came a little voice within herself. The truth came clear. She had been deluding herself if ever she thought she could marry Larimore, especially now, not when he would have to be bribed to marry her. Honor decreed there was only one course she could take.

"Take Donegal." She raised her chin high. "Send me to North Wales if you will, but I shall never marry Lord Sufton." There, the words were out. She commanded her knees to stop shaking, but they wouldn't.

Papa looked puzzled. "But why? You were at least considering Sufton yesterday."

"A dowry is one thing," Clarinda answered, "but a bribe is another. I have my pride. How could I spend the rest of my life with a man who had to be paid to marry me?"

A small smile of satisfaction crossed Mama's lips. "It's hopeless," she said to her husband. "Donegal must be sold immediately. Let us hope he fetches a good price."

Papa bestowed a look tinged with contempt at his wife, brought about, Clarinda surmised, by the subtle reminder of Mama's gambling debts. Then sorrow settled on his face. "You might wish to reconsider, Clarinda."

"I am positive."

"No, you think about it," Papa answered gently. "I only want what's best for you. By morning you may think better of your decision and change your mind."

"Oh, Papa!" Her heart leaped at the thought that her father might care, at least a little. But before he could answer, Mama spoke up.

"You are being much too lenient with her, John."

Papa sighed deeply. Clarinda's heart sank. She knew that sigh. It was the kind of sigh he always gave when, invariably, he caved under the influence of his iron-willed wife. "All right, Edwina, the horse shall be sold tomorrow. As for North Wales, tomorrow will be soon enough for a final decision. You had better go now, Clarinda."

Sick at heart, Clarinda went to the door. The specter of dreary years spent with dour Grandfather Montague in that dark, dank castle in North Wales hung over her. She couldn't even bear to think about losing Donegal.

She must try once more. In the midst of her despair she could see two faint glimmers of hope. First, she sensed that Papa wasn't eager to send her away. Did this mean he possibly had a shred of affection left for her? And if he did, could he stand up to Mama? He was not a coward, and, in fact, ran his estates with an iron hand. It was only in matters where the children were concerned that he always let Mama have her way. But perhaps, just this once, he could show some backbone.

And the second glimmer of hope . . .

At the door she turned. "Mama, Papa, if I could prove to you I did nothing wrong would you reconsider?"

Papa answered, "Of course, child."

She hardly dared hope that Rissa would ever admit the truth, yet it was worth a try. Without another word, she left the library and hastened to Rissa's bedchamber.

"Are you daft?" asked Rissa.

Estelle had been dismissed for the night. Rissa, in her voluminous white nightgown, golden hair falling loose around her shoulders, sat cross-legged in her bed with the covers pulled up. "What are you saying?" she asked, "that I had something to do with your scandalous conduct in the library with Lord Cranmer?" Giggling, she admonished, "Really, Clarinda, such an embarrassment! The worst of it is, it was Lady Lynbury and that mealymouthed Agatha who caught you. Now the whole countryside will know."

Clarinda sat carefully upon the foot of the bed. "I find no humor in this," she answered, suppressing her anger. *Forceful but calm*—that was the way to handle Rissa. "I want the truth. When Lord Cranmer walked into the library he called me 'Rissa.' It was clear he knew you from London and that something had gone on between you."

Rissa started to pout. "That's not true."

"It very well is true." Clarinda looked her twin directly in the eye. "Nobody's here except the two of us, so there's no need to lie."

Rissa shifted her gaze away. "I don't know what you mean."

"Yes, you do know." Clarinda shook her head in puzzlement. "I don't understand. Twins are supposed to love each other, help each other, but ever since we were children, you've resented me, for some reason, I don't know why."

"That's nonsense."

"Is it? Mama and Papa are taking Donegal away, all on account of you. It's breaking my heart, but do you care?"

"Of course I care," came Rissa's sullen reply, but her words were belied by a tiny flicker of triumph that flashed through her eyes. She yawned, stretching her arms high. "I'm sleepy now. Can't we talk about this tomorrow?"

"We'll talk about it now." Rissa was an expert at avoiding unpleasantness, but not this time. "I recall when we were children how close we were, but even back then, there were times I had to take the blame for something you'd done. Nothing's changed, has it? Sometimes I think you take great delight in seeing me come to grief."

"Of course I don't," came Rissa's weak reply. Eyes still averted, she started plucking at the covers.

"You've resented me all our lives, so why would you change now? You did carry on with Cranmer in London, didn't you?"

"What if I did?" Rissa bit her lip to stifle a grin. "You could never prove it."

"Perhaps not, but it's true, isn't it?"

Rissa's face lit. "I've been dying to tell you," she burst out. "Lord Cranmer is madly in love with me. When we were in London, he said he adored me and I drove him to distraction and he could not eat or sleep for thinking about me. Well, what could I do? I did permit a kiss or two, out of pity more than anything else . . . well, maybe a little bit more. You should have seen him!" Rissa giggled again. "He got all excited and was breathing like the bellows of a forge. Then he got so carried away he plunged his whole hand down my bodice and grabbed my—"

"Spare me the details," Clarinda quickly said. "How often did this happen?"

"Twice. Once at Lady Harlestone's ball, and the other time in the library at our town house in London. That's all. That's not so terrible, is it? Am I to blame if a man finds me so irresistible he cannot control himself?"

Clarinda stared aghast at her sister, who now sat with a smug look on her face, twirling a golden lock around her finger, as she waited for Clarinda's response. It was obvious Rissa had been dying to brag about her supposed conquest. Incredible though it appeared, she actually seemed flattered that Cranmer, that basest of rakes, had been after her.

"Cranmer's a viper," Clarinda declared. "You're a ninny if you think he's in love with you." In complete frustration, she slipped off the bed and started pacing. "Don't you understand? Cranmer is enamored of two things—himself, and anything in skirts who will kiss him back. And you think he adores you? Ha!"

Clarinda stopped her pacing. Hands on hips, she glared, astounded at her sister. "How could you be so foolish?"

With a satisfied smile, Rissa flopped her palms out. "But that's the best part. It's marvelous fun to do something deliciously naughty now and then. Of course, you have to be sure you won't get caught, and I wasn't, was I?" Thoughtfully she tipped her head. "There's the difference between us. You've always been the rebellious one, but you're openly defiant, whereas I have always been—"

"The sneaky one," Clarinda interjected with more than a little satisfaction.

"You're just jealous," Rissa lightly replied. "It all goes back to Jeffrey, doesn't it? You're still mad that I stole him away from you." Her mouth took on an unpleasant twist. "Which I deliberately did, you know, and it was *so* easy."

Clarinda was taken aback. "You deliberately stole Jeffrey?"

Rissa slapped a hand over her mouth, very much looking as if she'd caught herself saying too much.

"Speak up!" demanded Clarinda.

"That's all I have to say," Rissa replied, on the defensive, "except you can call my behavior sneaky if you like, but that's the reason I'm Mama and Papa's darling and you're the one who's been in trouble since the day you were born."

Clarinda gave her sister a cold, hard stare. "No, Rissa, you're not going to change the subject this time. Tell me about Jeffrey. What did you do?"

Rissa cried, "Oh, Clarinda, I was so madly in love with Jeffrey I was desperate!"

"What do you mean, desperate?" Clarinda asked coolly.

Rissa covered her face with her hands. "I told a lie," she whispered through her fingers.

"What lie?"

"But I only told it out of sheer desperation."

"What lie?"

Rissa looked up again. "If you must know, I pretended I was you and told Jeffrey I had fallen madly in love with someone else."

Clarinda sat stunned. Of course! Now it all came clear. No wonder Jeffrey, without warning had turned cold as ice, and then started courting her sister.

Apparently Rissa's distress was short-lived, for now she looked not in the least contrite. "Actually I was doing you a favor."

"And what might that be?"

"Jeffrey was so weak it was pathetic. I had been dying to capture him, but once I did, I discovered what a shallow pate he was. So I lost interest. I was amused the other day when you remarked on my 'brave' demeanor when Jeffrey died. The truth is, I really didn't care. You wouldn't have either, if you'd gotten to know him better."

"That's not true!"

"You can cry tears all you want over that old book of poems he gave you, and your withered rose, but the truth remains, Jeffrey was a milksop. The only reason he's a hero is because he's dead."

Clarinda's shock yielded quickly to fury. But what could she say? Jeffrey was gone, there was no going back. One thing she must make clear though. In a voice cold and exact, she said, "I won't forget this, Rissa. Don't you ever, ever pretend you're me again, do you understand?"

"But I was only—"

"Never, *never* pretend you're me!" She wanted to shout,

wanted to shake her sister until all that deviousness, and deceit, and selfishness were gone.

"But is Jeffrey the issue?" asked Rissa, assuming her wide-eyed innocent look.

Clarinda fought to calm herself. She would think of Jeffrey later. Right now she should stick to the point. "I can never prove Cranmer thought I was you, but considering the serious consequences to me, I thought just this once you might have the decency to go to Mama and Papa and confess."

Rissa shook her head. "I just can't. You know how delicate I am. I couldn't stand to have Mama and Papa mad at me."

It was hopeless. When Rissa got that obdurate look on her face, there was nothing she could do. But considering the dire consequences, she would give it one more try. Clarinda sat on the edge of Rissa's bed again and took her hand. "Please help me, Rissa."

Rissa made a face and jerked her hand away. "I told you no, and I meant no. Don't drag me into this."

"You said yourself you're Mama and Papa's darling," Clarinda went on. "You know as well as I, they won't send *you* off to North Wales, no matter what you do."

"But even so, they'd have to punish me, and you know how fragile I am."

"You're as fragile as a brick."

Rissa pondered for a moment. A crafty expression crossed her face. "What if I did tell the truth? It wouldn't help you the least bit."

"What do you mean?"

"Do you think Mama and Papa would believe me? Or would they think that I, the sweet, devoted twin, was simply trying to take the blame for her naughty sister?" Rissa regarded her triumphantly. "You see, I really cannot help you. You lose either way."

With a sinking heart, Clarinda realized her sister was right. "You win again," she answered, not attempting to keep the bitterness from her voice.

Rissa continued, "And since we're talking honestly, there's something else."

"Yes?" Clarinda asked warily.

"I have decided I shall marry Lord Stormont."

Clarinda felt a jolt at the sound of Stormont's name, which was strange, considering her hostile feelings toward the man. "I thought your heart was set on marrying Lord Sufton."

"Lawrence is as exciting as a bowl of porridge." Rissa broke into a childlike smile. "But Lord Stormont! Did you see how handsome he looked tonight? The man simply oozes excitement. When he danced with me I thought I should die."

"So what do you want me to do?" Clarinda asked abruptly. She was in no mood for Rissa's childlike gushing.

"I want you to stay away from him."

"Your request is hardly necessary. Do you think I could care for a man who plans to remove all the beautiful horses from Hollyridge?"

"Then you promise?"

Leave it to Rissa to pay no attention to concerns that did not involve herself. "Promise what? That I not throw myself at Lord Stormont's feet in hopes he will marry me?"

"Exactly."

What did it matter? Clarinda could easily promise, especially considering her feelings for the man. But considering Rissa's behavior tonight, it was galling she would have the nerve to ask for anything. "Take him if you can get him," Clarinda said with a shrug. "I really don't care." She managed to shrug and say offhandedly, "Besides, thanks to you I shall soon be in North Wales."

"I still want you to promise," insisted Rissa.

"I don't have to promise you anything," Clarinda snapped. She could stand no more of this. Not bothering to conceal her disgust, she strode to the door.

"Don't be mad!" Rissa called after her, all sweetness again.

At the door, Clarinda turned. "No, I'm not mad, but a word of advice—it might be marvelous fun to do something 'deliciously naughty' now and then, but someday your actions will come back to haunt you."

"Don't be silly," Rissa replied as she snuggled into her covers. "You're the one with the problems, not me. I lead a charmed life. Nothing bad ever happens to me."

*   *   *

Back in her own bed chamber, Clarinda wondered if she had been completely honest with herself. Aside from the obvious, did she have some ulterior motive for not making that promise to Rissa? She had to admit that despite Stormont's display of selfishness this evening, she found him most charming and devilishly attractive. Yet would she ever consider marrying him?

No, let Rissa have him.

The troubles of the day came flooding back. Why was she even thinking about Stormont when her world was about to fall apart? She should have known Rissa wouldn't help. No surprise there. Her heart sank at the realization there was no way out of her predicament. She was doomed, no matter what she did.

Rissa had only pretended to be sleepy. After Clarinda left, she lay wide-eyed in the dark, feeling irritable with herself, wishing she could have changed the events of the evening. She was sorry about that misadventure concerning Cranmer. Clarinda had been obliged to take the blame, which was really unfair, she supposed, but then, Clarinda was the strong one. *She can handle Mama and Papa's anger much better than I.*

Rissa recalled her sister's angry warning: "Don't you ever, ever pretend you're me again, do you understand?" Mercy, but she'd been upset. It was just a good thing Clarinda didn't know about those other times she'd been impersonated, like with Lord Westerlynn . . .

Again, Rissa thought about the keys. *What shall I do about the keys? I had better check and see if they're still there.* Rissa slipped out of bed and lit a candle. Holding it high, she went to her chinoiserie work cabinet, decorated with black lacquer and gilt, which was fitted with boxes for storing her sewing things. She raised the lid and lifted one of the boxes. Underneath lay the two ancient keys, still safe. What to do? She wished now she hadn't kept them. But she had, and now it was much too late to suddenly announce, "Oh, by the way, before Lord Westerlynn died, he gave me these keys . . ."

Ah, well, why should she care if Sara Sophia did or not have a fortune? She was curious, though. What doors would the keys unlock? It was most intriguing. Perhaps she should simply throw the keys away, but no, on second thought, she would keep them awhile longer. One never knew what might happen.

The leaves still glistened with morning dew as Robert guided Sham at a brisk pace along the riding path that followed the course of the river. Always an early riser, he had just spent over an hour in the well-appointed study, trying to make sense out of Hollyridge's accounts. Inexcusable, the way old Westerlynn had allowed the management of Hollyridge Manor to slide into what amounted to sheer chaos. Robert had decided he needed a break, which meant a highly enjoyable ride on Sham.

At the stables, he discovered Sara Sophia saddling two horses. "Good morning," she called, "I see you're also out for a ride."

After he greeted her, he casually asked, "And who is going riding with you?"

"Why, Lord Wentridge."

"Lucius?" He could not prevent his burst of gleeful laughter. "There must be some mistake. Lucius hasn't been up at this early hour since the day he was born—unless he'd made a night of it and was just coming home."

"We shall see," Sara Sophia said confidently.

Now, riding along the tree-lined trail, Robert reflected upon his inability to sleep last night. All that was Clarinda's fault. Thoughts of her had kept him awake far later than he cared to admit. Try as he might, he could not prevent the regrettable image of her in the arms of that nodcock, Cranmer, from flashing through his mind. He had tossed and turned, cursing himself for a fool, then asking himself over and over how a girl like Clarinda could have been so foolhardy. In the wee, small hours he concluded she could not have been. Surely there must be another explanation.

I shall not think of her, he commanded himself as he rode along. He was happy to be away from the musty account books for a while, and should concentrate on nothing else but guiding Sham and admiring the view. Idly he noted that somehow he had found the path to Graystone Hall. He wondered if he might possibly meet Lady Clarinda again, as he had yesterday. Not likely. There he went again. His thought was ridiculous, considering he didn't give a groat whether he saw her again or not.

But here she came! His heart leaped. Shafts of early morning sunlight slanting through the trees lit her path as she, riding astride, approached at top speed on Donegal. How beautiful she looked—not wearing that dull black riding dress of yesterday, but a gracefully draped gray riding gown, her golden hair streaming in the breeze, not covered by that ridiculous plumed hat. Spying him, Clarinda tightened her reins. The horse slowed and continued on at a more dignified pace. As they drew near, he could see that her cheeks did not hold yesterday's rosy glow. In fact, as she drew ever closer he was struck by her pale, drawn expression.

"Good morning, m'lord," she said, not slowing Donegal to a complete stop. It was obvious she planned to ride right by.

"Good morning, Lady Clarinda."

"Ah, he knows it's me," she said, rolling her eyes skyward, finally reining her horse to a stop.

"Of course I knew it was you," he replied. "Or does your sister also ride Donegal at a breakneck speed"—he lowered his gaze to where her legs hugged the horse's flanks and a good bit of trim ankle was showing—"and astride?"

She gave him a haughty glance, nudged her steed, and started off. Damnation! Never had he met such a stubborn chit. Suddenly it was of the upmost urgency he talk to her. "Don't think you're going to ride right by me, because you are not." He leaned and grabbed the gelding's bridle, thus bringing him to a halt again.

Apparently unperturbed, Clarinda simply gazed at him. In a dispirited voice she asked, "What more is there to say, sir? I told you what I thought last night. My opinion hasn't changed."

What is amiss? Stormont wondered. Where was the lively girl who had roundly set him in his place last night? "What's wrong?" he asked. "Don't tell me it's nothing, I can see it in your eyes."

She gave him a twisted smile. "Oh, it's something all right. They are selling Donegal. This will be my last ride." She lowered her gaze as she reached out a hand to stroke the horse's black mane. He waited. She did not look up but remained with her head bent, fingers lovingly entwined in Donegal's long, silky hair, silent, her face hidden from view. Then her shoulders shook and he knew she was trying to keep from crying.

Robert was at a loss for words. He thought to inquire as to why the gelding was being sold but stopped himself. He didn't have to ask. It was obvious her parents were taking Clarinda's horse away as a punishment. *How cruel.* He thought of the first time he'd seen her—only yesterday, but he'd never forget. It had taken his breath away—the sight of that young, spirited girl, laid out nearly flat on the back of her magnificent Irish hunter, the two of them streaking across the field, graceful as a swan in flight, almost as if they were flying. He remembered, too, before she mounted again, how she had pulled down Donegal's head and whispered something endearing. In acknowledgment, the horse had pawed the ground, nodding as if he'd understood, his ears fluttering like young birds. It was obvious Clarinda loved that horse nearly as much as life itself. Now, for reasons he was positive were unjust, her unfeeling parents were going to sell her beloved Donegal.

"I am terribly sorry," Robert said, then waited quietly, knowing the worst thing he could do was gush with sympathy.

Finally she raised her head, revealing tearstained cheeks. "Thank you," she said simply. He offered her his handkerchief. Gratefully she took it and blotted the tears away. "It's nothing anyone can do. I am being punished for my so-called indiscretions." He could hear the tears in her voice as she laughed bitterly. "I am such a naughty girl."

"Are you really?" he asked, knowing full well his question was beyond the realm of politeness.

She looked him square in the eye. "That was my feeble attempt at a joke. There was a misunderstanding. I have done nothing wrong. That's all I can tell you."

"If you say you are innocent, then you are." Robert felt a great relief. He had known her only briefly, but he sensed she wouldn't lie. "Might I ask, what's to be done with Donegal?"

"My parents are selling him, I don't know to whom." She looked so stricken he was afraid she would start to cry again, but she bit her lip and smiled bravely. "I shall never see him again, that's the worst of it. Oh, dear." She gulped and again dabbed at her tears with the handkerchief. When she raised her eyes, she was in control. "But I shall be fine, sir." She lifted her chin and eyed his hand, which still grasped her horse's bridle. "I must be on my way, that is, if you would not mind letting go?"

"As you wish." He dropped the bridle and watched as she signaled Donegal with a nudge of her knees. The horse started away. He called, "Good day, Lady Clarinda. I'm sorry for your troubles."

"Don't be," she said, looking back with her features deceptively composed. "Thank you for your kindness. I shall be fine, just as I always am. I don't want your sympathy." Her horse picked up the pace and disappeared down the trail.

Perdition! thought Robert, staring after her. How utterly unfair. He wished he could help, but what could he do?

Nothing, he firmly told himself as he turned Sham toward home. He must get all this nonsense out of his head and concentrate on those musty, muddled account books. Then he would go back to London—do a bit of gambling and also visit Selena. Strange, since yesterday he'd hardly given her a thought.

Shortly after Robert resumed his work in the library, Lucius strode in, dressed in his riding clothes. "Damme if she wasn't right," Robert commented. Lucius nearly always slept until noon, but here he was, not only up, but with a spring in his step and an eager spark in his eye.

As usual, Lucius retained his aplomb. "Not only am I up, my good fellow, but I am going riding."

Robert gave him an odd glance. "I never knew you to be so eager to take the morning air. Could it be a certain dark-eyed young female is involved in your decision?"

Instead of returning his usual caustic reply, Lucius nodded pleasantly. "There's a first time for everything," he said softly. "I find Miss Sara Sophia Clarmonte most attractive." Before Robert could answer, he raised his hand. "No further comment, please! She's a delightful riding companion, that's it, nothing more."

"I'm glad to hear you say it. What a disaster it would be if you—"

"If I fell in love with Sara Sophia?" Lucius laughed loudly—too loudly. "Ridiculous!"

Not ridiculous a'tall, thought Robert, not taken in by Lucius's so obviously false laughter. But there was nothing to be gained from further comment. He changed the subject by mentioning what was utmost on his mind: how he had met Clarinda on the trail and the sad news that her parents were going to sell Donegal.

"Damn shame," commented Lucius.

"The girl loves that horse. She will be devastated . . ." Robert let his words trail off, aware he was revealing more of his thoughts than he wished his friend to know. "Something should be done. What they're doing is a crime."

Lucius sized him up with a slanted glance. "My, my, such concern for a chit you hardly know? How unlike you, Robert. What do you care whether the girl loses her horse or not?"

His friend's indifference caused Robert to fume inside. Lucius simply didn't understand. "In the first place, the girl did nothing wrong."

"What about that business with Cranmer in the library? Are you sure she's innocent? Cranmer's an impudent dog, but he has a way with women." Lucius thought a moment. "It is more than likely she allowed him—"

"Silence!" Robert bellowed.

A heavy silence followed. Finally Lucius, much subdued, ventured, "Have they sold the horse yet?"

"How do I know?" asked Robert, also subdued. "Sorry I yelled. Why did you ask such a question?"

"Apology accepted." Undaunted, Lucius continued, "Why don't you find out if the horse is sold, and if it's not, buy it yourself? Then you could keep it here and let her ride it."

The idea jolted Robert. Why hadn't he thought of it himself? With caution, he ventured, "I suppose it's a possibility."

"Just an idea, Robert, but on second thought, not very practical. For one thing, aren't you going to sell Hollyridge?"

"I was planning to."

Lucius brightened. "I have it! Disrepair or not, Hollyridge Manor is twice the estate Oakley House is. Did you ever consider not selling Hollyridge? Why not move here? You'd be getting a beautiful river at your doorstep, plus there'd be much more room for your horses. Then you could keep Donegal here. Clarinda could still ride her horse, or at least take comfort from the knowledge her gelding was close by and well cared for."

"That wouldn't work," said Robert, shaking his head. "They are selling the horse to punish the girl. Like as not, they would not want her horse within a hundred miles of here."

"But on the other hand," Lucius persisted, "from what I hear, Lord Capelle is strapped for cash right now. He might consider your offer regardless, provided you sweeten the pot a little."

Robert looked puzzled. "What do you mean? Capelle's a wealthy man."

"Indeed he is," Lucius replied. "His holdings in the West Indies alone are worth a fortune, but not a ready fortune. Lady Capelle's the problem. From what I hear, her gambling losses have put them deep in the hole. Capelle may well accept your offer, provided it's an exceptionally generous one.

Robert lapsed into deep thought until Lucius impatiently inquired, "So what will you do?"

Robert brought his hand to his chin and mused aloud. "Money aside, that Irish hunter is a beautiful piece of horseflesh I would buy in a minute, whether or not he belonged to Clarinda."

"Then you may as well purchase the animal. If you don't, someone else will."

Lucius's remarks had set off a new, wild train of thought in Robert's head. The rest of the morning and part of the afternoon he mulled over various plans, all the while asking himself why he was going to such lengths. By late afternoon his plans were set.

"Jennings, tell the groom to saddle Sham," he ordered the butler. "I shall be visiting Lord Capelle."

Lucius overheard. "What are you planning?"

When Robert told him, Lucius burst into uproarious

laughter. "Are you out of your mind? They will never accept an offer as insane as that."

"Don't be too sure," Robert said confidently, although inwardly, he was not at all sure himself.

In the oak-paneled library at Graystone Hall, Robert sat across from Lord Capelle, each with a brandy snifter in his hand. *He's not a bad fellow,* Robert mused as they chatted. In fact, he had greatly enjoyed discussing horses with his tall, pleasant-faced neighbor at last night's ball. But that wife of his! Such a cold woman. He had seen her occasionally in London, usually playing whist at the home of Lady Archer or Lady Buckinghamshire. And losing plenty, as he recalled. She was no dilettante, though. She took her whist seriously—a bona fide, hard-nosed gambler. Hard to believe she was the mother of a girl as warm and charming as Clarinda.

Although Capelle was a gracious host, Robert noticed a certain tenseness in his neighbor's face, and that he kept up a nervous drumming of his fingers on the arm of his Roman giltwood armchair. Finally Capelle asked, "Well, Stormont? You said you came for business."

"I understand you have a gelding for sale."

Capelle was instantly alert. "Indeed I do, sir. An Irish hunter, sixteen hands, three years old. Great strength in his jumping quarters, as I'm sure you know. No finer specimen—"

"I want to buy him," Robert said.

"Really?" asked Capelle, faintly surprised at Robert's unquestioning resolve. "By gad, I don't see why you couldn't buy him, except . . . hmm."

"Is there a problem?"

"I am afraid so." Lord Capelle's normally friendly, open face clouded with concern. "There is a certain delicate matter to be considered here."

Robert deftly asked, "I understand the horse belongs to Lady Clarinda?"

"Yes, Donegal is Clarinda's. You must understand, certain, er, events have occurred which have compelled me to make this decision to sell the animal." Capelle stopped and cleared his throat, obviously reluctant to proceed. "Donegal must go. You're obviously a good judge of cattle, Stormont, so I don't have to tell you what a fine piece of horseflesh you'd be getting. Paid two hundred guineas for him, and a like amount for Dublin, Rissa's horse. Might I ask—?"

"Four hundred guineas for Donegal," answered Robert, "however, there is a condition."

Cappelle could not suppress a gasp. "That is more than generous, sir!" A satisfied smile lit his face, but quickly faded. "Uh-oh. I have just thought of an obstacle." He heaved a heavy sigh. "Not even knowing your condition, under ordinary circumstances, I would accept your fine offer immediately. However, circumstances compel me to . . . ahem! . . . consult with her ladyship."

"What obstacle is that, sir?" Robert asked.

"Er . . . it is a family matter."

Robert set down his brandy glass. "May I be honest?" Capelle nodded. "I mean brutally honest, and if you will permit me, with great reluctance, I am compelled to refer to that delicate family matter."

"Go ahead," said Capelle, also setting down his glass. He sat back, steepled his fingers, and waited for his guest to proceed.

Robert continued, "I take it you are selling Lady Clarinda's horse as a punishment. Am I correct?"

Capelle nodded affirmatively. "Not only that, we are seriously considering sending the girl to her grandfather's castle in North Wales."

No. Robert felt a jolt in his stomach. "I had not realized. But you say you are only considering such a move?"

Capelle sighed. A melancholy frown flitted across his features. "If it were up to me, I would consider the selling of her horse punishment enough. Actually too much, between you and me, but"—he rolled his eyes upward, doubtless toward the current whereabouts of her ladyship on the third floor—"mine is not the only opinion involved here." He smiled wryly. "They say a man is master of his household, but in some matters . . ." He gave a helpless shrug, then took another healthy sip of his brandy.

So, thought Robert, that shrew of a wife ruled the household, just as he suspected. Judging from Capelle's pleasant, easygoing nature, he was not surprised. He decided to go a step further. Risky, breaking all sorts of Society's silly rules, but he could always back down. "Forgive me for intruding on private matters, but I take it this punishment had something to do with the incident that occurred last night involving Lord Cranmer." To Robert's relief, Capelle did not become incensed at such a rude intrusion of the family's privacy, but rather, nodded glumly. Robert inquired, "Could there have been a misunderstanding?"

Capelle sadly shook his head. "She claims she is innocent, but, alas, the facts speak for themselves."

Facts can easily be twisted, Robert thought, but now was not the time to argue. "I had planned to sell Hollyridge immediately, but as fate would have it, my plans have changed. I shall keep the estate, and, in fact, have made preliminary plans for moving there."

"I am simply delighted," exclaimed Capelle. "Couldn't ask for a finer neighbor."

"Thank you, sir. Which leads me back to the condition I mentioned."

"And what might that be?" Capelle asked. He was still resting easy in his chair, but his shrewd eyes were alight with interest.

"That Clarinda be permitted to come to Hollyridge and ride Donegal whenever she wishes. Actually, she would be doing me a favor because the horse would be in need of exercise." Robert chuckled to himself. No need to mention the more than adequate number of stable boys he planned to employ.

"And for how long would this arrangement last?" asked Capelle.

The shrug Robert gave was as casual as he could make it. "Until she marries, I should think. You know how these young girls are. Soon her mind will be occupied with things domestic, and maternal. Meantime, I shall have a fine piece of horseflesh for myself."

Capelle sat straight. "I must confess, I am mystified. Considering you have hardly met Clarinda, your offer is beyond magnanimous. Might I ask why you're doing this?"

Why? Because I am an idiot. But he had best find a more suitable answer. "I met Clarinda on the riding path yesterday. It was easy to perceive her devotion to her horse. Perhaps I, also a lover of horses, feel a certain . . . affinity." Damme, this was hard. How could he explain his actions when he hardly understood them himself?

"I understand, sir," Capelle answered, "and may I say I am overwhelmed by your beneficence?" He rolled his eyes upward again. "I, personally, would accept your more than generous proposition, but there's Lady Capelle's feelings in the matter to consider. Alas, I suspect she will not take kindly to your offer. She feels Clarinda should be punished, and you must admit, it would not be much of a punishment if—"

"Shall we ask her?"

"Er . . . ahem . . . well . . ."

Robert grinned with confidence. "I shall win her over, sir. You can count on it."

"But you just don't know—"

"Let me handle it," Robert interrupted with an assurance he did not feel. *You're in for it now*, he informed himself. The worst part was, this uncomfortable situation was of his own doing, all caused by a saucy chit who could ride like the wind, who would not remove herself from his thoughts, who now had goaded him to the point where he was about to go out on a limb and quite possibly make a fool of himself.

Shortly after, having been summoned to the library, Lady Capelle swept in, looking her usual severe self in an unadorned morning dress of Devonshire brown and a plain white cap. After she was seated, Robert repeated his offer.

"Let her keep riding Donegal? Absolutely not!" Lady Capelle set her lips in a thin, obdurate line. "Clarinda must be punished and that's that."

Lord Capelle argued, "But Lord Stormont is willing to pay a most handsome sum."

"Absolutely not."

Lord Capelle cast a helpless look at Robert. "I am afraid we cannot accept your offer."

Capelle needed the money. Robert could see that he did from that disappointed look in his eye. Of course, persuading Lady Capelle to change her mind would not be easy, yet remembering her ladyship's love of money, it was worth another try. "Lord Capelle, would you be so kind as to have your butler summon my coachman? Tell him, bring the bag."

Soon, the coachman arrived carrying a large bag, obviously heavy. Robert took the bag, murmuring, "Thank you, Thomas, you may go now." He pulled the tie at the top of the bag, and in a swift, fell swoop, let the contents spill out with a loud clink, clank, and clatter upon the small table next to Lady Capelle.

"My stars!" she exclaimed, her hand to her heart as she gazed at the gleaming mound of golden guineas that now covered the table.

"I shall need to count them," Robert remarked casually. By twos he started shoving the coins into a separate pile. "Two, four, six—there's way more than four hundred here, wouldn't you say? Ten, twelve fourteen . . ."

By the time he reached four hundred, Lady Capelle was staring, near hypnotized. Robert saw her hand edge out slightly, then draw back. With great deliberation, he kept on. "Four hundred two, four hundred four—a marvelous Irish hunter, I must have him—four hundred six, four hundred eight—ah, madam, you would be doing me a great favor if you would but take the entire amount—around five hundred guineas in all, I do believe."

Lady Capelle had not taken her eyes off the growing pile of golden guineas. "The girl is extremely vexing," she grumbled.

"I do understand," said Robert, all sympathy.

"She has tried my patience since the day she was born."

"You must have had the patience of a saint."

"Indeed I did."

Was she weakening? Robert wondered. He watched as, frowning, she cast a glance at her husband. "Were we not going to send her off to North Wales?"

"That's entirely up to you, m'dear, but . . ." Capelle tugged at his lip, apparently in deep thought. "I suppose it wouldn't hurt to give the girl one more chance."

"Well, I suppose . . ."

Out shot her ladyship's hand, and this time—aha!—she scooped up a handful of coins saying, "All right, Clarinda may continue riding Donegal. But only with your express permission, Lord Stormont. I want it made crystal clear the horse does not belong to her anymore."

Robert bowed low, careful to hide his glee. "You are more than kind."

"You will never know how I've suffered with that girl." After a moment, Lady Capelle's expression softened and she gazed meaningfully at her guest. "She is so unlike her twin, whom you danced with last night. You do remember Rissa?" She sighed, and to Robert's discomfort, rattled on. "Please understand my chagrin, m'lord. Clarinda has been a rebel since the day she was born, whereas Rissa has been my sweet angel, so even-tempered, so amiable, so kind. You should see her embroidery—positively exquisite! You should hear her play the piano. It is music straight from heaven, simply divine."

How could he answer such nonsense? "Er . . . I am sure of it, madam."

Although as unenthused as he could make it, his answer spurred the woman on to new heights. She smiled, fluttered her eyelids, and inquired, "Might you not stay for dinner tonight, Lord Stormont? I am sure dear Rissa would adore seeing you again. Bring along Lord Wentridge if you like."

Robert thought fast. "I am deeply honored by your kind invitation. Unfortunately I have made other plans."

"Then next week? We are having a dinner party next Friday night."

Caught. He forced a smile. "We should be delighted." At least the evening would not be entirely wasted if Clarinda would be at dinner, too.

When Stormont departed, Lord Capelle walked him out. "I shall have the papers drawn immediately," he said. "Also, I shall tell Clarinda to ride Donegal over to Hollyridge first thing in the morning, if that will be satisfactory."

They reached Graystone Hall's grand hallway. Out of the corner of his eye, Robert saw someone coming down the stairs. Clarinda! To his chagrin, his heart quickened its beat. Smoothly he bowed and said pleasantly, "Good afternoon, Lady Clarinda." He saw she was pale and unsmiling.

"So you recognize me again, sir," she said in a voice devoid of enthusiasm.

"Uncanny!" Lord Capelle interjected. "My word, Stormont, you can tell my twins apart better than I. He addressed Clarinda. "I have sold Donegal, my dear, to—"

"Word travels fast, Papa. I have already heard." Clarinda gazed at Robert, stony anger in her eyes. "Do not think for a moment, sir, that I am grateful. If you bought Donegal, fine, but if you expect I shall come and ride him, or even see him, you are much mistaken, because I never shall."

"Clarinda!" barked her father. "That is most rude and unkind."

"Quite all right, sir," Robert assured Lord Capelle. He

regarded Clarinda with appraising eyes. "Never is a long time. Perhaps you'll change your mind. If you do, the invitation is open. You may come and ride Donegal any time."

Her eyes flashed with anger. "I think not, sir. In fact, I would rather die. Now if you will excuse me—"

Clarinda turned and retreated up the stairway, shoulders back, head held high.

"I must apologize—" Capelle began, but Robert raised his hand.

"Let her go. It's all right. Your daughter has lost the possession she loved most in all this world—family excepted, of course. I, too, would be distraught under the circumstances. I shall send my groom to fetch Donegal this afternoon, if that is satisfactory."

Soon after, as she expected, Clarinda was called to the library to face her parents. "We were appalled at your behavior toward Lord Stormont," Mama said.

Papa declared, "Stormont did you a favor. Why were you so rude?"

"Because . . . because . . ." Clarinda hardly knew herself. "I don't care if he did me a favor. I only know I shall hate having to ask permission every time I want to ride my own horse."

"He is not your own horse anymore," Mama pointed out.

Papa observed her quietly for a moment. "I suspect you would feel the same toward anyone who bought Donegal, am I not right, my dear?"

"Does it matter how I feel?" Clarinda cried.

"I have had enough of this," Mama exclaimed. "Listen carefully, daughter, I am going to tell you what your life will be from now on. Thanks to your father's and my kindness, you shall not be sent to Grandfather Montague's, at least not for now. Instead, while Rissa has her London Season, you shall stay home, watch over Alexander, and tend to your embroidery. You shall never have another Season again, as far as I am concerned. Should you decide to marry Sufton, we will allow it. Otherwise, no men will be allowed to come courting, nor will you be allowed out to balls or any other social events. Have I made myself clear?"

"I believe you have made yourself clear, Mama," Clarinda replied, smiling to cover her nearly broken heart.

Chapter 7

That evening, at dinner with Lucius and Sara Sophia, Robert recounted his visit to Lord Capelle.

"So you have yourself a new horse," Lucius casually commented, before taking a bite of his Open Tart Syllabub.

Sara Sophia had been listening with intense interest. "Poor Clarinda," she exclaimed, turning a stricken gaze to Lucius. "I fear you don't understand what a tragedy this is. Clarinda must be brokenhearted. If only there were something I could do, but there's not. I feel so helpless." She stood and pushed back her chair. "If you will excuse me, gentlemen, I shall retire early." With a bare nod she left the room.

"It appears we're not too popular with the ladies today," said Lucius.

Thoughtfully, Robert took a sip of his Burgundy. "Not popular hardly describes Lady Clarinda's animosity. It was bad enough when I announced I was removing Hollyridge's horses. Now I've changed my mind, but to no avail. I've made a bad situation a thousand times worse by buying the young lady's prized gelding."

"But you were only trying to help," Lucius declared indignantly. "If it weren't for your kindness and generosity, she might never have seen her horse again. Only heaven knows what its fate might have been." Lucius frowned and nodded emphatically. "Lady Clarinda should realize that and be properly grateful."

"Ha!" Robert's dark brows drew together. "The girl detests me. My own fault, of course. I should have foreseen she'd be distraught at losing her beloved horse in such a humiliating fashion. Of course, her parents are the ones to blame, but I suppose it's only human nature that I'm the one she despises, despite my good intentions."

"I doubt she despises you," Lucius commented, none too convincingly.

Robert ignored his comment. "The worst of it is, my efforts were all for naught. I had thought she could come and ride Donegal, but she won't."

"She'll come round."

"I doubt it. She said, and I quote, 'If you bought Donegal, fine, but if you think I'll come and ride him, or come see him, you are much mistaken, because I never shall.' " Robert took another generous sip of his Burgundy. "Does that sound like a woman likely to change her mind?"

"She will," Lucius declared staunchly. "I'd wager twenty pounds on it."

"She won't." Robert finish off his wine and signaled the footman for more. "Twenty pounds? Done. You're going to lose, Lucius. Now let's talk of something else." He shrugged elaborately. "Actually, I'm not in the least concerned. Why should I give a groat what some silly chit thinks of me?"

Oh, Jeffrey. Clarinda sat atop her coverlet, in her lap the book of poems Jeffrey had given her.

> ". . . Had we never lov'd sae kindly,
> Had we never lov'd sae blindly!
> Never met—or never parted,
> We had ne'er been brokenhearted . . ."

If only he had lived, was her anguished thought as she clutched the book tight to her bosom. He would never have been hers, yet even had he married Rissa, she would have felt comforted by his presence, especially now, during the most humiliating time of her life. Unexpectedly, thoughts of Lord Stormont crept into her head. How different Lord Stormont was from dear Jeffrey, who had been kind, sensitive, and gentle, whereas Stormont . . .

There was no comparison. The man was rough, crude, and overbearing. Why she would waste one extra thought on him, she didn't know. It was strange, though, how, when she did think of him, her pulse raced. *There must be something wrong with me.*

She closed her eyes and tried to picture the one time

Jeffrey had kissed her. Just one precious kiss in the rose garden, his lips barely grazing hers, so sweet, so gentle. Somehow her vision of that tenderest of moments was blurred today.

The door opened and Rissa burst in. Clarinda quickly tucked the book beneath a pillow.

As was her custom, Rissa plunked herself down on the foot of the bed. "Why so gloomy?" she asked. "It was just a horse. At least they're not sending you to Wales."

Clarinda thought to protest, but what was the use? Rissa would never understand how wretched she felt. "You are so right, dear sister." She swung her feet to the floor and pulled on her shoes. "I should be grateful for the little things, shouldn't I?"

"Yes, you should." Rissa smiled triumphantly. "Guess what? The boring Lords Sufton have left for London."

"Have they really?" Here, indeed, was good news.

"Yes!" Rissa giggled with delight. "Just imagine, all that money we could have had! Well, they're gone, and good riddance. You didn't want Larimore, whereas I shall happily relinquish Lawrence now that I have another prospect in mind."

Thoughtfully Clarinda regarded her twin. "You think you have a chance with Lord Stormont?"

"Of course." Rissa slid off the bed, half danced to the mirror, and turned this way and that, running her hands lovingly over the indentation of her tiny waistline and the smooth curve of her hips. "He and Lord Wentridge are coming to our dinner party next Friday night. What shall we wear?"

Clarinda wondered if she would even be allowed to go to dinner in her own house, but she supposed she would. "I really don't care what we wear. You choose."

A wary look crossed Rissa's face. "You do remember what I said, don't you?"

Clarinda looked away in disgust. "Stormont is all yours, Rissa. Only a few minutes ago I made it quite clear to Lord Stormont that I didn't find his company agreeable."

"Good." Rissa looked relieved, then frowned. "But what about your horse? Won't you want to visit Hollyridge Manor to see him?"

"I informed Lord Stormont I would never visit Donegal."

But did I mean it? Clarinda asked herself after Rissa had left. Thinking of Donegal, her misery was so acute it was like a physical pain. It was awful, knowing her beloved Irish Hunter was only a mile from Graystone hall and that, in a moment of pique, she had declared she would never see him again.

How can I stay away?

The following Friday morning, Robert went to the stables early. His purpose was to take an early morning ride, or so he told himself, but he also felt the urge to check on Clarinda's gelding, as he'd done every morning since the horse had arrived. That stubborn girl, he thought as he entered the stable. Apparently she'd meant what she said. Nearly two weeks now, and no sign of her. *Even if she doesn't like me, she could at least . . .*

He heard a noise and stopped abruptly. Looking down the row of stalls, he saw that the slatted door to Donegal's stall was slightly ajar. He stood listening and heard a woman's voice. Faint, but he knew. Clarinda had come to see her horse! *Thank God.* His pulse leaped. *You fool, you mustn't let her know how happy you are to see her.*

In a stern voice he called, "Who's there?"

Clarinda had awakened early. As usual, thoughts of Donegal weighed heavily on her mind. She had stayed away long enough. No question, she had to see him. Casting aside her vow to Stormont, she threw on her old gray riding gown and in the dawn's first light walked the mile to the stable at Hollyridge. She was feeding Donegal a carrot, delighting in humming sweet nothings in the gelding's ear, when, all of a sudden, Stormont's voice boomed out loudly.

What is that? she wondered, nearly jumping from her skin. Quickly she shoved the remainder of the carrot into Donegal's eager mouth. Telling herself she must stay calm, she stepped into the aisle, where at least fifteen horses, their heads poking over their stalls, regarded her solemnly.

"Ah, Lord Stormont, what a surprise," she said, pleased that her voice sounded perfectly normal.

"Good morning, Lady Clarinda," Stormont replied, equally composed. Dressed in plain riding clothes, he was standing, hand on hip, in the aisle, where shafts of sunlight from windows high above struck the hay-strewn, wooden plank floor. His other hand rested lightly atop a stall gate; his booted foot was at a point, crossed casually over the other. "I see you've changed your mind," he said with a trace of a smile. "You have cost me twenty pounds."

"Do tell," she said, indicating with a toss of her head that nothing could concern her less. She picked up a bucket of oats and held it beneath Donegal's nose. "I trust your invitation still holds."

"That you could come here any time?" Stormont got a gleam of mischief in his eye. "Of course you can, although if memory serves correctly, you most emphatically said you would—how did you put it?—rather die?"

"You should have known I didn't mean it." She had tried to keep a straight face, but burst into laughter. "All right, you win. That was silly of me. How could I stay way from Donegal knowing he was only a mile away?" She grew serious and regarded him curiously. "Why did you buy Donegal?"

He shrugged. "Just think of me as a friend who wishes you well."

She might have believed him but for the questioning, sensuous light that smoldered deep in his dark brown eyes. He moved closer, so close that amidst the earthy horse-and-hay aromas of the stable she could detect a faint smell of honey water coming from his person. Just a friend? Send her to Bedlam if she believed for a moment this man closing in on her, radiating his fascinating charm, was after friendship alone. Her heart beat faster. Catching her breath, she tried to recall if Jeffrey had ever made her feel this way and had to answer, no, he had not, nor had any other man. She must strive for nonchalance, though. She must bear in mind she didn't like this man at all. He must not know how he was affecting her. She tried to feign a deep preoccupation with Donegal's chewing of his oats. The trouble was, she didn't dare look up for fear Stormont would detect the quickness of her breathing and her racing pulse.

"How lucky you are, Donegal," he said, reaching over her head to stroke the horse's nose, "you can throw your mistress off your back and she doesn't think *you're* detestable, but as for me, ah well, it seems I cannot win."

Clarinda also addressed the animal. "Donegal, kindly inform his lordship that I cannot endure any man who plans to remove all of Hollyridge's horses for no other reason than his very own greed."

"Donegal, inform your mistress that I have reconsidered such a move."

Taken by surprise, she swung around to face him, dropping the oat bucket to the ground. "Are you serious?"

"Quite."

"But you seemed so set on selling Hollyridge. Might I ask what changed your mind?"

He smiled down at her. "Who knows? It appears I am developing a fondness for Hollyridge Manor. There's no reason why I can't leave the horses here, and spend part of my time here, if it suits me. I might even sell Oakley House and move all my horses here."

She asked, "What about Bottom and Nicker?"

"They can stay."

She broke into a relieved smile. "That's wonderful!" Amusement flickered in her eyes. "Perhaps you're not the knave I thought you were."

"Perhaps." He moved closer still. Her pulse raced faster. She should start brushing Donegal, but Stormont was staring down at her with such intensity she couldn't look away. How overwhelmingly masculine he was! Not like quiet, sweet Jeffrey, but rather like a man who knew he could take what he wanted whenever he wanted it. Frantically she searched for something—anything—to say to break the spell. "Sara Sophia will be pleased to hear your news." She turned, picked up Donegal's brush, and started brushing. "Sara Sophia loves these horses. Sara Sophia—"

Ah . . . his hand was touching her. She felt first the light tracing of his fingers along her upper arm. Then his grip slowly tightened. *Back away,* she told herself. It wasn't too late. But she could not. It was as if her whole being was held captive. She felt his clasp tighten, heard the quickness of his breath. She hadn't looked at him, but now she knew she must although her heart pounded even harder at the thought of what she knew she would see. Pulling her gaze from the gelding, she turned slowly and looked into Stormont's eyes. Ah, as she had guessed. The amusement was gone. In its place was a burning look of desire—need—

lust—passion. "I had best put the oats away," she murmured, but stood rooted to the spot.

"Later," he said. "Ah, Clarinda . . ." She could feel his uneven breathing on her cheek as his arms went about her. "Beautiful Clarinda."

Like a moth to the flame, she dropped the brush and bent toward him, only faintly aware of the distant coo of a dove, the indifferent whinny of a horse from down the aisle, the shaft of sunlight that struck a bright spot on Donegal's shiny coat. She thought of Jeffrey and tried to pull back. "Sir, I am in mourning for another, and I really don't think—"

"Then don't think," he answered roughly. His lips came down on hers. At first his kiss was slow, thoughtful, gentle, like Jeffrey's. But then he smothered her lips with demanding mastery. She found herself responding, slipping her arms around his neck, returning his kiss with reckless abandon. Blood pounded in her brain as his lips pressed harder, as he rocked her in his arms in a grip so tight she felt every hard inch of him. Then, just when she began to wonder if she had lost total control, he pulled his lips from hers. Thrusting her slightly away from him, he kissed her in the hollow of her neck, on her nose, her forehead, the top of her head. He stepped away and looked down at her. Hoarsely he murmured, "Say you didn't like that, Clarinda."

It took a moment for her to regain her senses. *What am I doing?* she thought with horror. "This is folly!" she cried. "I cannot do this, not after last night. What if my parents saw me? I would be sent into exile for the rest of my life." Firmly, she backed away. "I am not supposed to . . . this mustn't happen again."

"Of course not." He was in control again, the passion faded from his eyes. With an amused quirk of his eyebrow, he said, "You're a beautiful woman, Clarinda. Do forgive me if I was carried away."

"I don't know that I should," she answered with an indignation she didn't feel. Her knees were still weak, her senses still reeling, but he must not know how his kiss had affected her. "I can only hope you will allow me to come here to care for Donegal without . . . what just happened."

He gave her a devilish grin. "I suppose you have my word."

She was in no mood for silly games. "Really?" she snapped. "Well, according to my parents, I'm damaged goods, so if you have plans to indulge yourself again, you had best take up with my sister."

"That is absurd," he replied, instantly sober.

Clarinda picked up the brush where she had mindlessly dropped it and began brushing Donegal. Over her shoulder, she flung, "Rissa likes you, so why not? We are exactly the same, you know." She gave Donegal an extra-vigorous stroke and tartly added, "Just two peas in a pod."

Stormont seemed to stiffen. "I think it best I leave you now." He smiled, if faintly and wryly, and said with a slight, mocking bow, "Stay as long as you like. I shall see you at dinner tonight. Rest assured, I shall know which twin you are." He turned and was gone.

When Clarinda stepped into the cobblestone courtyard, Stormont was nowhere to be seen, but Sara Sophia had arrived, warm eyes full of delight at seeing her friend again. After a hug, she said, "I think it's terrible, your losing Donegal, but how wonderful he'll be close by."

"At least I shall get to see him," Clarinda told her. "Apparently Lord Stormont plans to stay. Isn't that wonderful news? That means you won't have to leave and be a governess. You can stay right here and keep on taking care of the horses."

To her surprise, Sara Sophia did not appear overjoyed. "I shan't stay much longer in any event," she said. Clarinda started to protest, but Sara Sophia sadly shook her head. "Don't you see? It's time I made my own life, away from here. Of course Lord Stormont would allow me to stay, but only out of charity. I must go where I am truly needed. If I don't, I shall feel useless in this world."

"Please reconsider. I would miss you so." Clarinda's heart ached at the very thought she might lose her dearest friend.

"I cannot stay. There are other things to consider, like . . ." Sara Sophia hesitated, and to Clarinda's surprise a blush bloomed on her cheeks. "I feel it best to get away from . . . certain problems in my life."

Clarinda was baffled, then suddenly it all came clear.

"It's Lord Wentridge, isn't it?" She felt a sudden anger. "Has he made advances? Because if he has, I shall inform Lord Stormont immediately."

Sara Sophia looked horrified. "Oh, no, nothing like that. Lord Wentridge has been the perfect gentleman. It's just that . . ."

Clarinda waited patiently while Sara Sophia hesitated, obviously debating with herself whether or not to tell all. "We've gone riding together every morning since he arrived," Sara Sophia began, a dreamy look of pleasure in her eyes. "We talk and talk and talk."

"What of?"

"Everything and nothing. Poetry . . . art . . . music. Horses . . . the cost of hay. We could talk all day, all night. He is a truly brilliant man, and so very knowledgeable."

"I would have thought him just another dandy."

Sara Sophia vigorously shook her head. "I know he appears vain and arrogant, but that's all for show. Underneath, he's kind, considerate, and very much the gentleman." A look of deep sorrow crossed her face. "I am falling in love with him. Such folly, for I am such a nobody. Even if he loved me, he could never in this world take me for his bride."

"Does he love you?" Clarinda asked softly.

"Who knows? Sometimes he looks at me in such a way that I think, yes, I can see love there, deep in his eyes. But then I think, you foolish girl! Lucius is a first son. He must marry well." Sara Sophia gave a bitter little laugh. "What a catch I would make! No dowry and a bastard to boot. To say the least, he would be marrying poorly if he married me. His parents would disown him."

"Sara Sophia, don't you dare say that about yourself," exclaimed Clarinda, wishing with all her heart that what her friend said wasn't true. Yet she couldn't argue. The facts spoke for themselves.

"Don't feel bad," Sara Sophia went on, patting Clarinda's hand. "I've started searching for a governess position. The sooner I leave here, the better." She managed a faint smile. "Now what about you? Were you talking to Lord Stormont just now? I saw him leave in rather a hurry, looking none too happy, I might add. Don't tell me you were arguing."

Clarinda's first impulse was to divulge everything. And yet, Stormont's kiss was so fresh, so earth-shaking, she needed to keep it secret within herself, at least for a time. To revel in the memory of his kiss? she wondered. To condemn herself? She wasn't sure, she only knew that for now she could not reveal her feelings, even to her dearest friend. "We did argue," she said. "I find him to be a most disturbing man, much too rough and uncouth."

"Well, he's certainly not Jeffrey," Sara Sophia said with a curious lilt to her voice. Clarinda was not sure what she meant but didn't ask.

After her talk with Sara Sophia, she finished with Donegal and hastened back to Graystone Hall. Tonight was Mama's dinner party. Stormont would be there, not that she cared. Rissa would care, though. Clarinda dreaded the rest of the day, wherein Rissa, intent on making herself The Most Beautiful One of All, was bound to be in such a bird-witted state of agitation that the whole house would be in an uproar.

Rissa . . . Lord Stormont.

What if he did decide he liked Rissa? Despite her protestations, an unwelcome, most surprising pang of jealousy struck Clarinda's heart.

When Clarinda arrived home, she found Rissa and Estelle in her bedchamber, rummaging through her clothes. "What do you think?" asked Rissa. Unabashed, clutching a gown of white lace over ruby satin, she glided to the mirror and held it up to herself. "Marvelous! Shall we wear this tonight?"

How Rissa could show such excitement over a silly gown was beyond her. "It looks fine to me," she said with a weary sigh.

"Fine! Estelle, go to my closet and get mine out."

After the lady's maid had left the bedchamber, Rissa perched on the bed. "I know where you went this morning. Did you see Lord Stormont?"

"Only briefly." Clarinda laughed to herself, picturing what Rissa's reaction would be if she knew the truth.

"Did he mention me?"

"Not that I remember." At least that much was true.

"Did you see Sara Sophia?"

"Rissa, really! Why all of a sudden are you so inquisitive?"

Rissa gave an elaborate shrug. "No reason, I was just concerned about her, that's all."

Clarinda eyed her sister with incredulity. "You've never cared one whit what happened to Sara Sophia. Why all the interest now?"

With shameless audacity, Rissa continued on. "Is she really poor? Have you any idea who her parents were? What will she do now?"

"She's a poor orphan who plans to be a governess. Nobody knows who her parents were. Now are you satisfied?"

Rissa ignored her question. "Do you know, I have lived next to Hollyridge Manor all my life but have rarely seen the inside?"

"Whose fault is that?" Clarinda asked sharply. "You could have come with me to visit Lord Westerlynn many a time." What was Rissa up to now? she wondered, detecting a suspiciously crafty expression in her sister's eyes. No one else would notice, but Clarinda did.

Rissa pointedly ignored her last comment. "Hollyridge Manor is awfully old, isn't it?"

"Built somewhere around 1530, I believe."

"I have heard talk of secret rooms and passages at Hollyridge, haven't you?"

Clarinda thought a moment. "I heard someone mention them once, I believe old Lord Westerlynn, but I'm not sure. At any rate, I've never seen any."

"So you wouldn't know if there are any there, would you?" Rissa asked, the craftiness still lingering in her eyes.

"Of course not." Clarinda frowned. "Why are you asking? I can't imagine any reason why you'd want to know if Hollyridge had secret rooms and passages."

Rissa shrugged. "I had better see to my dinner gown." She arose and left the room.

What is she up to? A feeling of unease came over her. More than anyone, she was aware there was never anything spontaneous about her sister. She was the most devious of schemers and calculated everything she did. When Rissa said, "No reason—just curious," it was a glaring signal she was up to no good.

But what? Clarinda wondered. She had no idea.

Chapter 8

Alone in her bedchamber, Rissa opened the chinoiserie work cabinet and once again took out the ancient keys Lord Westerlynn had pressed into her hand the day he died. She could not get them out of her mind.

"What the devil are you for?" she muttered, glaring at the keys as they lay in the palm of her hand.

A fortune awaits. Look for the room in . . .

The old man's last gasping words kept nagging at her. What room? And where? It was infuriating, knowing that but a mile away, in that musty old mansion, there existed some kind of a fortune hidden in a room someplace. A secret room? Was it a cache of gold coins perhaps? Was it a trove of precious jewels? If only she could sneak into Hollyridge Manor and look around. But how? Now she was sorry she had never made friends with Sara Sophia as Clarinda had done. But then, how could she have associated with such a low-class girl? This was all Clarinda's fault. She probably did know of a secret room and was simply not telling. This wouldn't be the first time Clarinda had plagued her. If people thought it was nothing but fun to be a twin, they were sadly mistaken. It was humiliating, having someone so exactly like herself, only she did everything faster. Clarinda had walked first, talked first, learned everything easier and quicker. She was even born first, by only two minutes, but just the same . . .

Rissa tossed the keys back in the cabinet and dropped the lid. Somehow, someway, she must think of an excuse to get into Hollyridge Manor, search for the secret room, and find the fortune, whatever it was. When she did, that mealymouthed little orphan would not get a penny. Everybody knew the poor were poor because God wanted them that way. If there was a fortune to be found, she, Lady

Clarissa Capelle, of impeccable wealth and lineage, deserved all of it, not that little tallow-faced Sara Sophia.

Rissa turned her attention to the gown she was planning to wear tonight. She would look so stunning Lord Stormont would fall at her feet, she was sure of it. Twenty were expected for dinner, including Lady Constance Lynbury, her son and daughter-in-law, and, regretfully, old Lord Skeffington, the most wearisome man on earth, whose passion for dull old medieval mansions caused him to drone on about them, ad infinitum. Indeed the guests would be a tedious lot, but welcome, nonetheless. They would fill the space between Lord Stormont and Clarinda, who, mercifully, would be sitting at the far end of the table, as far from Stormont as possible. And if her dear sister so much as batted an eyelid at him . . .

"She had better not," Rissa muttered. She picked up the etched ivory fan she intended to use at the dinner. Facing her mirror, she raised the fan to her face, so that only her eyes showed above. With a tinkling laugh, she practiced, "Why, how amusing you are, Lord Stormont." She would make sure she carried the fan in her left hand, a signal she was desirous of his acquaintance. But would he understand? Every dandy in London would know, but she wasn't sure if a man as rugged and independent as Stormont would be much concerned with the language of the fan. It was worth a try, though.

She had never understood why Clarinda never flirted that way. In fact, Clarinda had not the grace to flirt at all, besides not caring all that much about her clothes and her hair, and smelling of horse much of the time. That's why she couldn't work up much sympathy for Clarinda. That's why all her life she had known she was much more deserving than her twin.

How much longer?

Seated at Lord and Lady Capelle's dinner table, Robert had never been so bored. Worse, for at least the last ten minutes he had been forced to listen to Lady Constance Lynbury's steady stream of vitriol. Good God! He now knew more useless trivia about the neighbors than he would have wished to know in a lifetime. But what was his alternative? On his other side sat Lady Rissa, waiting to pounce.

"What delicious salmon," exclaimed Lady Lynbury. "Do you not agree, m'lord?"

"Hmm . . . what? Oh, indeed it is delicious," Robert answered, once Lady Lynbury's question had finally penetrated his churning thoughts. He flicked a glance toward the far end of the table where sat Clarinda, looking absolutely dazzling. How unfortunate he had not been seated closer, but then, he warned himself, he was not going to get involved with her, so what did it matter how close he sat?

I must stop this foolishness, he admonished himself. This morning's kiss in the stable had caught him completely off guard. All day he had been wondering why he had kissed her in the first place. He had most certainly not intended to. It must have been the lure of her golden hair in the early morning light, and those big blue eyes that regarded him so solemnly, not with that silly flirtatiousness of most girls that always put him off.

"I hear your stay here will be short, Lord Stormont, and that you intend to sell Hollyridge Manor."

Now seemed a good time to set things straight. "I plan to stay, Lady Lynbury."

" 'Pon my word!" cried the stout dowager, regarding him with avid interest. "The ladies of the countryside will be thrilled, my good sir." She wagged a finger at him. "Wait till you see the beauty of our local belles! Your bachelor days are numbered. We shall get you married, and soon, naughty boy."

Damnation! Despite what he had been telling himself, there was only one person he wanted to talk to tonight, and that was Clarinda. Not much chance of that, though. Not once all night had she met his eye. He felt a slight nudge against his knee. Turning with reluctance, he looked into the wide, flirtatious eyes of Lady Rissa.

"I am so glad you intend to stay, Lord Stormont," she gushed. "We shall get to know each other much better."

Damnation again. "It would be most pleasant to become better acquainted with *all* your family." He hoped she got the hint.

Undaunted, Rissa continued, "And I would just adore to see Hollyridge Manor, which I haven't seen since I was a little girl. It's such a beautiful old mansion, I would adore it if you would give me a tour."

Before Robert could answer, stuffy old Lord Skeffington, who had been one of Westerlynn's cronies, spoke up from across the table. "Yes, yes, Hollyridge Manor—a fine example of Elizabethan architecture built over structures of earlier date—dismantled abbeys, abandoned castles and the like."

Robert groaned inwardly, suspecting all at the table were doing the same. Given the chance, Sir William, a devotee of the architecture of old English mansions, would ramble for hours, boring all with his references to trussed rafters, corbels, crenellations, and heavy-molded purlins.

Lady Rissa spoke up. "How utterly fascinating, Sir William. Tell me, was Hollyridge converted from one of the old monasteries that Henry the Eighth destroyed?"

Sir William, flattered by the attention, sat straight and cleared his throat, obviously preparing for a lengthy discourse. "Hollyridge Manor is an outstanding example of the sixteenth century conversion of a castle. The original castle, much in ruins, was bought in 1540 for seven hundred fifty pounds by Sir Jonathan Lavery, the third earl of Sharrington."

"Is there much of the original castle left, Sir William?" Rissa asked with an expression of avid interest.

"A small portion remains. Perhaps the best example is the gatehouse. Above it rises a tower of thick gray stone that supposedly was used for defense in those olden times when the castle was in danger of attack. You won't see it from the front. That entrance is no longer used. The gatehouse stands in a remote corner of the estate. Just as well, perhaps, considering beast heads snarl and grimace like medieval gargoyles directly below its Renaissance parapet." He chuckled. "Gargoyles hardly fit with your Elizabethan architecture."

"How remarkable," exclaimed Rissa, "do tell us more."

Robert was incredulous. The whole table was yawning, yet the feather-headed Clarissa was urging Sir William to greater heights of tedium.

Clarinda spoke up from the far end of the table. "Sara Sophia and I used to play around the gatehouse when we were little. We were dying to see the inside, but could never get in."

"Of course not," said Sir William, regretfully shaking his head. "The entrance has a heavy oak door that's locked tight. Tried to get in myself once, but no luck. Need the key."

Rissa still appeared fascinated. "Tell me, Sir William, if Hollyridge was built around an old castle, might it not have any secret rooms or secret passageways?"

Sir William cleared his throat. "I don't believe so. Unless . . . If any place, you'd find a secret room in the gatehouse—above it, in the tower. That would have been the place for medieval skulduggery." He rewarded his remark with a kind of ancient cackle, then went on, "But getting back to . . ."

From her place at the far end of the table, Clarinda listened to the conversation with growing astonishment. She knew her sister as well as she knew herself, or up to now had thought she did, but Rissa's sudden interest in architecture was baffling. What was Rissa up to? She never did anything without a reason, always a selfish one. Clarinda had no idea what it could be. Secret rooms and passageways, how silly! But one good thing: focusing her attention on Rissa gave her a chance to sneak an occasional look at Lord Stormont, who sat next to her. Had he forgotten what occurred this morning? All evening he had not so much as glanced in her direction. She, however, had been able to ignore him only with the greatest difficulty, especially after that kiss. There they went again—those little quivers in her stomach every time she thought of the wonderfully powerful way he had swept her into his arms this morning and kissed her soundly, not giving her a chance to demur and say no. Certainly not like Jeffrey, who had asked permission first. When she'd said yes, he had brushed her lips lightly, almost timidly, as if she were a delicate flower that might crumble and blow away. Compared to Stormont's, Jeffrey's kiss was tame as tepid milk. *But what am I thinking?* she wondered, struck with guilt. *How could I have been so disloyal?* Jeffrey had died a hero's death at Trafalgar. She had vowed to mourn him all her life, yet here she was, so disturbed by Stormont's kiss she could not stop thinking about it. That rogue had stirred her passion as it had never been stirred before. But in memory of Jeffrey, it must not ever happen again. Besides, what if they had been caught? She felt unnerved just thinking of the consequences if word of their passionate embrace in the stable had reached her parents. And yet . . .

Her gaze kept straying toward Lord Stormont, catching mostly a view of his clear-cut profile as he listened attentively to the loquacious Lady Lynbury. She felt a ripple of excitement just looking at him. All day she had been thinking about him. She liked how that lock of dark hair fell over his forehead. She liked—

He glanced her way. Their eyes locked. Oh! She wanted to look away but the intensity of his warm, expressive gaze held her captive. They were seated at opposite ends of a long, crowded table, yet it was if they were alone together, the message his dark, insolent eyes were sending unmistakable: *I want you in my arms again. I want to kiss you again.*

"You seem rather quiet this evening, Lady Clarinda."

What was that? Oh, yes. Lucius, Lord Wentridge, seated next to her, had just spoken. She switched her gaze and gathered her wits. "If I am quiet, I'm not the only one, m'lord. You seem rather quiet yourself this evening."

Gossip had it that Lord Wentridge was not much more than a Bond Street fribble, but to her surprise he bluntly replied with heartfelt emotion, "I have been thinking of Sara Sophia. What a crime she cannot be here."

"I do agree." She frowned in puzzlement. "Forgive me, but I can't help but wonder why a man of your standing would give a fig about a girl like Sara Sophia."

"I wonder myself," Lucius replied with an odd look of bitterness on his thin-nosed, aristocratic face. "Were we to become involved, such a situation would be hopeless."

What a strange thing for him to say. She had no reply. Later, when she managed another glance toward the other end of the table, she caught Lord Stormont in an animated conversation with Rissa, who appeared all atwitter, waving her hands with great animation. *If she keeps that up, she will fall off her chair*, Clarinda thought, bemused.

It wasn't all that funny, though. Rissa had announced she was going to marry Stormont. What if she did?

I would not like that.

No, she would not like that at all. But she must stop

thinking this way. She must keep reminding herself that her heart had been broken when Jeffrey died and she would never love another man the same. Besides, even if she did fall in love with Lord Stormont, what chance would she have? Rissa wanted him, and Rissa always got what she wanted—Mama and Papa would see to that.

Of course, she had never promised Rissa she'd stay away from him . . .

No matter. The price for showing her feelings for Lord Stormont was too high. Mama and Papa would not hear of it if they knew that Rissa wanted him too. She laughed to herself, thinking how quickly she would be packed off to Grandfather Montague's.

Jennings, the butler at Hollyridge, let Lucius in when he arrived home from the dinner party, early and alone.

"Is anyone awake?" asked Lucius.

"She is in the north drawing room, sir."

"Thank you, Jennings." Lucius headed for the drawing room, musing upon the remarkable perceptiveness of servants, who sometimes knew a thing before he knew it himself.

Sara Sophia was sitting on a couch by the cavernous stone fireplace, her small face rosy in the glow of the fire. She was working on her embroidery. Hearing him, she raised her soft, luminous eyes and smiled sweetly. "Good evening, Lord Wentridge, home early are you not?"

How beautiful she looks, thought Lucius, *sitting there, her small, delicate white hands busy at their task.* Her expression was peaceful, as if she accepted without complaint the hapless circumstances of her life.

"I left early, Miss Clarmonte." He knew he shouldn't, but anger welled within him and he had to express himself. "It's an outrage you weren't there."

Her tinkling laughter filled the air. "But I was not invited. You knew that."

"It is still an outrage." Loosening his cravat, he slung himself into a chair next to the settee. "I cannot understand why they would not invite a lady of your quality. Why, you are more genteel, more intelligent—"

"It is all in the luck of one's birth," Sara Sophia interrupted with a slight shrug. "You, sir, were born to a life of wealth and privilege, whereas I have never possessed more than a few farthings and have only the vaguest idea who my parents were. But please don't concern yourself. I accept who I am." She bent her head over her stitching. "I shall be leaving soon. I have two offers of employment as a governess. Now it is just a matter of picking which one."

Lucius bit his lip and stared upward, unseeing, at the climbing cherubs that decorated the baroque chimneypiece. "I have enjoyed our rides," he finally said.

"So have I."

"No, really . . . Damme!" He leaped from his chair and started pacing. "I have never enjoyed riding so much, is what I meant to say. What I mean is—"

"Lord Wentridge, please do sit down." When he returned to his chair, Sara Sophia dropped her embroidery into her lap and regarded him thoughtfully. "When I first met you, I thought you were extremely arrogant."

"I was. I am still, but not with you."

"Oh, I know." Her expression softened. "On our rides by the river I got to know you better. I could see that underneath that satirical facade of yours hides a man who is compassionate and kind."

He tilted his brow and looked at her amusedly. "I can name a lady in London who doesn't share your opinion." He laughed ruefully. "Actually several."

She ignored his attempt at wit. "You said you enjoyed our rides. May I tell you why?"

"Yes, of course, though you could not possibly know—"

"Oh, I know all right," she said with a wise little smile. "It has been said of me that I am honest, sometimes unnecessarily so, but that's my nature and I cannot change."

"Nor would I wish you to."

"Then I'm glad you understand." Sara Sophia's took a deep breath. "Dear Lord Wentridge—"

"Lucius."

"Lucius, then. I, too, have hugely enjoyed those morning rides we take, and stopping to rest on the riverbank and just talking. Those are moments that have become so precious to me I can think of nothing else."

"I, too, can think of nothing else." With an eagerness unlike him, Lucius slid from his chair to kneel beside her. Gently he lifted her small hand and covered it with both of his. "I want you, Sara Sophia," he said, desperation—despair—resignation ringing in his voice. "I am mad for you. I think of nothing but you day and night." He unfolded her fingers and kissed the open palm of her hand.

Sara Sophia pulled her hand away and laid her palm gently along his cheek and gazed into his eyes. "This can never be," she said softly, "you know that."

"I want to marry you."

"Never. You know we cannot."

"I know no such thing," he vehemently replied. "I shall inform my parents you will be my bride. If they refuse to understand, they can keep their bloody fortune. We'll run off to Gretna Greene."

Sara Sophia sadly shook her head. "You have led a rich and satisfying life. Why would you want to waste the rest of it on a nobody like me?"

"Rich life?" Lucius laughed ironically. "Oh, yes, I was the rake of London. Gambling . . . drinking . . . other things I am not so very proud of. You've made me see how empty it all was."

Firmly she shook her head. "No, Lucius, this is the end of it. That's what I meant to tell you. No more early morning rides together—no more conversations by the river. They would be too tempting for the both of us. I am not a suitable girl for you and I shall never be."

"Do you know what irony this is?" Lucius asked. "Over the years, I could have married half the belles in London. Not that I flatter myself—my wealth and title were what they were after. I turned them all down. Now, for the first time in my life I have fallen truly in love, but can we be together?"

"No," she finished for him in a voice so unbending his heart sank because he knew she meant it and would never change. "Your parents would never approve of me. You think now that you would be happy with just me. You would, for a while, but later, after love's first bloom had faded, you would resent me for having robbed you of your fortune, your title, all that you hold dear."

"Not true," he stoutly declared, but she shook her head. "I shall be leaving soon, to work as a governess. Until I go, please, don't come riding early anymore. If I see you on the path, I swear I shall turn and go the other way."

"Of course," Lucius answered in a voice full of pain. "If

that's what you want." He paused to collect himself and rose to his feet. One corner of his mouth curved into a slight smile. "I have just one request."

She looked up at him, misery in her eyes. "I would do anything for you."

"Except marry me," Lucius answered wryly. "Will you kiss me? Is that too much to ask? I shall never love again, you know," he said as he drew her to her feet. "Just once. One kiss that must last me a lifetime."

Her silence was her acquiescence. He drew her close. His breath came fast as he ran his fingers through the softness of her silky hair and over the milky softness of her cheeks. He had kissed many a woman, but only as a prelude to his own selfish needs. How different this was. He could feel himself trembling, but he didn't care. With a groan, he crushed her to him and covered her lips with his, his heart hammering in his chest. He felt her eager response. They clung together, as if melted into one, until he felt her hand push gently on his shoulder. He broke away, burning with desire, aching with the need for more, but she pressed her fingers to his lips and whispered, "No more. It breaks my heart, but we are done, Lucius."

How could he ever let her go? "I love you, Sara Sophia," he said. "My heart will be forever empty without you. We could have had so much together . . ." He could say no more because his voice broke. He felt a surprising moisture in his eyes—Good God, what would they say in London!—and, embarrassed, turned away.

"I shall leave for London in the morning," he said, his back to her.

"But there's no need—"

"Yes there is." He turned to face her, his mask of cynicism restored. "Things do get rather dull in the countryside. London calls. For the best, right? Farewell, Miss Clarmonte. I shan't trouble you further." He left her then, agonizingly aware he had left his heart behind.

In the morning, Clarinda walked the mile to the stables at Hollyridge. "Ye could ride Lady Rissa's horse," Morris had told her when she passed by Graystone's stables, but her heart rebelled. If she could not ride Donegal, she preferred to walk.

At Hollyridge, Clarinda found Sara Sophia hard at work brushing one of the thoroughbreds. "Lord Stormont isn't riding today?" she asked.

When Sara Sophia turned to face her, Clarinda was shocked to see her face, pale to begin with, was a sickly white. Her eyes were red and held a stricken expression, as if something terrible had happened.

"Dear God, what is wrong?"

Shoulders sagging, Sara Sophia replied, "Lord Wentridge—Lucius—is leaving as we speak. He's returning to London. I doubt he'll ever return."

"But why? You two were getting along so well."

Sara Sophia managed a tremulous smile. "Too well, I'm afraid. I love him with a passion, you know, and last night he told me he loved me. But what could we do? I had to tell him . . ." Sara Sophia fought back tears. "I shall never see him again, and that's so hard."

"I am so sorry," Clarinda said, putting her arm around her friend.

"Don't be. I shall be fine." Sara Sophia pulled out her handkerchief and wiped her eyes. "My whole life, I've been happy to be who I am. Only now"—she gave a desperate little laugh—"if only I could have been born *somebody.* Not a princess, or a duchess, or a countess—just a viscountess would have done, or even a baroness would have suited. Just *somebody,* good enough for Lucius's family."

Clarinda nodded in grim agreement. "I would wager they would have accepted even the daughter of a knight, if Lucius insisted. But as it is . . ." She regarded her disconsolate friend with concern, searched desperately for something uplifting to say. "Try not to feel bad. I'm sure you'll meet someone else someday and you'll forget all about Lucius."

"No, never," Sara Sophia declared as if her heart would break. She pulled back her shoulders and put on a brave face. "Ah, well, I am what I am and nothing will change it. Will you ride Donegal today?"

Clarinda wished she could comfort her friend, but realized, bleakly, there was nothing more she could say. "Indeed, I shall ride Donegal." Despite herself, her gaze wandered toward the mansion. "It is my fondest wish that Lord Stormont stay away." Sara Sophia began to laugh, causing Clarinda to ask with mock indignation, "What? Is that funny?" Underneath, she was happy to hear her friend laugh again.

"I know you too well, Clarinda. You like Stormont better than you care to admit."

"What's the point even if I did?" asked Clarinda. "Mama has decreed no man except Lord Sufton can come courting. I am under strict orders to stay away from him."

"Stay away from whom?" came a male voice.

Stormont. He had startled them both. There he stood, crop in hand, looking absolutely smashing in his plain but exquisitely tailored riding clothes. Clarinda was so taken aback she didn't know what to say until she decided, why not the truth?

She drew herself up with dignity. "I am to stay away from you, sir. Do not ask why."

A muscle twitched in Stormont's jaw, the only sign that he could be annoyed. With a raise of his brows, he said, "Quite all right, Lady Clarinda. I daresay, this estate is so huge, and there are so many places to ride, that we can easily arrange separate paths. Are you planning on riding Donegal today?" She nodded. "Which way?" he inquired pleasantly.

"I think . . . perhaps I shall take the path that circles around the estate."

"Fine. I shall take the path by the river." He bowed nicely and looked about for the groom. "Fetch Sham's saddle, will you, Pitney?" he called. "Good day, Miss Clarmonte, Lady Clarinda. May you enjoy your ride." After a smart bow, he disappeared into the stable to get Sham.

Clarinda stared after him, finding herself keenly disappointed.

"Do you feel bad you can't ride with him?" asked Sara Sophia.

"I could say no," said Clarinda. A pain squeezed her heart as she thought of him. "But that would be a lie."

Chapter 9

Morris was feeding a horse in the courtyard of Graystone Hall's stables when he heard a noise, looked up, and blinked in surprise. "Yer back already, Lady Clarinda?"

Horrid old man. Rissa glared at him. "I am not Lady Clarinda. I am Lady Clarissa and I have come to ride Dublin."

"Sorry, mum." The old man looked confused. "So shall I get him for you, or—?"

"Of course, get him, and put the saddle on him, and whatever else you're supposed to do."

Rissa tapped her foot as she stood waiting, snapping her riding crop impatiently against the side of her never-before-worn black riding gown. This was Clarinda's doing. Everyone knew a lady of class and refinement would never dream of saddling her own horse. Not her beloved twin, though. Judging from Morris's confusion, Clarinda, who cared nothing for the appearance of things, was crass enough to do it herself.

"Give me a boost," she commanded Morris after he had readied Dublin for the ride. As she settled into the sidesaddle, the gelding snorted, threw his head back and danced about. Alarmed, Rissa clung to the saddle and let out a yelp.

Morris grabbed the reins and settled the horse. "Careful, mum, Dublin's a mite frisky today." He frowned. "Ye don't have the experience riding like Lady Clarinda does. Per'aps ye shud ride old Buttercup."

The gall! Fury almost choked her, but Rissa managed to declare, "That won't be necessary, Morris. Now stand back."

How anyone could find pleasure in riding on an animal's

swaying, sweaty back was beyond her, Rissa mused, as she carefully guided Dublin along the river path to Hollyridge Manor. If it weren't for the necessity of keeping her mission a secret, she would never have thought to ride Dublin. She had no choice, though. She had planned this out last night—in the middle of the night, actually, when, half asleep, she had been struck by a startling revelation. The old gatehouse—the locked oak door—Westerlynn's keys!

Of course! She had sat bolt upright in her bed, her mind racing. The secret room was in the gatehouse tower. The more she thought, the more excited she became. Not only was the tower the obvious hiding place for the fortune, but the best part of all, it was not part of the house and could be accessed from the outside. She would not even have to invent some ruse for getting herself inside the old mansion! All she had to do was go to Hollyridge, circle around until she found the deserted gatehouse, open the oak door with the key, and . . . Ah! Her heart skipped a beat, just thinking of the fortune that could be awaiting her inside.

The only problem was, how to get there. She could walk, she supposed. It was only a mile to Hollyridge, but after she got there, she would be compelled to creep about that huge estate, through brambles and thickets and thick forest, and heaven-knew-what. Much easier by horseback. Besides, if she were caught walking, she would have no excuse, whereas someone on horseback could ride where they pleased with impunity, simply claiming they had lost the path.

Only she hated horses. For a time, she had debated whether she could bring herself to ride Dublin, but curiosity won, plus the compelling appeal of Lord Westerlynn's final words on this earth: *A fortune awaits Sara Sophia.*

Not Sara Sophia, *me,* Rissa thought as she turned Dublin from the river path to cut directly to the estate. For a while she carefully guided Dublin through the thick forest that backed the estate, the horses's hooves muted on the forest floor, over dips and hollows, hillocks and mounds, all up-holstered in spongy moss. At last she came to the area she hoped would be closest to the gatehouse. She was right. As she rode Dublin out of the woods, she was pleased with herself for having guessed so closely. Directly ahead, she spied the top of the old gatehouse tower that stood not far from the rambling estate, the bottom of its ancient gray stone walls only slightly visible beneath the overgrowth of shrubs and thickets. Ivy vines grew up the tower's surface, clear to the leering gargoyles beneath the parapet three stories above.

Rissa slid off Dublin to the ground. Heaven only knew how she would get back on the wretched animal, but she would worry about that later. She tied the reins to a tree branch, then reached down the bodice of her riding gown. She shoved aside her gold necklace and pulled out the two ancient keys, warm from their resting place between her breasts. Clutching the keys tightly, she looked carefully around. It wouldn't do at all if someone saw her. Not much chance of that, though. This part of the estate appeared deserted.

When Rissa was positive there was no one else about, she made her way to the gatehouse, where a large, sturdy oak door was built into an arched recess. It was so old and weathered it looked as if centuries had elapsed since last it was opened. Rissa looked up. From the parapet on the tower above, one of those horrid medieval gargoyles snarled directly down at her, its stony eyes clearly signaling, *If you trespass you die!* She fought the urge to flee, telling herself she could not possibly leave now, not when she was so close to finding the fortune. "You had better open," Rissa muttered as she slid the key into the lock. She turned the key. Nothing. It wouldn't budge. She turned it again. Nothing. She pulled the key back, just a trifle, tried again, and—oh yes!—with a screeching creak the ancient bolt released.

She had unlocked the door! In triumph, Rissa caught her breath. But suddenly she wondered, *what if I find something dreadful inside?* What if there were hideous skeletons lying about, or some evil force waiting to harm her, or bats flying out at her—only didn't they do that just at sunset?

She felt a shiver of panic. How could she cope with acting on her own like this when all her life she'd been surrounded every waking moment by nannies, governesses, lady's maids, and tutors? She was more frightened now than she had ever been in her life, yet a driving force compelled her to continue. There could very well be a fortune inside. *My fortune.* With bated breath, her heart pounding in her chest, Rissa pressed down on the latch and pushed. Nothing happened, it was stuck. She had to use her shoulder, backed by all her strength, to shove open the ancient, squeaking door.

"Why, Lord Stormont, what a surprise."

Clarinda drew Donegal to a halt. She was heading home after her ride and had slowed her mount to a sedate gait when she heard clopping hooves along the path behind her and instantly knew who it was. "Fancy finding you here," she said, tongue in cheek, as Stormont rode up beside her. Pointedly she added, "Especially after we agreed to take separate paths."

The corner of Stormont's lips pulled into a slight grin. "You knew I would find you."

"I did no such thing."

He swung off his horse and reached for her reins. "Get down. I want to talk to you."

"I see no need," she said, flinging her hair back.

His eyes raked her boldly. "Well, I do. Come, get down."

The man was much too forceful. She should nudge Donegal and ride away. That would show him. But somehow she didn't want to do that. On the other hand, she hated to be told what to do. She'd had enough of that at home. "I do not like being ordered about."

"Do tell." With an exaggerated bow, Stormont declared, "My deepest apologies, madam, for not having the sensitivity to perceive that you are an independent young woman who thinks for herself." With an irresistibly devastating grin he regarded her. "Now, get off your horse, or shall I lift you down?"

"My, my, so masterful!" With a laugh she slid from Donegal, not minding in the least she had capitulated. A thickness of tall oak and hornbeam trees, hawthorn bushes, green grass, and buttercups edged the trail where they had stopped. A fallen log lay in thick grass mixed with periwinkles and forget-me-nots. Laughing, they made their way to the log and sat down.

Arranging her riding skirt about her, Clarinda asked, "Now tell me what you wanted to talk to me about. I cannot imagine what it could be, especially since you know I'm supposed to stay away from you." Apprehensively, she looked around. "I could be in a great deal of trouble if we're seen together."

He looked puzzled. "I know they took your horse away, but there's more?"

With reluctance, she related all the ways she was being punished for her supposed shocking transgression with Lord Cranmer. When she finished, she was tempted to tell Stormont about her sister's plans to capture him, but decided she could not because that would be disloyal. He most certainly deserved to know, though. Rissa didn't know how lucky she was not to have her predatory plans revealed.

She was startled when Stormont asked suspiciously, "Does Rissa have anything to do with this?"

She gave Stormont an impish smile, determined to dodge the issue. "What does it matter? Rissa and I are so alike you would be as happy with one of us as the other."

"You're being absurd again," Stormont answered with a frown, not in the least sharing her humor.

Clarinda said bluntly, "Don't forget, Rissa has liked you from the beginning, whereas I started out not liking you very well."

"Because I was making off with Hollyridge's horses, as I recall."

"Yes, and because you bought Donegal, only now . . ." She could not help a slight grin. "Now that I've thought about it, I'm grateful to you for letting me ride him."

"Does this mean I'm totally forgiven?" he said with a gleam of devilment in his eye.

She looked down her nose at him. "Not entirely."

"Crushed again!" he said lightly, then turned serious. He took her hand in his and looked her square in the eye. "I liked kissing you yesterday at the stables. Take warning, I have plans to do it again."

"That's honest enough," she answered, "but if you're so inclined, why don't you go kiss Rissa? I said we were exactly the same, didn't I? Well, I was wrong." From under her long lashes she glanced at him mischievously. "We're not entirely the same. She likes you more than I do."

"Stop throwing Rissa at me," Robert said, bridled anger in his voice.

"Sorry." She knew she'd gone too far.

Appeased, Robert continued, "Yesterday you said you were in mourning for another. I want to know what in blazes you meant by that."

"I don't have to tell you every little thing," she protested, then, chagrined, caught herself. That sounded sickeningly coquettish, just like Rissa. He was looking at her, patiently waiting, as if he knew she would soon come to her senses and act like a reasoning adult. "All right, but what I shall tell you is in the strictest confidence."

"Of course."

With a little sigh, Clarinda told Robert of her deep, abiding love for Jeffrey.

When she finished, Robert was stony-faced and silent. Finally, "You two were not betrothed?"

She hesitated, reluctant to admit the truth. "Actually he was betrothed to Rissa."

"Indeed? I should like to know how that came about, but I shan't pry." Something lively sparked in Stormont's eyes. "So did your handsome poet ever kiss you?"

"Once," she grudgingly admitted.

"Then tell me, was it a brotherly kind of kiss, or was it . . . shall we say, similar to the one you received yesterday morning?"

Clarinda tried to keep her composure, but she could feel herself blushing. Ignoring it, she fluttered her eyelids in a Rissa-like manner and asked, "Was I kissed yesterday? If so, I have completely forgotten."

He gripped her shoulders in a movement so swift she gasped. "You haven't forgotten," he told her, purpose gleaming in his eyes. "You've been thinking a good deal about it, as have I."

"I have not!"

"Then it appears I must refresh your memory."

A devilish smile played on Stormont's face as he drew her closer. She knew she should push him away, and she most definitely would, in just a minute, but for now his masculine nearness was overwhelming. A delightful shiver of wanting ran through her. She *must* push him away, and soon, but right now she wanted very much for him to kiss her again. Then she thought, *Jeffrey. I can't do this.* Shaking her head, she placed her palm on Stormont's chest and pushed hard. "No, please don't," she said.

*   *   *

Her heart thumping madly, Rissa stepped into the musty-smelling bottom floor room of the gatehouse and looked about. Empty. What a relief! No bats, no skeletons. There was just a big, empty room, dimly lit by thin shafts of light from small slits in the wall far above. Nothing stood on the rotting wooden floor or hung from the gray stone walls.

A rough, uneven, narrow stone stairway was built against the wall, leading to the second story high above. Fearful again, Rissa climbed the stairs and found another locked door, smaller this time, at the top. She chose the smaller key, inserted it, and heard the bolt snap back. She pushed the door and nothing happened. Again, she had to shove her shoulder against it. The harsh sound of creaking hinges grated against her eardrums as, finally, it opened. When it was wide, a whiff of fetid air greeted her as she stepped inside, to a room in which the only light came from the high, slitted windows.

In the dimness she could see the room was not empty. Her pulse quickened at the sight of crates stacked around the wall. Surely the fortune was inside. She hastened to the nearest crate, pulled the top off easily, and peered in. There was something . . . what was it? Why had she not thought to bring a lamp or candle? Finally in the faint light she could make out rolled canvases. *Paintings?* She picked one up, laid it on the floor, and partially unrolled it, to where a nude woman lying in a prone position came into view. *Well, really.* How could anyone possibly be interested in a big-bellied woman with no clothes on, all stretched out with her hand behind her head? The woman was sort of smiling, looking as if she thought she had something to show off, which she most certainly did not. Rissa checked the corner that had some kind of signature. *Rubens,* it looked like, whoever he was. Oh, well. Was this all there was? She unrolled a few more canvases, plucking them from the various crates. There was a dreary painting by someone named *Van Eyck*; a dark portrait of a sour-faced old lord signed by someone called *Reynolds;* and some engravings by another name she'd never heard of, *William Hogarth.* Aside from more nude women—all of them fat and displaying themselves in a disgusting manner, there were paintings of pretty flowers, landscapes and the like, all signed with artists' names she did not recognize, and no wonder. She had paid little attention when she and Clarinda took lessons in art. Clarinda had been interested, but she, Rissa, had drifted unhearing through the lessons, daydreaming about more important things like gowns and coiffeurs, and beaux. How disappointing! All this effort for nothing except some stupid old paintings. Even if they were worth something, which she highly doubted, there would be no way in the world she could dispose of them in secret, all by herself.

Was there nothing more? She looked around. In the middle of the room stood an extraordinary stone table, supported by stone fauns carrying buckets of fruit. On the table sat what looked like a gilded jewelry casket. It wasn't large, but it was her last hope. As she walked toward it, she fancied a cache of gold, silver, diamonds, pearls, rubies.

The casket had a rounded top hinged at the back. It was not locked. Rissa pushed the top back and eagerly peered inside. How disappointing. There was nothing inside except several pages of aged-looking parchment covered with a fine handwriting in—she peered closer—of all things, French. "This isn't fair," she cried aloud. Her words echoed back to her from the cold stone walls, ringing tauntingly in her ears.

She grabbed the papers and came close to throwing them across the room. Nothing to be gained from that, though. Her next impulse was to simply leave them behind, but she was curious. She couldn't read them here, there was not enough light. Even if there were, she would have to take them home to translate. Like every refined young lady of the Polite World, she was supposed to know French, but unfortunately, her grasp of the language was abysmal. She wished now she hadn't daydreamed her way through all those boring French lessons.

The papers tucked in the bosom of her dress, Rissa left the tower, after straining to close and lock the heavy oak doors behind her so that no one would ever know she'd been there. All that effort for nothing! There was a sour feeling in the pit of her stomach as she led Dublin to the handy stump of a beech tree. Not without a struggle, she hoisted herself back atop the horse, grateful no one was around to witness such an awkward spectacle. This was all Lord Westerlynn's fault, she thought resentfully as she started toward home. What had the old fool been thinking of when he called a bunch of musty old paintings a fortune?

Halfway to Graystone Hall, Rissa saw two horses ahead of her, tied to tree branches beside the path. She halted Dublin and heard laughter coming from somewhere close. One of the horses looked like Donegal. The other—*was it Stormont's?*

The thought froze her brain.

Clarinda had promised she would keep her distance from Lord Stormont. Well, she hadn't exactly promised, but Rissa had made it clear she wanted Stormont for herself. *How dare Clarinda. But perhaps I am mistaken. Perhaps those horses belong to someone else.*

A burning curiosity overcame her. She had to know. Her first thought was to simply ride right up to Stormont and Clarinda, if indeed it was they, and confront them. But after further thought, she decided a much better plan would be to sneak up and see whatever there was to see. She slipped from Dublin—such folly! How would she ever get back up again?—led him off the path and tied his reins to a tree. Moving stealthily through the thick brush and brambles that bordered the path, she drew close, stopped, and listened. Nothing. She drew closer, grateful the foliage was heavy here, and peered through the thick branches of a hawthorn bush.

Shock flew through her. There they were—Stormont and her dear twin—sitting upon a log, and he was trying to kiss her, but she was saying something that sounded like, "No, please don't," and pulling away. "I must go," Rissa clearly heard Clarinda say.

"We must meet again," Stormont replied.

"I cannot."

"Why not?"

"You know why not. And besides, I am not ready for this." Clarinda stood and gazed down at him. "You should not have kissed me this morning."

"Do tell." Stormont appeared unperturbed. "I must leave for London tomorrow, then on to my home in Kent. While I am gone, give some thought to your dear, departed Jeffrey. Ask yourself if you really want to spend the rest of your life mourning for a man who preferred your sister."

"How calloused!" she cried.

He stood quickly and was on her like a cat, gripping her arms. "Can Jeffrey warm your bed at night?" He shook her slightly, his head bent, his face only inches from hers. "Can he make your pulse race? Can his kiss make you burn for his touch?"

"Get away!" Clarinda called, her fists beating on his chest. "Can't you see, my heart belongs to Jeff—"

Her words were smothered by his mouth, which came down on hers so hungrily Rissa heard her sister give a whimper. Rissa watched, transfixed, as Stormont continued the kiss with barbaric fervor, and Clarinda—oh, this was hard to believe!—continued her struggle to get away. Just watching, Rissa felt a wild swirl in the pit of her stomach. She could almost feel her own mouth burning with the fire kindled by Stormont's unleashed passion. *Clarinda, you're a fool,* she thought, as from a distance she felt her own limbs tremble as Stormont's hands slid upward, ever upward, from Clarinda's waist until they pressed against the sides of her breasts. *I surrender, Robert, I am yours,* she silently called. His touch sang through her veins. She could scarcely believe it when Clarinda broke from the kiss to declare, "Please, enough!" and Stormont let her go and backed away.

The two stood staring at one another, the only sound coming from Stormont's heavy, uneven breathing. At last he bowed and said lightly, "My apologies. Again I seem to have gotten carried away."

Clarinda appeared dazed and shaken, unable to say a word.

"Upon my return, I want to see you again," Stormont declared.

"I don't think I—" Clarinda began in a weak voice, but Stormont interrupted.

"Think about it while I am gone. I shall be back the Saturday before Christmas. Meet me Sunday morning, early—the stables at Hollyridge."

Still sounding as if she was in a daze, Clarinda repeated, "The Sunday before Christmas—early—the stables at Hollyridge."

"Don't forget," Stormont admonished as he swung onto his horse. "Good day, Clarinda." With an amused twinkle

in his eye, he touched his hand to his forehead in a mock
salute and rode away.

Swiftly, practically reeling from the stunning sight, Rissa
retreated as silently as she could and returned to where she
had tethered Dublin. Shock yielded quickly to fury. How dare
they! she thought over and over again as she stood off the
path, hidden behind a tree, silently waiting until she looked
down the path and Clarinda and her horse were gone.

At least they hadn't seen her.

To further compound her ire, Rissa could not find another tree stump to climb upon so she could get back atop
her horse. On foot, leading Dublin, she walked the rest of
the distance to Graystone Hall, her thoughts alternating
between anger that she had to walk, and rage at her sister.
Clarinda would pay for this. How, she wasn't sure yet, but
without doubt her twin would live to regret this act of
treachery.

And there was something else to occupy her mind . . .

Rissa pressed a hand to her bosom. Good. The keys and
papers were still there. Translating from French would be
an arduous task, but she simply must grit her teeth and do
it. She could hardly wait to find out what secrets, if any,
those pages in French revealed about Sara Sophia.

As for what to do about Clarinda, that would require
some thought. Best not to reveal she had seen her sister in
the arms of Stormont, although keeping her silence would
not be easy. Her impulse was to vent her rage at Clarinda,
then tell their parents, who would surely, and at long last,
dispense the ultimate punishment. But what of Stormont?
How deeply did he care for Clarinda? Might he not go
after her if she was sent away?

There had to be a better way.

An idea began to form in Rissa's head. If it worked, not
only could she wreak revenge, she could cool that fiery
passion she had witnessed between Stormont and her sister.
Their romance would turn as cold as the ice on the Northern Sea.

If she carried through with her plan, it would be tricky,
downright daring, but if it worked, what sweet revenge.

Thoughts of Robert Stormont kept crowding Clarinda's
mind. All day, and now into the evening, she had thought

of nothing but their encounter, feeling her heart swell whenever she thought of that long, passionate kiss he had given her while they were standing by the log. She caught her breath, just remembering the warmth of his hands through her dress, how they had started at her waist, then slid slowly upward . . .

Strange. He had been the one to break away.

A quick knock on the door. Estelle entered. "M'lady, what are you wearing for dinner this evening?"

She had totally forgotten, thanks to Lord Stormont. But this was a surprise. Usually Rissa was the one to choose, and she, not caring, merely went along with her sister's choice. "What does Lady Rissa want to wear?"

"Lady Rissa ees working at her desk and does not weesh to be disturbed."

"Are you sure?" Rissa hated to read, hated to write. Up to now, her lovely harlequin desk was mainly just for show.

Estelle rolled her eyes. "*Mon Dieu!* I swear eet's true. For the last hour she has been pouring over a French-to-English dictionary, translating some document on parchment."

"What could it be?" Clarinda asked.

"She wouldn't let me see."

Clarinda rose purposefully from the settee. "I shall be right back."

The minute Rissa had returned home, she hurried to the classroom that had once been hers and Clarinda's, but was now Alexander's. Rummaging through stacks of books, she finally found the tattered copy of a French-English dictionary. Gripping it tightly, she hastened to her bedchamber, straight to her desk, where with prodigious effort, and much looking-up of words, she translated the letter. After she was done, she shook her head, hardly believing the astounding words she had just put into English. Gingerly she picked up the letter. Unbelievable! Whoever would have guessed? She would read it again, just in case she had been dreaming.

To my dearest Sara Sophia,
It is with a heavy heart that I must leave you this sad missive. Collette, my faithful lady's maid sits by my bed,

writing my words down as I speak, for I, too weak to lift my hand from the counterpane, am deathly ill, not likely to recover. But before I depart this earth, I have one compelling task which, above all else, must be completed. I must explain to you who I am, who you are, and the circumstances which led your dear father and me to our tragic fates in a series of events too painful to relate, and yet I must relate them.

I, your mother, was born Louise Marie de Polignac in Saint-Cloud, France, in the year of our Lord, 1762. Daughter of the Comte de Polignac, I grew up accustomed to privilege and luxury. In 1780 I sealed my marriage with your father, Louis-Armand, Comte de Clarmonte, a man of great honor, charm, and wealth, whose vast estate at La Rochelle was noted for its fine collection of art and antiques. When I met Louis-Armand, he was a member of the French diplomatic service, serving the Sardinian court as ambassador to Russia. We fell in love immediately. Later, after we married, he served as an advisor to Marie Antoinette and was active on behalf of the French monarchy. This position proved to be his ultimate downfall, for the peasants revolted during this time and murdered thousands of members of the nobility who had remained loyal to the Crown.

Your dear father was among them.

Even now, as I lie in my sickbed, I find the tragic events that lead to his death excruciating to recall, but for your sake, my beloved daughter, I shall recount them. In 1793, during the Reign of Terror, your father was arrested as a monarchist by the National Convention. He was imprisoned for a time, then brought before the Revolutionary Tribunal on December 14, 1793. The trial was a mockery. After only minutes, he was condemned as a counterrevolutionary. Two days later, he was forced to ride in a tumbril through the streets of Paris, hands tied behind his back. Along the route, he was jeered at, spit upon by the unruly mob, until he arrived at the Place de la Liberté where that ghastly device, the guillotine, awaited him. For his sake, I was there, in disguise, blending with the bloodthirsty crowd that cheered each time that swift, cruel blade dispatched yet another innocent victim. Forcing myself, I watched as your father, his head held high, walked unaided up the steps to the platform. I heard him bravely decline a blindfold. I watched his lips form the words, "I love you," as he knelt to receive his fate and knew that those, his last words on earth, were meant for me. I watched the blade come down, and his head . . . ah, I can say no more on the matter, having never fully recovered from the near-unbearable agony I experienced that terrible day as I watched the only man I ever loved put to a horrible death.

During the time of his imprisonment, your father was selfless in thinking of his wife and child first while his efforts to save himself were always second.

To that end, he contacted his old and dear friend, Lord Westerlynn, with whom he had done business for many years. It was through Westerlynn's brave and selfless assistance that your father was able to smuggle much of his precious artwork from his chateau at La Rochelle to Hollyridge Manor. At the time of your father's death, I, too, was in dire peril of being arrested by the Tribunal. Thus, you and I were forced to flee France, taking only the clothes on our backs. Arranged by Lord Westerlynn, it was an arduous journey, fraught with peril, though I doubt you remember since you were barely four years old at the time.

I shall always be grateful to Lord Westerlynn for risking his own life in order to save us and bring us to England, where he gave us this haven, here at Hollyridge Manor.

At present we live in dire peril, should those members of the Tribunal discover where I am and come after me. Since it is my heartfelt wish that your childhood be without fear, I appealed to Lord Westerlynn that he pledge himself to secrecy and not reveal the true circumstances of your birth until your eighteenth birthday, at which time he would give you this letter. By then, I trust your life will no longer be in danger and that the world can know that as an only child you have, in your own right, inherited your father's wealth and title.

Know that you are Countess Sara Sophia Alexandrine de Clarmonte.

Know that although your father's entire estate was confiscated, his brave efforts salvaged enough art, mainly in

the form of paintings, to enable you to live in luxury the
rest of your life. Lord Westerlynn has found a safe place
to store the artwork that was smuggled at great peril
across the Channel to England. This is one of the things
he will tell you about on your eighteenth birthday, at
which time you will find yourself a countess, and very
wealthy indeed.

And so farewell, my daughter. I leave this cruel world
with joy in my heart, for soon I shall be reunited with
your beloved father. My only regret is that I shall miss
seeing you grow to womanhood. I know already of your
sweet disposition, and how bright you are, and I can see
by your eyes that you will also be beautiful. May God
shine his mercy upon you, and may you lead a rich,
happy, worthwhile life.

> With heartfelt love,
> Your mother, Louise Marie de Clarmonte

Astounding! Rissa dropped the letter to her desk and sat
back in awe. Who would have ever thought that drab of a
girl was a genuine countess?

Sara Sophia would be the toast of London if the *ton*
found out.

But they won't, not if I have anything to say about it.

And she definitely did. Rissa felt a glow of triumph. It
was indeed satisfying to know that she was in control, that
the fate of Sara Sophia—wrong!—*Countess* Sara Sophia Alexandrine de Clarmonte lay in her hands. She owed nothing
to Sara Sophia. In fact, given a title and a fortune, the chit
would then be a rival for the affections of Lord Stormont,
or even that decadent Lord Wentridge. That simply would
not do. Of course, it would be a pity when the poor girl
left for her dreary position as a governess, never knowing
the glory that was truly hers. But life was like that. If God
had planned for Sara Sophia to find that letter, then she
would have found it.

God meant that letter for me.

Rissa wondered if she should burn the letter. That way,
for a certainty, no one would ever know. She touched the
letter to the flame of the beeswax candle on her desk, then
quickly drew it back, frowning in deep thought. Such an
irretrievable step—perhaps she had better not. One never

knew. Perhaps the letter might come in handy later on. She would keep it, tucked away at the bottom of her sewing chest, along with the keys.

As for those paintings, it appeared they were worth something after all. But how to sell them? She would have to think about it. Surely there must be a way.

A knock sounded on the door, then it opened. *Clarinda*. Rissa felt a surge of anger. She wondered if she could keep her vow not to say anything about the shocking scene she'd witnessed. *But perhaps I should confront her*, she suddenly realized. *Perhaps I can use the knowledge to my advantage*.

Rissa quickly closed the dictionary and set it atop the papers. Placing a smile on her face, she turned to face her sister.

Chapter 10

What is Rissa up to? thought Clarinda as she entered her sister's bedchamber. How strange to see Rissa sitting at her desk, acting the studious scholar, papers stacked in front of her, as well as the tattered French-English dictionary they had used for their French lessons so long ago.

Rissa's face had an odd expression, as if she had been caught at something naughty. "You startled me," she said with an nervous smile. "I was, uh, just brushing up on my French."

"How commendable," Clarinda answered pleasantly. She could not resist adding, "In fact, quite the miracle."

Rissa appeared to take a moment to digest Clarinda's needling remark. But instead of replying in kind, as she normally would, she shifted her eyes away, a sure sign she was hiding something.

But what? Clarinda didn't know and knew it was useless to try and find out. "Estelle wants to know what we plan to wear for dinner tonight."

Her twin, composure quickly restored, regarded her with critical eyes. "You really should toss out that awful old riding gown."

Ah, the old Rissa again. "Just pick something to wear for dinner. Something simple."

"The bottle-green cotton batiste should do."

"Fine." Clarinda was turning to leave when Rissa asked, "Incidentally, has Sara Sophia made her plans?"

"Regarding what?"

"Regarding leaving Hollyridge Manor." Rissa's forehead creased in a frown. "Surely she's not staying?"

Why all this interest in Sara Sophia? This was the second time Rissa had asked pointed questions about her friend. "Sara Sophia is considering two positions as governess. She will choose one or the other quite soon, and then be gone. I shall miss her terribly."

"Hmm, but of course." Rissa made no attempt to conceal the look of relief that crossed her face. Again Clarinda turned to leave. "What are you doing tomorrow?" Rissa asked.

"Just the usual. Why do you wish to know?"

Rissa gave an elaborate shrug. "No reason. You don't intend to go visiting or anything?"

"You know very well I am supposed to stay home and repent my many sins." Since when did Rissa care about her plans for next day? She was planning something. It could not be good. "What are you up to?" Clarinda asked bluntly.

"Nothing." Rissa stood and faced her with a look of deep concern. "Oh, Clarinda, I am worried about you."

"May I ask why?"

"I was on the river path today."

"Really? I am astounded. Don't tell me you were actually riding Dublin."

"That's exactly what I was doing." Rissa glared resentfully. "You needn't be so high and mighty. You think you're the best at everything—well, don't forget I had riding lessons too."

Clarinda realized that she had been unkind. "I did not mean—"

"It's quite all right," Rissa said with a martyred air. "But what I was trying to tell you was that, quite accidentally, I saw you with . . . oh, dear." Rissa rolled her eyes upward, as if she were suffering from some acute malady.

What is Rissa up to? whispered a warning voice in Clarinda's head as she asked, "Are you talking about Lord Stormont?"

"You know very well I am talking about Lord Stormont." Rissa looked as if she were about to cry. "I am so concerned! What if Mama and Papa find out? You know what they'd do."

Clarinda smiled wryly. "This comes as a surprise. You mean you would actually care if I was packed off to Grandfather Montague's?"

"Of course I would care. You're my twin. You mean the world to me, despite . . . ." Rissa hung her head. "I do regret that business about Lord Cranmer. That was wrong of me. I am most concerned for your welfare, so much so, that today, when I saw the two of you by the riding path embracing, for all the world to see, I was most upset and vowed I would speak to you. How terribly reckless! Anyone could have seen you, and then what if they went and told Papa? You would be sent off . . . Oh, I cannot bear to think of it!"

"Why, Rissa, I am touched," Clarinda replied, completely baffled. Could Rissa be sorry for what she'd done? And even more amazing, did Rissa actually harbor some remnants of affection for her? Despite Rissa's selfish tantrums, they had been inseparable when they were little. Only in recent years had they grown apart. Clarinda had wondered if their alienation had in any way been her fault, but no, she knew in her heart she had done her best to keep the bonds between them close. It was Rissa who was full of jealousy, not her. But if now she felt differently, how wonderful.

"Rissa, it's my heartfelt wish that we be close again, just as we were when we were children." Clarinda smiled wistfully. "I miss those days."

"I too," Rissa answered.

If so, you've done a fine job of hiding it these past few years. But perhaps she shouldn't be so cynical. "Then we're off to a new start?"

"Of course we are, and you might begin by vowing to stay away from Lord Stormont," Rissa answered sweetly. "You seem to have forgotten he is mine and you promised to stay away from him."

Clarinda felt a crush of disappointment. She might have known Rissa's gesture of friendship was too good to be true. "I did not make such a promise. If memory serves correctly, I told you to take him if you could get him, I really didn't care."

Rissa's smile had disappeared. "That was then—this is now. You do care, don't you?"

Did she care? Clarinda recalled Stormont's passionate embrace today. The very thought of it sent a thrill through her. *I do care. I did enjoy that kiss.* But what of Rissa? Clarinda could almost guess her sister's next words.

"I could tell Mama and Papa myself," said Rissa, not in

the least to Clarinda's surprise. "It would be for your own good. They would believe me, you know, even if you tried to lie."

She was right. Suddenly Clarinda found herself looking into a bleak future. "I don't tell lies, Rissa. You should know me better than that."

"Hmm . . ." Feigning deep thought, Rissa rested her chin on the tip of her finger. "But of course I don't have to tell them."

"No, you certainly don't have to tell them. But if you don't, I suspect you would expect something in exchange."

Rissa smiled brightly. "I want only one thing—that you keep that promise you said you didn't make. It's simple. I want to hear you vow you shall have nothing to do with Stormont ever again. In exchange, I won't mention your moment of recklessness to Mama and Papa."

Clarinda thought of Stormont's marvelously self-assured demeanor, his blunt masculinity, those dark, mocking eyes, that sensual mouth that could curve down in disdain or up in faint amusement. The man was devastatingly attractive, so unlike all those fops and dandies she had known before. She recalled the first time they met when she fell from Donegal, and how concerned he'd been as he bent over her. She thought of how she had been in his arms today and caught her breath just thinking of how he had pressed her against his hard, strong body. At the thought, a flickering flame stirred deep within. It was a feeling no man had ever made her feel before, not even Jeffrey.

Rissa was speaking. ". . . and besides, aren't you being disloyal to Jeffrey's memory? Where is that great love you said you had for him?"

Jeffrey.

Something clicked in her mind. Suddenly she saw her feelings for Jeffrey for what they really were. Saw that out of the real Jeffrey she had constructed Hero Jeffrey, who, she was devastated to admit, only existed in her wildest fantasies. Hero Jeffrey was her dreamy-eyed poet whose works ranked with Robert Burns and Thomas Moore. Real Jeffrey wrote mediocre verse which even at the time had sounded juvenile and insincere, though she had been loath to admit it. Hero Jeffrey was the most tender of lovers, who would, when the time came, transport her to the heights of

passion; Real Jeffrey had given her nothing but an old book
of poems and a rose. Not only that, he had aroused her
not one iota that one time he had kissed her, not like . . .

Stormont. She had backed away from him today because
of her supposed Great Lost Love, as well as Mama's orders.
But not next time! She could hardly wait to be pressed
tight in his arms again. Oh, how different things would be!

"Well, Clarinda? Why are you staring into space?"

Clarinda realized she had better set her mind to the problem at hand. Would she toady to her sister? Never! "Tattle
if you must. I find I have feelings for Lord Stormont, so I
can make no such promise."

"Are you sure?" Rissa asked, her voice glacial.

"Yes I'm very sure, so do what you have to do, although
I hope you meant what you said about wanting us to be
close again." Clarinda smiled. "Of course, I still hold the
deepest of affection you. Nothing will ever change that.
Can we still be friends?"

Rissa smiled sweetly. "But of course. I had no idea you
felt so deeply about Lord Stormont. Now that I know, he
is all yours. And you can rest easy. I wouldn't dream of
telling Mama and Papa. Your secret is safe with me."

"How wonderful that you understand," said Clarinda,
hugging Rissa tight. But even as they hugged, she had a
nagging feeling something wasn't right.

None but the servants were awake the next morning
when Clarinda walked the mile to Hollystone Manor to
ride Donegal. When she arrived, she was not surprised to
see Sara Sophia, always the early riser, grooming Sham in
the cobblestone courtyard. "He's gone?" Clarinda asked,
distressed by her friend's pale face and strained expression.

Raw hurt filled Sara Sophia's eyes as she nodded. "I
shall miss him." She laughed bitterly. "Call that a slight
understatement. My heart aches for him. I have just lost
the only man in the world I'll ever love. Oh, I try to be
optimistic—you know me—but I know what my life holds
from now on. I shall always be alone, and lonely, living in
someone else's home, never my own, until I get old and
die—probably in the middle of the night, all alone."

"Oh, Sara Sophia, that's not true!" Clarinda cried, putting comforting arms around her despondent friend. "I

have never seen you in such a state. You'll find someone else, I know you will. And meantime, you can work as a governess, which should be vastly entertaining, and most interesting, and very worthwhile, and—"

"No, it won't." Sara Sophia pulled away, grimly shaking her head. "Do you know what the life of a governess is like? No, how could you? Well, let me tell you, it's a dreadful life. When you are a governess you are neither fish nor fowl"—she laughed bitterly again—"which I am anyway, so nothing will change. Only I shan't eat with the master in the dining room, as I do here, I'm not good enough. Neither shall I eat with the servants because *they're* not good enough. So I shall eat alone in my room like an outcast." She buried her face in her hands. "I loved him, Clarinda," she whispered. "I shall never forget those rides we took, the poetry he read me. He loved me, too. He told me, and I could see it in his eyes. Oh why must I be such a nobody! He wanted to marry me, regardless of my status—run off to Gretna Greene. But I couldn't have that. What could I do but tell him I would never see him again? What could he do but leave?" Finally she looked up. "My heart is broken. I shall never love again."

Clarinda had listened, helpless, searching in vain for something comforting to say. But Sara Sophia drew herself up bravely. "Sorry. I must stop torturing myself. Don't be concerned, I won't make a spectacle of myself again. I've decided which position I shall take."

"You have?" Clarinda asked tentatively. After Sara Sophia's outburst, something she'd never heard her do before, she didn't know if this was good news or bad.

"I shall be governess to the eight children of Thomas Rich, the Earl of Middlestone, at a place called Rondale Hall. It's in Northumberland, near Alnmouth on the River Aln."

"But so far away!"

Sara Sophia nodded sadly. "It's not likely I shall see you for while."

More like forever. Clarinda searched for words of reassurance that it wouldn't be so bad, but nothing came to mind. Sara Sophia *did* face a dismal life. She *was* a nobody, at least in the eyes of the world. "I shall never forget you," she said softly. "You will always be my dearest friend, even if we never see each other again."

Sara Sophia gazed back, a wealth of warmth and affection in her eyes. "You shall always be my best friend, too. I do admire you so, Clarinda. You're so bright and witty, and compassionate and kind, and you can ride a horse like nobody else I've ever seen. I just wish your parents saw you as I do. You deserve nothing but the best in this life."

"I'm afraid that's not likely to happen . . ."

Clarinda proceeded to describe her meeting with Stormont on the riding path yesterday—the embrace, which, luck would have it, Rissa had witnessed. "She wants us to be friends again and says she won't tell Mama and Papa. I assume she means it."

"Are you sure?"

"Rissa said she was sorry about Lord Cranmer. I believe her."

"Should you?"

"She admitted she was wrong. Of course I believe her." Clarinda noted Sara Sophia's skeptical little smile. "Besides, even if I didn't believe Rissa, what more harm could she do?"

That afternoon, Lady Rissa Capelle, elegantly attired in a pink velvet spencer over an embroidered white silk afternoon dress, sat in the back of the family curricle which was proceeding at a brisk pace toward the home of Lady Constance Lynbury. Perched on the high seat in front, Timmons, the chief coachman, dressed in crimson livery, guided the two high-stepping matched bays. A footman, attired in the same gold-and-red livery, stood on the back step.

What a fine picture we make, thought Rissa as the equipage turned into the long, circular driveway that led to the fine Tudor mansion of Lady Constance Lynbury. A breeze caught the curls that lined her forehead. "Slower, Timmons!" she called. Drat the man. Estelle had worked for an hour to create her fine coiffeur, only partly covered by her best ribbon-and-silk flower-trimmed bonnet. She did not want it mussed.

Rissa felt a nervous clenching in her stomach as she wondered if she'd thought of everything. The necklace? She touched the gold filigree pendant that hung prettily around her neck, running her finger over the "C." She had thought sneaking it away from Clarinda would be the most formidable task of all, but it had proven the easiest. Clarinda always took the necklace off during her bath. It had been easy as breathing to enter Clarinda's bedchamber while she sat in her cast-iron hip bath, chat pleasantly for a time, all the while searching surreptitiously for the spot where Clarinda had left her necklace. Rissa had finally spied it atop the bedside table. The switch was simplicity itself, accomplished when Clarinda, for a brief moment, turned her head away.

As for the rest, Mama and Papa had left for London, so they were nothing to worry about. Clarinda was in her room, and likely to remain there for the rest of the day. All went smoothly when Rissa, her pulse beating erratically, swept downstairs and announced to Manning, "Tell Timmons Lady Clarinda wishes to go visiting. He's to put on his best livery and bring the curricle around." *Well done!* she had congratulated herself. Despite an inner tremor, her voice rang out strong and sure. If Manning was suspicious, he did not say, as well he shouldn't, being he was only a servant. The same with Timmons, who, when assisting her into the curricle, had warned, "Watch your step, Lady Clarinda." Was that a strange look he gave her? Perhaps. Clarinda had never in her life had the least inclination to visit the ladies of the countryside, especially by herself. In fact, she always had to be dragged along. But Timmons was a servant, too. If he was suspicious, it mattered not one groat.

Rissa's plan was running so smoothly she could hardly believe it. At first, she'd had butterflies in her stomach, but now they had stopped their fluttering. By the time the curricle reached the main portico, she brimmed with confidence.

From this moment on, I am Clarinda, even to myself.

After Timmons reined in the horses, he turned and asked, "Do you wish to send in your card, m'lady?"

"Of course." Rissa withdrew her mother's card from her pink-tasseled reticule. Across the back she had written "Clarinda Capelle" in a large, firm hand. She handed the card to the footman. "Ascertain if Lady Lynbury is at home, and if so, ask if she is receiving."

Would Lady Lynbury ever be surprised! This was not

her regular at-home day. But of course she would be at
home, Rissa thought confidently, especially when the
daughter of an earl came visiting. She sat back to wait,
watching the footman carry the card to the door, ring, and
hand it to the Lynburys' butler as if it were a precious
jewel. From time to time she gazed up surreptitiously at
the main drawing room window on the first floor. Aha!
Almost imperceptibly the drape pulled back. The old cow
was peering down at her, no doubt all atwitter that Lady
Clarinda Capelle, daughter of the esteemed earl, who never
came visiting of her own accord, was actually on her doorstep, waiting to be invited in.

As Rissa predicted, the door soon opened. The butler
whispered to the footman. The footman marched ceremoniously down the steps and announced in a solemn tone,
"Lady Lynbury is in and would be delighted to receive
you."

In no time Rissa was seated on a faux rosewood and gilt
sofa in the vaulted main salon, in her hand a porcelain,
silver gilt cup full of Ceylon's finest tea. After some small
chitchat, she remarked, "I am delighted, as well as grateful,
Lady Lynbury, that you, in your most gracious benevo-
lence, condescended to see me."

From across, the ample Lady Lynbury smiled magnani-
mously. "But, my dear, of course you are welcome,
despite . . . well, there are some things it is best not to
discuss."

"But we must discuss it!" Rissa bowed her head and
lowered her eyelids, knowing how pretty her long, dark
lashes looked lying against her rosy skin. "Ah, how painful
this is! You are well aware of my indiscretion with Lord
Cranmer which you had the misfortune to witness."

At Rissa's honesty, the loquacious Lady Lynbury was
stunned into silence, and she spilled a spot of tea upon the
ample bosom of her gown. "I am so ashamed of my wicked
behavior," Rissa humbly continued. "You must have been
so shocked. Can you ever forgive me? You may rest assured I shall never, ever, be so reckless and unthinking
again."

"Well, of course, I . . . I," Lady Lynbury began, flustered
as she dabbed her napkin at the unwelcome spot. Regaining
some of her composure, she went on, "But of course it was

a shock. When I think of the flawless deportment of your dear sister Rissa—"

"Ah, Rissa!" Rissa gave a sorrowful shake of her head. "How I wish I could be more like my sweet angel of a sister. Her grace . . . style . . . behavior are so perfect in every way, whereas I . . ." Rissa tried to force a tear, but her eyes remained dry. She bit her lip instead. "I could spend a lifetime trying to be as perfect as my sister, and never come close, but at least I shall try."

"Well, my dear, that's all you can do," Lady Lynbury answered, grandly magnanimous. "I do forgive you. In fact, I admire you for admitting your tendency toward . . . shall we say, unladylike behavior. I can only hope you have the fortitude to abide by your new resolve."

"You forgive me?" Rissa clasped her hands with joy. "Ah, Lady Lynbury, how kind, how generous you are! As for me"—she hung her head again—"I have vowed that in future my behavior shall be impeccable, although"—she sighed and shook her head unhappily—"it will not be easy, what with a certain problem I face." She sighed again. "But that is a cross I must bear. I shan't burden you with the loathsome details."

Lady Lynbury blurted, "But of course you must!" Then, apparently realizing she had sounded a bit too eager, and had, in fact, edged noticeably forward in her chair, she sat back and continued in a calmer voice, "I mean, perhaps if you confided in me, there might be some way in which I could assist."

"Well . . ." Rissa appeared to reconsider. "You must promise me that what I am about to tell you is in the strictest confidence and shall not go beyond these walls."

"No need to worry on that score. My lips are sealed, as they always are."

Rissa looked stricken. "Oh, dear, I did not mean to imply. . . . Everyone knows you are the soul of discretion."

"So?" asked Lady Lynbury, her eyes alight with eagerness.

"It is that dreadful Lord Stormont who is causing my torment," Rissa answered simply.

"Lord Stormont?" Lady Lynbury looked genuinely flabbergasted. "Why . . . why, I find that hard to believe. Stormont is rich as Croesus—a first son—titled—handsome—charming. 'Pon my word, a fine catch for any girl in the countryside!''

"So one would think," Rissa chirruped after a slight silence.

"You mean—?"

"I mean, Lady Lynbury, that looks can be deceiving, and there are times when the true nature of man is not readily revealed."

"Really?" By now, Lady Lynbury was nearly bug-eyed, and literally perched on the edge of her seat. "Do go on."

"He won't leave me alone," Rissa cried, trying once more to squeeze a tear from her eye but to no avail. No matter. Her words were having their desired effect anyway. "Whenever I ride he appears out of nowhere, constantly annoying me. Why just yesterday . . . well, perhaps I should not repeat—"

"Please continue!"

"He tried to kiss me. It was while I was taking my daily ride along the river path, well out of screaming distance of the house. I was terrified."

"But did he—?"

"Fortunately I was able to break away, but even so, I live in fear of next time. Such a loathsome man!"

Lady Lynbury sat speechless, shaking her head, clicking her tongue. "But I never would have guessed," she finally exclaimed. "He's such a handsome man and so exceedingly eligible. Do you not find him the least bit desirable?"

"Desirable?" Rissa glanced around the vaulted room. Ah, the timing was perfect. Not only was the white-gloved butler present, but also a footman and a maid. She bent forward, as if to emphasize the confidentiality of her next remarks. "Lady Lynbury, would you be shocked if I were to offer you my true opinion?"

"Not a'tall, my dear."

"Then I shall tell you what I think." Rissa lowered her voice, but not too much. "My parents are insisting that I marry him. You can understand, of course—his wealth, his title." She heaved a tragic sigh. "I, being the dutiful daughter, will obey my parents' wishes, but I can assure you, it will be a loveless marriage. I could never love a man like Lord Stormont. How I shall dread sharing his bed! He's such a . . . a . . . toad!"

"Upon my word!" Rissa's astonished hostess, who had just lifted her teacup, set it down again with a clatter. "One never knows, does one?"

Rissa smiled sweetly. "But remember, you promised not to tell."

Lady Lynbury drew herself up. "I have known you since childhood, Clarinda." She nodded toward the necklace. "I don't need that 'C' on your lovely gold necklace to know it's you. As always, I have your best interests at heart. Rest assured, you have my promise. All the wild beasts in the jungle could not drag one single word from me concerning your true feelings about Lord Stormont."

The next morning, when Clarinda went to put her necklace on, she noticed it had an "R" instead of "C."

"Rissa's necklace?" she asked aloud. Quickly she went to Rissa's bedchamber, where her twin was at her dressing table. "Do you have my necklace?" she asked. "It appears I have yours, although I can't imagine how they got switched."

Rissa appeared quite startled. She looked down at her own necklace, which, of course, had a "C." "I can't imagine either," she said, looking Clarinda innocently in the eye. "It must have been the servants. Shall we ask Estelle?"

The lady's maid denied any knowledge of how the necklaces could possibly have gotten switched.

"How strange," said Rissa, appearing completely baffled. She removed the "C" necklace and gave it to Clarinda.

"How very strange indeed," replied Clarinda, dropping the "R" necklace on Rissa's dressing table.

"I guess we shall never know, shall we?" asked Rissa.

"I guess not."

Clarinda decided it would be best just to forget about it.

Chapter 11

Early morning, the Sunday before Christmas.

Never in her life had Clarinda been more anxious for Christmas to arrive, not even when she was a child and went to bed every night with visions of Yule cakes and mistletoe dancing before her eyes. There wasn't much different now, except instead of Yule cakes, visions of Robert, Lord Stormont, crowded her mind. Each night as she fell asleep, she saw his dark, proud eyes beckon her with hungry longing, just as they had that day on the river path. His arms reached out for her, only now she didn't try to break away but willingly allowed herself to be swept into his embrace where she, held tight, could feel every contour of his long, lean body. *Ah, Robert.* Because of Jeffrey she had backed away. Now that she had come to her senses, her supposed lost love was but a dim memory. She could hardly wait to see Stormont again.

The Sunday before Christmas finally arrived. Clarinda awoke from a restless sleep before dawn. Throwing her covers off, she slipped from bed heedless of the chill in the air and the darkness outside. Robert had returned. She had learned the news from Estelle, that reliable font of gossip gleaned from all the servants of the countryside. Lord Stormont, accompanied by his friend, Lord Wentridge, had arrived at Hollyridge Manor yesterday afternoon, accompanied by a large entourage of servants, household goods, and no less than ten of his finest horses from Oakley House. "*Mon Dieu,* m'lady! He ees settling een and plans to stay."

Clarinda had rejoiced at the news. Now, trying to slow herself down—she must not appear too eager—she dressed in a dark wool serge gown, wide-skirted for easy riding, and embroidered with pearls. Over it, she donned her new brown redingote. She peered at herself in the mirror, á la Rissa, she thought with silent mirth, and decided she was not bad-looking by half in this latest of fashions borrowed from the stage drivers' Carrick coat. The redingote had multiple capelets banded with black velvet, as well as smart tabs for buttons down the front and more bands of black velvet around the bottom. *I do want to look pretty for him.* She donned the matching bonnet.

By the first light of day, Clarinda was at the stables slipping a harness and side saddle on Dublin, who needed riding, and besides, Rissa would never know. The weak winter sun had barely cleared the horizon as she brought Dublin to a slow trot along the river path, this time riding sedately on her sidesaddle. These past few months had been dreadful, she mused as they went along, but for the first time in ages she felt blissfully happy—fully alive. She had hardly dared think of the possibility that Stormont might propose, but what if he did? She knew now that she loved him. Today, if things went as she hoped, she would tell him so straight-out. She would not be coy. If he loved her, if he proposed . . . her heart welled at the thought of how perfect their life would be. Once her parents realized he loved her, not Rissa, they would be so ecstatic they would forgive her for everything. No question, they would grant her their blessing. At last she could get away from her twin and be her own person. At last she could marry a man she loved— and, oh, the joy of it!—a man who loved horses. They would raise children, and thoroughbreds, and Arabians, and be blissfully happy the whole rest of their lives.

She touched the reins to Dublin. Her wish was like a beautiful fairy tale, too good to be true, and it would be best not to think about it. Yet it could really happen. With spirits high, she eagerly turned her horse off the path toward the stables at Hollyridge Manor. She wondered if Stormont, too, had arisen at the crack of dawn, beside himself with eagerness to see her again. She would wager that he had. She would wager, too, that he would be at the stables waiting, anxious to hold her in his arms once again.

She was wrong. Stormont was not waiting at the stables, nor did he ever come.

She had waited, and waited, and waited some more. She

had yearned for Sara Sophia, but, alas, her friend had left for the far northern reaches of Northumberland. She had fed and groomed both Donegal and Dublin—swept hay, heedless of her brand-new redingote—greeted Pitney when he arrived to begin his work for the day. He was both surprised and happy to see her, but had no comment other than to mention that more stable help would be needed now that his lordship, who had arrived yesterday, had brought with him ten additional horses. Not that she had asked if he had arrived. She had too much pride.

The sun was high in the sky when she, at last despairing, declared, "My, my, how the time flies, Pitney. I must go home now." With a proud tilt to her head, she rode Dublin sedately until out of sight of the stables. It was not until then she halted Dublin and bowed her head in despair. Robert had not come. There could be no excuse. Either he had forgotten, or, worse and more plausible, he had deliberately chosen not to keep their rendezvous.

Only a few tears flowed before she wiped them away and resolved not to cry anymore. Her swell of pain was beyond tears. What good were tears when her life was over and her heart broken? With a moan of distress, she whispered, "Let us go home, Dublin." She had left Graystone Hall with her hopes high. Now, with Sara Sophia gone, her parents' harsh disapproval hanging over her, and this latest—Stormont's desertion—she must return to continuing misery. She desperately wished she could look forward to some semblance of happiness in her life, but a bleak, black future lay before her.

But what did I do? she wondered. Robert had seemed so eager. What has changed him? She racked her brain, but could think of no reason.

"Coming for breakfast, Robert?" asked Lucius, addressing his friend, who was staring moodily out the many-paned library window.

"Hmm? Oh, go ahead without me, Lucius, I find I'm not very hungry this morning."

Lucius frowned. "Whatever is the matter with you, Robert? You were in high spirits yesterday when you arrived home, but now you look as desolate as a tomb."

"I am in fine spirits," snapped Robert. "I've no idea why you would think otherwise."

Ignoring his friend's barbed comment, Lucius inquired, "I say, does this have anything to do with that rumor the servants are bandying about?"

"What rumor?"

Lucius chuckled. "It's silly, really. It seems your Lady Clarinda was visiting Lady Lynbury the other day and in the course of the conversation called you a toad. How droll! My valet told me, who got it from the butler, who got it, I surmise, from the Lynburys' butler. Her exact words, if I can repeat them correctly, were, 'I could never love a man like Lord Stormont. How I should dread sharing his bed! He's such a—' "

"Enough!" Stormont had ground the word out from between clenched teeth. "Get your breakfast. I shall be down later." Without another word he left the room and proceeded to his bedchamber, where he closed the door, dropped into a chair, and let his head fall into his hands. Damn the woman! And to think, he had been about to propose. Luckily the cursed web of servants' gossip had reached him in time, through his valet, who, though red and stuttering with embarrassment, had mustered up the fortitude to tell him the appalling truth.

Toad? How could she have said such a thing? He had thought she felt as he did. Of course, that first kiss had taken her by surprise, giving her no chance for objection. But on the river path that day, had she not come close to falling into his arms? He had certainly thought so. In fact, up until now what woman had not fallen into his arms when given the opportunity?

Stormont strode to his mirror and struck a manly pose, chest out, fists resting on his hips. Not bad. Surely she could not find him repulsive. But then, perhaps she could. "You are an arrogant fool, Stormont," he said aloud, grimacing at himself. Lesson learned. Jeffrey, Lord Landsdale, might have been a mediocre poet, and only an accidental hero at Trafalgar, but they said love is blind and they were right. Nodcock or no, Jeffrey was first in Lady Clarinda's heart and likely to remain so.

Very well. This humiliating rejection was all it took for him to realize that in future, he should confine his romantic notions to his London ladybirds. There, for the cost of a few trinkets, he could find all the love needed.

As for Lady Clarinda, just the thought of her . . .

Robert gave a choked, desperate laugh as a raw, primitive grief overwhelmed him. He had lost her. For a brief moment he thought he could not go on. Only for a moment, though. He was nothing if not strong. With luck, he would not see her again, although that was doubtful now that he lived on the adjoining estate. He simply would not think of her—pretend she did not exist.

Stop being an idiot, he informed himself. Of course he would think of her again. These past weeks he had thought of nothing else.

That night, Clarinda, trying to hide her anguish, looked around the long, crowded dinner table at Graystone Hall. There were aunts, cousins, grandparents, and other relatives of the Capelles', who had gathered from far and wide for the Yuletide celebration. Mama, actually looking cheerful for a change, remarked, "I do hope it snows tonight. It is more like Christmas if there is snow on the ground when we bring in the Yule log."

Mama's remark reminded Clarinda of all the years past when she, her family, guests, and servants, had traipsed merrily into the woods to haul home the log that had been selected months before. It was always a huge one, massive as it could be and still fit into the main salon fireplace. At first, oxen and horses, all draped with garlands of Yuletide greenery, would drag the log from the woods, the whole assembly following, singing carols, shouting, sounding loud horns. But once at the front door, all together would triumphantly push and pull the huge log into the main salon. After it had been settled into the fireplace, and lit ceremoniously from the remnants of last year's log, there would be music, dancing, a banquet, and many toasts proposed from around the wassail bowl.

What a joyous occasion it had always been! *But not this year*. Clarinda dreaded tomorrow. She would have to laugh and sing, act as joyous as the rest, while all the time her heart was breaking and she felt nothing but despair. She would hide her true feelings, though. Never would she dream of dampening the family's holiday spirits.

"Everything all right, Clarinda?" asked Papa from the head of the table. He was gazing at her with concerned eyes.

"Of course, Papa, I am fine." He had noticed! She was torn between chagrin and gratefulness that Papa, for the first time in weeks, had spoken kindly to her. She had lost Stormont, but if she had regained her father's love, at least in part, she would be greatly thankful.

From the foot of the table, her mother spoke again. "Oh, by the way, Arthur, I have invited our new neighbor to participate in tomorrow's festivities." To the gathered relatives she explained, "Robert, Lord Stormont, has just taken over Hollyridge Manor, which borders Graystone Hall. He is quite the handsome bachelor and wealthy, besides. Of course, I'm only inviting him out of kindness, since he is new, and not yet acquainted with the gentry of the countryside, and yet"—she cast a quick sidelong glance at Rissa—"one cannot overlook the possibilities of an alliance with one of our lovely belles, can one?"

"Mama, please," admonished Rissa, blushing, though obviously pleased. "You know very well I have plans for another London Season, and yet . . . well, I do find Lord Stormont attractive." She turned to Clarinda and pointedly asked, "Don't you?"

"Indeed," Clarinda answered. Keeping her voice light had been difficult. She felt sick inside. How could she bear to see Stormont tomorrow, knowing he had spurned her? Tomorrow would be a dreadful day, unless, of course . . .

Tomorrow would they have a chance to talk? And if they did, could he possibly have some reasonable explanation for his unfathomable behavior?

The day dawned bright, clear, and with snow on the ground. Clarinda, for once under no edict to dress like her twin, had chosen to wear a blue cashmere shawl over a plain wool dress, black leather lace-up boots, and warm bonnet.

Soon she was trudging through the snow, surrounded by laughing friends, servants, and family, while she, filled with sadness, fought to keep a smile on her face. It was not easy. Stormont and his friend, Lord Wentridge, had arrived early, both appearing to be in excellent spirits. So far, whether by design or accident, hers and Stormont's paths had not crossed. He had ignored her completely, and to make matters worse, if that were possible, he was now walking behind the log with Rissa, chatting amiably.

Papa, rosy-cheeked from the brisk air, appeared beside her. "You seem a mite downcast," he remarked after they had walked for a while. "That's not like my Clarinda."

She gave him a rueful smile. "It has not exactly been a good year."

Papa clasped her shoulder and squeezed it affectionately. "I know. We've been hard on you. Your mother . . . well, enough of that. Clarinda, I sense you've not been happy. Won't you reconsider marrying Lord Sufton? If you did, I would buy back Donegal, if Stormont agreed. Think how happy your mother would be—all of us, the whole family."

She cast him a skeptical look. "You mean Mama would forgive me?"

"Leave that to me."

Marry Larimore? What a depressing thought! How could she? And yet, she felt heartened that Papa had noticed how unhappy she was and was trying to help. Little did he know of how she yearned for Robert Stormont.

From ahead, she heard Stormont's booming laughter—saw him bend his head in some obviously amiable conversation with Rissa.

Clarinda felt Papa's warm, comforting hand on her shoulder and wanted to cry.

"Oh, Lord Stormont, you are so very droll!" Rissa cried prettily with a flutter of her eyelashes. She knew she looked her best, with her face framed by her fur-lined hood and her cheeks flushed pink from the cold. She looked up at the tall, handsome man walking through the light covering of snow beside her. "Now you must promise to sit next to me at dinner tonight. I shan't take no for an answer."

Stormont smiled down at her. "I am honored, Lady Rissa."

Her heart glowed with satisfaction. Not once today had his eyes sought out Clarinda. "How do you know I am Rissa?" she asked coyly, fluttering her eyelashes once more.

"Rest assured, I know who you are," he said, in a tone

she could not quite fathom. But why worry? Obviously the details of her visit to Lady Lynbury had reached Stormont's ears. Rissa laughed to herself, thinking of her close call with the necklaces. She had thought Clarinda would not immediately notice, but she had, unluckily before Rissa had a chance to switch the necklaces back. No harm done, though. Honest, high-minded Clarinda was satisfied one of the servants had done it. She would never have guessed the truth in a million years.

Later that night, the height of the celebration was reached when everyone gathered around the large wassail bowl. All evening Clarinda had wondered if Stormont might speak to her, but so far, he had not. What could be wrong? she wondered over and over. Why had he seemed so passionate that day on the river path, but now so cold? Finally, as the butler ladled the mixture of ale, cider, and wine sweetened with sugar into the serving cups, hers and Stormont's gazes locked. He stared at her, eyes like granite, then turned away.

All hope was gone. *It's over*, she thought with a sinking heart. Truly over. Disinclined to make a spectacle of herself, she kept a smile pasted on her face, but inside, she felt disconsolate and heartbroken. She needed to get away, far from the gaiety and laughter. When no one was looking, she slipped from the grand salon and hastened to her bedchamber. Estelle was downstairs, celebrating Christmas with the rest of the servants, so she undressed by herself. Untying the back of her dress was awkward, but she managed. Down to her chemise, she unclasped the gold necklace and held it in the palm of her hand. How she hated it—this burdensome symbol of her fettered life as a twin. Quickly she dropped the necklace into her jewelry box. She wished she could get up the courage to tell her parents she would never wear it again. But no, she must try to do their bidding. She felt better about Papa. He had asked her to not be rebellious, to reconsider a betrothal to Lord Sufton.

Perhaps she should.

What was left to her otherwise?

To think, only two nights ago she had fallen asleep dreaming of the wonderful life she could have with Robert, foolish enough to think that yesterday he might even pro-

pose. Such folly. She dreaded the thought of marrying Larimore, but if she did, Papa would buy back Donegal. What
a wonderful thought! Wonderful, except for the price she
would pay, having to live with boring old Larimore the
whole rest of her life. But then, having Donegal back just
might possibly be worth it.

A frigid January went by, too cold and snowy for riding,
as was February and at least half of March. Clarinda stayed
away from Hollyridge during that time, assured that Pitney
and his newly hired staff would take good care of Donegal.
She rode Dublin a few times, but with the weather so cold,
never stayed outdoors for long. Besides, every time she
rode, she thought of Sara Sophia and the rides they used
to take, and that made her even sadder.

To her surprise, Stormont visited Graystone Hall a time
or two, but she had presumed it was out of politeness to
her parents and Rissa, and had stayed in her bedchamber
and not come down.

As for Lord Sufton, she could not make up her mind.
She would soon be compelled to do so, though. Papa was
getting impatient, she could tell.

In the middle of March, a letter from Sara Sophia finally
arrived. Clutching it tight, Clarinda took it to the library,
where a warm fire blazed in the marble fireplace. Settling
into the recessed velvet window seat, she opened it.

My dearest Clarinda,

Months have passed since I left Hollyridge Manor, but
not a day has gone by that I have not thought of you
and fervently hoped that you and your family are well
and in good spirits.

As for myself, I am now firmly established as the governess for eight children, ranging in age from six to sixteen. Alas, they are a rambunctious lot, not a one
dedicated to serious study. I do try. In all modesty, I feel
I have a natural bent for teaching, but what I told you
before I left most certainly applies. Since the lord and
lady of the manor treat me like a servant, and a lowly
one at that, how can I expect their offspring to respect
me? Suffice to say, they do not. Not a day passes but
what I am hard put to keep my patience when one or

the other of the children misbehaves, sometimes, I fear, just to goad me. They do so with impunity, for they know that no matter what they do, they will not be punished.

Ah, well, I do not mean to complain and should dwell more on the optimistic. I have a room to myself, thank goodness. It is quite small, dark, and rather on the cold side, but adequate. I take my meals there alone, just as I predicted. Sometimes I think that out of sheer loneliness I would prefer eating with the servants, but Lady Rich would not allow it. She is a stern woman, much on the haughty side, who is a great one for obeying rules and running Rondale Hall strictly by the clock. Meals—lessons—visits, are all scheduled to the minute. There is a set hour for my young lady charges to play the pianoforte. There is a thirty-minute period in the evening for all the children to exchange pleasantries with their parents. Otherwise, I must keep them out of sight.

There are extensive stables at Rondale Hall, and many fine horses. Alas, I am not permitted to ride. I am informed my one and only duty is to the children. Further, I am obliged to put all thoughts of my own amusement out of my head.

You will forgive me for not writing sooner, but as I am sure you understand, it is difficult to write when one's heart is heavy and when one has little of a happy nature to report. Oh, I hate being such a pessimist! But, Clarinda, I miss you—and Sham—and Hollyridge so much that each night I cry. And when I think of Lucius, and how I have lost my dear love forever, I see naught but a bleak future ahead. Sometimes black thoughts overtake me in the middle of the night. I see myself growing old here, and dying here, and no one will care. But enough of this self pity. I shall try my best to be cheerful and find a purpose for my life.

Again, please forgive me. I promise my next letter will be more cheery. If it is not, then I shan't send it! I miss you horribly, dear friend, and yearn for those happy times we spent together that will never come again.

Ever your fondest,
Sara Sophia

Clarinda pressed her hand over her eyes as she let her friend's letter fall to her lap. How could it be that a woman like Sara Sophia, who could light up the room with her tender smile, who was both witty and wise, could be doomed to a life of drudgery and sadness? Talk about injustices in this world!

She gazed through the arched Venetian window, to a dreary gray sky that hung over the winter-barren garden, and was assailed by a terrible sense of bitterness as she watched snowflakes begin to swirl. Sara Sophia did not deserve such a fate. How Clarinda wished she could help somehow, but there was nothing she, or anyone, could do.

Chapter 12

A chilly March gave way to a sunny April bursting with the promise of spring. Clarinda hardly noticed. She was still caught up in a melancholy mood that would not go away. Sara Sophia's plight lay heavily on her mind. Clarinda had written to her several times, but since that first sad letter, she had not heard from her friend again.

Clarinda's estrangement from Lord Stormont still hurt so much it was difficult to get through the day without a hopeless feeling overcoming her. Through gossip, she had learned he was making great progress in his renovation of the neighboring estate, as well as augmenting the stables with the finest thoroughbreds. She yearned to see them but had stayed away, not once returning to Hollyridge Manor since that fateful day he had not kept their rendezvous. Though she missed Donegal dreadfully, she had her pride. Nothing she could imagine could drag her back to the stables at Hollyridge.

As yet, Clarinda had made no decision about marrying Larimore, although not a day passed that Mama didn't plague her. Now, part of her day was taken up with riding Dublin. Sometimes she took Alexander along, when he wasn't sick. He adored riding Captain, his Shetland pony. The two would have great fun riding the many paths around Graystone Hall, but only the paths that led nowhere near Hollyridge Manor.

At first, she feared her parents would object to her riding any horse, but Mama scarcely noticed, she was so taken up in getting Rissa ready for the upcoming Season. As for Papa, of course he noticed, but remained silent, appearing to tacitly approve. When she wasn't riding, she was either reading, playing games with Alexander, or, when Mama insisted, working on a detested sampler.

Meanwhile, Rissa grew more radiant every day. Lord Stormont had called twice! Mama, ever cautious, had warned her they were probably just courtesy calls, but as usual, Rissa heard only what she wanted to hear. Stormont was calling on her and her alone, she just knew. "I have him eating out of my hand, Mama. I doubt I'll need another Season. I expect a proposal soon."

Would he propose? Clarinda wondered. On both occasions when Stormont had called, she had pleaded a headache and not gone downstairs. She had no desire to be the object of his glacial stare again.

Now, on a sunny afternoon in April, Clarinda and Rissa were in Rissa's bedchamber being fitted for new gowns when Mama poked her head in.

"Quick, girls! Lord Stormont has come to call. Rissa—?" Mama looked confused. "You are Rissa, are you not? 'Pon my soul, twenty years and I still cannot tell."

"Of course I am Rissa," Rissa snapped.

Unremorseful, Mama actually looked pleased for a change. "This makes three times he's come visiting—far beyond the necessary for courtesy calls. You were right, Rissa. Lord Stormont is most definitely a suitor." In a rare show of emotion, Mama clasped her hands together. "I am most pleased. You have succeeded, Rissa. A fine title! Twenty thousand pounds a year! I am beside myself with joy." Her expression changed to disapproving as she looked toward Clarinda. "You must also come down."

"I think not, Mama."

"Why ever not?" Mama inquired indignantly. "Twice you have made excuses, don't think I didn't notice. If you refuse to come down again, you are being most rude, especially since Lord Stormont might soon become a member of the family." As an afterthought, Mama added, "Besides, Lord Stormont specifically asked to speak to you."

"He did?" Clarinda's heart took a leap.

"He wanted news of Sara Sophia."

"Only you would know," Rissa interjected with a smirk.

Clarinda's spirts plunged again. "Very well, Mama, I should be happy to tell Lord Stormont the latest news of Sara Sophia, not that there's much to tell." She didn't want to see him—would much have preferred to stay in her room, but she was curious. Why would Lord Stormont want news of an insignificant orphan who had no standing and was poor as a church mouse?

Soon, Clarinda and Rissa were dressed alike in gowns of white muslin with a tartan belt and band around the hem. For once, Clarinda was glad she looked exactly like her sister. She looked forward to their entrance into the drawing room. Despite Stormont's boast he always knew who she was, this time she would take pains to ensure he would not be able to tell them apart.

When they finally entered the drawing room, Clarinda was exactly in step with Rissa, and her head was tilted exactly the same. Let him just guess which was which! How she would love to see him fumble.

Spying them, Stormont set down his teacup and stood. As he rose to full height, Clarinda was reminded once again of how splendidly tall he was, and how magnificently tailored. But no matter. She could hardly wait to see the embarrassed look on his face when he couldn't tell them apart.

Stormont bowed to her sister. "Lady Rissa," he said without hesitation, "how lovely you look today." He bowed again, this time to her. "And, Lady Clarinda," he continued, looking her directly in the eye. "You cannot imagine how devastated I was to hear of your headaches. I trust you're better now." Only a slightly raised eyebrow gave his amusement away.

How dare he tease her! But what was most astounding, how did he know Rissa was Rissa and she was she? Astonishing, considering even Mama could not tell them apart. She wanted to ask how he knew, but no, she would not give him the satisfaction. He would not be privy to her feelings in any way.

She dipped a slight curtsy and gave him a radiant smile. "I am most grateful for your concern over my headaches. They're much better now. It is the most amazing thing, how I seem to get a headache every time you come to call."

"Clarinda!" Mama began in a shocked voice, but Stormont starting laughing.

"Alas, it appears I have that effect on some young ladies," he said lightly. He motioned toward the settee. "Come, sit down, shall we? Were you told, Lady Clarinda, that I wanted news of Sara Sophia?"

After they were seated, Clarinda related some of Sara

Sophia's letter—only the good parts, though. Sara Sophia was much too proud to want anyone to know the travesty her life had become. "And so she is doing quite well at Rondale Hall, m'lord. May I inquire why you ask?"

"I was not asking for myself," Stormont replied, "although of course, I'm concerned for her welfare. It was . . ." He paused, seeming reluctant to say more, finally continuing, "My good friend, Lucius, Lord Wentridge, has an interest in her. He will be pleased to hear Sara Sophia is doing well."

"Well enough, I suppose." *Bite your tongue, you foolish girl.* She had just implied Sara Sophia was not doing well. Most men would not pick up on such a subtle insinuation, but she suspected Stormont would. Those dark eyes of his, so sharp and assessing, were focused on her now.

"Only well enough?" he asked, confirming her suspicion.

"Sara Sophia can take care of herself wherever she goes," she answered firmly, hoping that would assuage Stormont's curiosity.

It did. Or so she thought. Nothing more was said concerning Sara Sophia. The rest of Stormont's visit was taken up with frivolous conversation, led by Rissa, who preened, giggled, and did everything but stand on her head to keep Stormont's attention. *How I would love to dump a pitcher of cold water over her head,* Clarinda mused idly as she watched in disgust. Despite herself, she felt a growing anxiety. Stormont appeared more than attentive to Rissa's blandishments. He seemed to be quite taken with her. *You don't give a fig,* she told herself. But whom was she fooling? Of course she did.

When their visitor had left, Rissa clasped her hands in delight. "He likes me. Don't you think, Mama?"

"Most definitely."

Rissa addressed Clarinda. "What do you think? Does he like me?"

"It would appear he does," Clarinda answered, a heaviness settling around her heart. There had been no warmth in Stormont's eyes when he looked at her. He had, in fact, been only as polite as courtesy decreed, and no more. Again, for at least the thousandth time, she wondered what had gone wrong and why Stormont, who once had trembled with passion as he held her in his arms, could now, it appeared, hardly stand the sight of her.

A heaviness weighted Robert's shoulders as he swung onto Sham and started home. *Perdition*. He had failed miserably, all the way around. Was there anything he had not mucked up? He thought of poor Lucius, beside himself in London. "Sara Sophia said she wouldn't write and she hasn't," he had cried. "I have no idea how she is. Robert, can you at least find out if she is happy and in good health?"

Robert shook his head as he rode along. Lucius's transformation from high-living dandy to lovesick clod was astounding. Well, not clod. That Lucius had a truly deep, abiding love for Sara Sophia was beyond all doubt. One could not fault him for that. But dear God, how the man had suffered for his hopeless love! To their friends' astonishment he had become practically a recluse, eschewing Tattersall's—White's—his old taverns of choice—and most astounding, all enticements from his various lady loves. Now former lady loves. Lucius had lost his charming, acerbic wit. He hardly ate anymore, and to Robert's amazement now led a celibate life. *He might as well become a monk,* Robert thought dismally.

He had told Lucius, "Rest easy. I am returning to Hollyridge tomorrow. The first thing I shall do is visit Graystone Hall. Surely Lady Clarinda will know how Sara Sophia is faring."

And so he had, but instead of gleaning reassuring news of Sara Sophia, he had ascertained just the opposite. He must find out more news of Sara Sophia. That meant talking to Clarinda.

Clarinda.

He had spent the past months trying to convince himself he most definitely did not love her. Indeed, heeding his father's advice, he had vowed long ago not to love any woman until he was ready, and he most certainly was not. His life was too comfortable, too well arranged, to allow a woman in to ruin it. Time and again he recalled his parents' miserable marriage: the screaming—carping—name calling—constant complaints. No. His father had it right. "Do not marry under any circumstances before you are forty,"

Papa had admonished him, "and when you do, find some young chit who's attractive, but more important, quiet, docile, and uncomplaining. Even a large dowry is unnecessary, my son, you don't need the money. A small dowry will work to your advantage. She will be so everlastingly grateful you married her, she will never complain."

Papa was absolutely right, Stormont assured himself for at least the thousandth time as the gables of Hollyridge came into view. Although . . .

An astounding thought struck him. Why, he was as bad off as Lucius!

Father, did the juices of hot passion never flow through your veins? Did you never want a woman so badly you could not eat—sleep—think straight? Did you never want a woman as much as I want Clarinda . . . ?

Curse the woman. With a moan, Stormont pulled Sham up short. Before this visit today he had vowed he would remain aloof to Clarinda's charms. As far as appearances went, he had succeeded. His behavior had been impeccable. He had even managed, God knew how, to show a decent interest in her ninny sister. But inside . . .

I do not love her, he told himself again, but his words rang hollow. The trouble was, even if he did love her, what was the use? He started to laugh—a bitter, haunting laugh that went on so long that Sham turned his head and regarded him with one big, brown, curious eye.

His laughter stilled. Stroking the horses's mane, he softly inquired, "Sham, how could I love a woman who called me a toad? Complete folly, would you not agree?"

He did love her. No sense fooling himself. But it was hopeless. The worst of it was, for the sake of his desperate friend he would have to see Clarinda again—find out the truth about Sara Sophia.

He must be careful. She must not think he had any purpose in mind other than to find additional news about her friend. Never should she know she was ruining his sleep at night because he could not stop thinking of her. Never should she know he loved her as he had never loved another woman in his life.

How could he see her and talk to her alone? He thought to pay another visit but immediately realized Mama and the sister would be hovering like vultures, not giving them one moment by themselves. Besides, she would likely plead a headache again and not come down. But perhaps he could contrive to meet her elsewhere. He thought to write a letter, but concluded, too risky. Writing notes to single young ladies was an exercise fraught with peril, especially if her parents found out. But he had to see her. There was only one way, he finally concluded. He was sure she still rode, probably Dublin, and probably, now that the weather had warmed, every day, no doubt early. And where would she ride? That was easy—in the exact opposite direction of Hollyridge Manor. *In order to avoid me,* he thought with irony.

The next morning, Clarinda, riding sedately sidesaddle on Dublin, was traveling along the river path when she saw an approaching horse and rider. Her pulse leaped. Even at a distance one could not help but admire the tall, straight carriage of the rider atop his noble stallion. It had to be none other than Lord Stormont riding Sham.

How awkward. She had taken great pains to avoid him, yet here he was, cantering toward her at a fast clip. Her mind raced, wondering how best to handle what could be a troublesome confrontation. She decided she would nod curtly as he rode by, but not slow Dublin, thus making it clear she had no desire for conversation.

"Ah, Lady Clarinda, what a surprise!" he called as he approached. "How delightful to find you out riding early, and on Dublin, I see."

To her chagrin, her plan to ignore him was thwarted when Stormont stopped Sham in the middle of the narrow path, thus blocking her attempt to pass him by. She reined Dublin to a halt. "Good morning, m'lord." With a lofty toss of her head, she continued, "I often ride this early, and on Dublin."

"To the neglect of Donegal," he commented.

Her anger spurted. She opened her mouth for a sharp retort but he laughed and raised his hand.

"Forgive me. That slipped out. I confess, this meeting is not accidental. I had a fair idea you'd be out riding this morning. I need to talk to you."

"What could we possibly say to each other?" Clarinda asked. Dublin chose that moment to do a little dance along the path, so the frosty glance accompanying her words was lost. After she settled the gelding, she declared, "I must return home. Will you kindly clear the path, sir?"

"Return home?" he asked skeptically. "Why the urgency?" She regarded him scornfully. "I must work on my sampler."

Stormont did not move. Instead, he frowned at her, directing his gaze to her sidesaddle. "Ah, I see we have become a lady now. No more racing full tilt across the field, legs astride."

Infuriating! "How I ride is none of your concern," she retorted, making no attempt to conceal her indignation. "Now I must insist—"

"You are not getting by." Stormont dropped his reins and crossed his arms. "Not until I talk to you. By God, you're stubborn." He was silent for a moment, apparently lost in his thoughts, his face a reflection of some inner turmoil that appeared to be raging inside his head. "I have not come here to argue with you," he finally said, his voice restrained. "Instead, I've come to beg a favor."

Her pique subsided. It was difficult to be angry with a man who'd come begging. "And what might the favor be?" she asked.

"I want to know the truth about Sara Sophia."

"I told you—"

"No, you did not. Yesterday at tea you were dispensing pap. I read between the lines." Stormont leaned forward in his saddle. "I shall be honest. I said my friend, Lord Wentridge, had an interest in Sara Sophia, which is true. What I did not say—and would not say because it is no one else's business—is that Lucius has fallen madly in love with Sara Sophia, and she with him. Their situation is hopeless"—Stormont threw up a hand—"but nonetheless, he is in London pining away for the girl, in a state of—how shall I say?—extreme love sickness?"

Stormont looked uncomfortable, but carried on. "The man cannot be consoled. I promised I would find out what I could, for what good it might do. I had thought that perhaps if I brought him news that she was well, and reasonably happy, he might be able to carry on with his life, but because of your little—shall we say, hesitation?—yesterday, I felt compelled to get you aside and ask for the truth."

So that was it. She felt hideously deflated, realizing he

had only sought her out because of his friend. "I shall tell you what I know . . ."

She proceeded to relate everything she had read in the letter from Sara Sophia, plus what Sara Sophia had not said, but could be read between the lines. ". . . so as you can see, she's miserable, and her situation is not likely to improve."

"Wentridge asked her to run off to Gretna Greene with him," Stormont commented. "Perhaps she should have."

"She was tempted, yet her sense of honor compelled her to say no. It's terribly sad. My heart aches, just thinking about them."

Stormont nodded his agreement. "Surely a romance doomed from the start." He heaved a disappointed sigh. "Perhaps I shan't tell Lucius the truth after all," he mused aloud.

She nodded grimly. "In this case, it might be better to pretend you don't know." With a great show of casualness, she gathered up her reins. "Is that all, sir?" The words had almost stuck in her throat, so miserable was she that their meeting was about to end. She longed to tell him how she missed him, how she dreamed each night of those brief moments she had been in his arms. It was obvious, though, he was not going to give her the opportunity. Not a word of a personal nature had he said. Furthermore, his eyes, though friendly, contained none of the passion she had seen that day he kissed her on the riding path. Naturally they wouldn't. For reasons she would never understand, he no longer cared. She had better stop torturing herself and accept his indifference. And more, she must show him that she, too, did not care. Thank goodness, an aching heart did not show.

Stormont gazed at her with guarded eyes. "That's all," he replied. "I am in your debt, and if you hear anything more of Sara Sophia—?"

"I shall keep you informed." She knew she could achieve a graceful exit if she tapped Dublin with her riding crop and left this instant. But somehow she could not move. Their gazes locked. Was it her imagination or was there a faint glint of raw hurt deep in those dark eyes?

As if they had a will of their own, almost before she

knew what she was saying, the fatal words slipped from her mouth.

"Why did you not come that day?" She held her breath, waiting for his answer.

Stony-faced, Robert continued staring at her. For a moment she thought he might ask, "What day?" but he did not. She should have known he was too blunt, too honest to pretend he didn't know.

He looked away, looked back, regarded the sky, looked back again. "The words you spoke at Lady Lynbury's had wings," he said sardonically. "Have you not learned by now not to speak your mind in front of the servants? Let alone Lady Lynbury, who reigns supreme as the purveyor of gossip throughout the countryside."

"What are you talking about?"

"Your remark to Lady Lynbury," he responded with biting sarcasm. "Perhaps you remember?" He laughed wryly. "Not exactly flattering to a man."

Her mind was reeling. "You mean you think I said something insulting about you?"

"You did say it. Don't deny it. Servants don't lie, at least not about something such as this." With a supposed easy laugh he continued, "But never mind. As you can see, I am not Lucius. My heart is far from broken. As to your question, naturally I was not eager to keep our rendezvous once I heard your opinion of me." His eyes turned hard and cold as ice. "You had best reconsider, though, before you make such a remark again."

"I never made any such remark," she cried, feeling sick in her stomach at his sudden hostile demeanor. "There must be some mistake."

"You brought it up," he said harshly. "I haven't asked for an apology, nor do I expect one. I heard of your remark through two different sources—the servants, and Lady Lynbury herself, who called on me personally." He laughed bitterly. "You can imagine her distress at having to impart every tiny detail of your visit—your pink velvet spencer, your white silk dress, even your gold necklace with the 'C'." He shot her a twisted smile. "It was you all right. Do not do me the discourtesy of lying to me now."

"But I—"

"It would appear there's nothing more to say," he said

coldly, backing Sham away. "You will let me know any news of Sara Sophia despite our differences?"

"Of course," she replied, matching his coldness with her own.

"Then good day, m'lady." Stormont touched the reins to Sham and started away.

With rising dismay Clarinda watched the man she loved urge Sham to a trot and disappear down the path toward Hollyridge. *But I have not gone to visit Lady Lynbury for ages—long before Lord Stormont arrived.* In a state of complete bewilderment she wondered how Lady Lynbury could have told such a lie. But the servants, too? They couldn't all be lying. Perhaps they had just thought they had seen her. Or perhaps . . . ?

There is something about the necklace . . .

She recalled the day she had discovered hers and Rissa's necklaces had been switched. Rissa had denied all knowledge of how it could have happened, other than it must have been a servant who had switched them. Clarinda had thought it strange at the time, but there was nothing more she could do. Suddenly the undeniable and dreadful fact struck her hard. Of course! There was only one way those necklaces could have been swapped. It was . . .

Far down the path she saw clouds of dust fill the still morning air as a horse's great hooves pounded against the earth. Stormont hove into view, approaching fast as light. When he reached her, he reined so hard Sham snorted, reared, pawed at the sky. In a twinkling, Stormont slid off. With powerful strides he approached her, a lethal calmness in his eyes.

"It was Rissa," he said.

"I can't believe it, yet who else could have done this but my own sister?" She looked down at him from atop Dublin, not knowing whether to laugh or cry. "Why didn't you tell me? If only I had known!"

"Because I was hurt. Because I was a fool." Stormont leaned his palms against Dublin, one on either side of Clarinda as she sat upon her sidesaddle. He looked up at her, his face twisted with emotion. "This had to be deliberate. What a hellish thing for her to do."

"What exactly did she say?" asked Clarinda. She had to know.

"I am loath to repeat it."

"Please do."

He smiled wryly. "She said, 'I could never love a man like Lord Stormont. How I should dread sharing his bed! He's—' "

"But that's not true!" she blurted. "Why, I have often thought—" Realizing what she'd just said, she felt herself turning red. "Just wait until I confront Rissa!"

"Hush!" Stormont commanded. "We shall discuss Rissa later, but now . . ."

With a joyous hoot, he wrapped his hard-muscled arms around her knees and drew her from the saddle, held her high, and whirled her around, not placing her on the ground. "So you've thought of going to bed with me," he said lightly, gazing up at her.

"Young ladies do not discuss such subjects," she answered primly, but with a smile.

"They don't?" For a moment he buried his head in her skirt. She felt him tremble as he let her slide down an inch or two, close as hand in glove against him. Scandalously close. Mama would definitely not approve. His compelling eyes riveted up at her again, then glanced at Dublin, who was busy nibbling grass from the side of the path. "What do you think, Dublin?" he called. "Does the young lady need to be kissed again? Or"—still holding her high, he joyously swung her clear around again—"perhaps your mistress prefers to get back to embroidering her sampler, in which case, I shall not kiss her at all, especially if she's thinking of the hero. What was his name? Hmm, I seem to have forgotten it."

Laughing, she gripped his shoulders. "Dublin," she called, "he knows full well it was Jeffrey." She tried to think clearly, but it was difficult, what with Robert's arms wrapping even tighter around her legs and his masculine scent of leather mixed with honey water wafting up at her. "But about Rissa—"

"Forget Rissa. You and I have some making up to do."

"Put me down."

"In good time."

He allowed her to slide down his chest a trifle more, then tightened his grasp again. How solid and sinewy his body felt! *I should not be doing this,* she thought. Again, she felt her face flush. "We really shouldn't," she said, thinking how weak that sounded. She made a feeble attempt to wrench away, but stopped immediately, knowing she had no wish to escape his embrace.

"We really should," he said. Still holding tight, he let her slide all the way to the ground, with infinite slowness, planting kisses as he went, at her waist—her midriff—between her breasts—the hollow of her neck, her hair. When they were exactly eye level, he whispered, "Or would you really rather go home and embroider your sampler?"

"No." Her arms slid around his neck.

He regarded her with burning intensity. "Or would you rather think about Jeffrey?"

"No!"

"Well, then." His lips feather-touched hers with tantalizing persuasion, as if she needed any! A torrent of emotions flowed through her as he pressed his mouth hard to hers. He cared! He wanted her! The dismal, bleak winter months were gone, and with them the terrible hurt she'd felt that he had rejected her. Her emotions whirled and skidded with the wonderful shock of it all.

Suddenly he broke off the kiss and put her away.

"Why are you stopping?" she asked.

"Because I'll take you right here if we don't stop," he said through ragged breathing. He walked to Sham, who though not tethered had not wandered away. "Good boy," he said, and patted the horse's rump, quietly, for some moments, as if he were collecting his thoughts. When he looked back at Clarinda, he was in control again. "We have much to discuss."

She nodded. "There's Rissa."

He bit his lip, in deep thought. "She's a danger to you."

"Oh, I hardly think—"

"She's a danger," he said in a voice that did not invite argument.

She spread her palms. "But she's my sister. I hardly know whether to confront her or not."

"Let's think on it a few days, shall we?" Leading his horse, Stormont came back to her and kissed her on the cheek. "Meet me tomorrow at Hollyridge—the stables, early morning. I have things to discuss with you that have nothing to do with Rissa." Gently he ran his hand across her cheek, through her hair until a shuddering sigh of wanting ran through him and he pulled his hand away. "Oh, God, you're beautiful," he said, almost in a moan, "and I—I—" He regarded the sky, then backed away and mounted Sham. "Until tomorrow," he said brusquely and rode away.

Chapter 13

What had happened to Clarinda?

All day, Rissa's suspicions grew. Clarinda had bounced in from her morning ride, cheeks flushed, eyes sparkling. During the day, the house rang with her infectious laughter, a sound no one had heard for months. She was smiling a lot, a far cry from the melancholy expression she had worn of late.

Was it Stormont? Was Clarinda seeing him again? But that would be impossible, Rissa decided. Surely word of her visit to Lady Lynbury had long since reached Stormont's ears. Still . . .

Stormont is mine, Rissa thought with mounting indignation. She had fallen deeply in love with him. She wanted him and she would have him. Nobody on this earth would stand in her way, most especially her twin sister, who had always gotten the best of everything all their lives, but not this time. By all that was holy, Clarinda would not win Stormont, the ultimate prize.

But first I must find out if what I suspect is true.

Early the next morning, in a lighthearted mood, Clarinda walked the distance from Graystone Hall to Hollyridge Manor. Robert was there when she arrived. He was saddling Sham. Donegal was already saddled. Pitney was there, too, along with a stable boy, so when Stormont gave her a formal bow and said, "Good morning, m'lady," in a cool but courteous voice, she knew his formality was for the benefit of the stable hands.

Continuing in the same vein, Stormont asked, "Would you care to accompany me today? I'm headed down the river path."

"I shouldn't mind," she said, as offhanded as he.

They rode slowly, chatting of this and that, she, sedately correct on her sidesaddle, until they reached the very log beside the path where once he had kissed her. Stormont brought Sham to a halt. "You might remember this spot." His mouth quirked with humor.

"Somebody kissed me here," she replied mischievously, "but I can't remember who."

She expected him to laugh, but instead, with a look of determination on his face, he swung off Sham, gently lifted her down from her saddle, and set her on the ground as if she were a delicate porcelain figurine.

"You think I cannot dismount by myself?" she protested with a laugh. "I am not a fragile flower."

"We must talk," he said, ignoring her protestations.

He seemed so intent on his purpose that she said no more and allowed herself to be led to the log they had sat on before. Immediately he turned to face her, took her hand and cradled it in his own. "I love you, Clarinda," he began. Joy shot through her. She tried to speak, but he continued, "No, don't say anything more, not yet. From the day we met—remember when you flew off your horse? I lost my heart when I looked at you, lying on the ground, the breath knocked out of you, your skirt"—his eyes twinkled with remembrance—"bunched up around those shapely limbs of yours. I never knew the meaning of the word smitten until that day. God knows, I tried to fight this attraction I have for you"—he smiled ruefully—"but I could not. I dream of you constantly." He bit his lip and looked away, shaking his head in disbelief. "I never thought a woman could do this to me." He turned back to look at her, a gleam of purpose in his eye, took both her hands and pressed them to his chest. "My dear Lady Clarinda, I am madly, passionately in love with you." He had said the words lightly, but she could hear the dead seriousness that lay beneath. "I had vowed not to marry until I was forty, but that was before I knew of your existence. Will you marry me? I'm warning you, if you don't, I am likely to pine away like Lucius." He laughed, but she knew he meant his words.

"I love you too," she said. Words to describe her love welled within her, but when she tried to speak again, he silenced her. "No, don't say anything. I don't want your

answer now. You must think on it. Much is involved here."
Stormont frowned. "I am aware of your current situation
with your family. And then there's Rissa."

"Rissa will not be pleased," she said, thinking that was
indeed an understatement.

"I fear Rissa has misinterpreted my attentions to her,
which, I can assure you, have been merely friendly at best.
Her visit to Lady Lynbury, impersonating you, is appalling.
We must make sure she won't do us any further mischief,
if mischief is the word." Stormont gazed deep into her eyes.
She saw love there, and compassion, and longing. "Think
about it tonight. Tomorrow I shall pay you a proper visit
and receive my answer."

"Of course." *And my answer will be yes,* she wanted to
cry, but if he wanted her to wait, she would. After all this
time, where was the harm in waiting one more day?

Walking home, Clarinda felt a sense of wonderment at
the turn her life was taking. She had been lost in darkness
and despair for so long that the very idea she could be
happy again was difficult to grasp. Stormont loved her! She
felt like dancing down the path. He was worried about her
family problems, but, really, they were minuscule. Papa
would go along with whatever Mama said. Mama, of
course, would protest that Rissa had some claim on
Stormont, but in the end she would approve, once she knew
whom Robert really loved. As for Rissa . . .

Clarinda had told Stormont, "I don't think Rissa will be
a problem anymore." She believed what she said. After all,
what more harm could Rissa do?

Seething with a mixture of hurt, resentment, and jealousy, Rissa retreated to her bedchamber the moment she
returned from her walk along the river path. It had been
easy to follow Clarinda, and step out of sight when Clarinda
and Stormont dismounted at the very same spot where they
had embraced before. A handy spot for spying, Rissa
thought with grim irony. She had managed to keep herself
well hidden, yet close enough to hear each one of Lord
Stormont's perfidious words.

She had been shocked beyond all measure. Robert had
called at Graystone Hall several times, surely just to see

her. He had not, in fact, shown the least regret that Clarinda had pleaded a headache and not come down to join them. What Rissa couldn't understand was, how could he possibly love a girl like Clarinda? She was stubborn and rebellious. She was outspoken and freely expressed her own opinions. Men deplored such traits in a woman, which was why she, Rissa, had gone to such lengths to demonstrate her skills in music, watercolors, and embroidery. Surely Stormont must have observed how she excelled at light conversation and the pouring of tea. Why would he not think she would make the perfect wife? She, who aside from being beautiful, was cheerful and obedient, with naught but frivolous thoughts in her head?

He doesn't love Clarinda, he only thinks he does, Rissa concluded. Given a little time, she was sure she could change his mind, but she had only until tomorrow when Stormont came to call. Clarinda would surely say yes, and when she did, he would go directly to Papa and ask for her hand. There could be no going back after that, they'd be good as married. Rissa pictured herself standing next to Clarinda at the wedding. Oh, the humiliation! How could she smile and act happy for her sister when underneath she would know that Clarinda had won again, just as she had done all their lives?

Rissa raised a clenched fist and fervently vowed, "She won't win, not this time!" There must still be a way to win Stormont. She must think of it and act quickly.

Rissa flung herself on her bed and for a long time stared at the ceiling, hands behind her head. She considered countless schemes, discarding them all, until at last—ah! Why had she not thought of this before? She had found the perfect plan.

Clarinda was in her bed chamber, staring out the window when Rissa knocked and entered. "Yes, Rissa?" she asked coolly. Despite her euphoria, she had not forgotten her sister's trickery.

"Come sit down," Rissa replied, ignoring her sister's hostility. "I must talk to you."

After Clarinda settled on the edge of the bed, Rissa on the settee, Rissa said, "I have a proposition for you."

"What kind of proposition?" Clarinda asked, full of suspicion.

Rissa settled back, relaxed and sure of herself. "You've known Sara Sophia all your life, have you not?"

"Of course. You know that."

"And you love Sara Sophia, don't you, and consider her your dearest friend?"

A lot more so than you, Clarinda thought. "Yes, she is my dearest friend, but what is this about?"

Rissa peered at her thoughtfully. "I simply wanted to make sure that Sara Sophia means a great deal to you. Do you feel bad, now that she's gone to work as a governess?"

"Bad is hardly the word. Sara Sophia was happy and content with her life at Hollyridge. Now she's working as a governess in a place where they treat her little better than a servant. Remember how she loved horses? Now they won't even let her ride. Then, too, she had developed a great fondness for Lord Wentridge, and he for her. It's hopeless, of course. My heart aches every time I think about what's happened to her, but what can I do?"

"There's something you can do," Rissa answered with a triumphant little smile, "something so magnificent, so totally astounding and incredible, that Sara Sophia's life will be changed forever."

"But what?" cried Clarinda, astounded at Rissa's words. "Tell me!"

"All in good time." As if trying to put her thoughts together, Rissa stood up and started pacing the floor. Nervously she pursed her lips and pressed her hands together as if in prayer, until finally she stopped and said, "Listen to me," and sat next to Clarinda on the bed. "Sara Sophia is not what she seems. I have written proof."

"Of what?" Clarinda was completely bewildered.

"Sara Sophia is a countess, and wealthy besides. It's a long story, but it's true."

"But I don't understand. How would you know—?"

"I just know," Rissa answered petulantly, "and I can prove it, but I must ask you something first."

Clarinda fought to stay calm, not easy with this shocking news concerning her friend. "Then get on with it," she demanded, none too politely.

In characteristic fashion, Rissa made a little moué. "No

need to get testy. Let's say, for instance, you have a friend whom you have known all your life and love dearly, and this friend has fallen on bad times and needs help."

"All right, let's say that." *Lord give me patience,* Clarinda prayed silently.

Rissa went on, "And let's say, for instance, there is a certain man you have fallen in love with." Rissa's voice hardened. "Mind, he's not just any man, he's titled, rich, handsome, and personable." The inharmonious change in Rissa's voice chilled Clarinda's heart. She wondered what her twin could possibly be up to. Whatever it was, it boded ill. "And let's say," Rissa continued, "just for instance, that this man you have fallen in love with has asked you to marry him."

She knows, Clarinda thought with fearful clarity. She felt a shock run through her. There was only one way Rissa could know of Stormont's proposal—she must have spied on them. Appalled, she slid from the bed and glared, hands on hips, at her sister. "You were on the path this morning, weren't you? What a despicable thing to do. How low! Where were you—hiding behind a bush?"

Rissa gave a disdainful shrug. "What if I was? Do you want to help Sara Sophia or not?"

"Of course I want to help, but—" Clarinda silenced herself and sank back down on the bed. However incensed she might feel about Rissa's blatant spying, she realized Rissa had the upper hand. "Do go on," she said, her voice tight.

Rissa regarded her with utter unconcern. "That's smart of you, sister. As I was saying—"

"I have heard enough of what-ifs," Clarinda cut in. "Just tell me what you want."

Rissa raised her brows as if amazed. "When will you ever learn your manners? All right then, what I want is this. Sara Sophia is a countess, and rich besides."

"You said that before, but that's hard to believe," Clarinda said. "Are you sure?"

Rissa retorted, "Of course I'm sure. I have positive proof. Can you imagine what this proof would do for your poor little orphan friend? She would not have to be a governess anymore. She could own all the horses she ever wanted and live in comfort the rest of her life. Best of all, Lord Wentridge's parents would be thrilled to have her in the family. Think of it, Clarinda, your dear friend could marry the man she loved, ride horses all the day if she liked, and lead a gloriously happy life until the day she died."

Clarinda sat shaking her head. How wonderful, to think Sara Sophia could be happy again! And yet, Rissa's claims were incredible. She was filled with doubt. "But I just don't see—"

"You will. I told you I have proof which I shall be happy to provide you on one condition."

Here it comes, thought Clarinda. She knew her twin too well not to know such wonderful news would come with a price. "What's the condition?" she asked, and braced herself.

"I shall give you all the proof you need that Sara Sophia is indeed a countess. Written proof, by the way, and I shall lead you to a certain treasure that is hers. In return for helping your friend—" Rissa paused and regarded her sister with flat, hard passionless eyes. "You will swear on a bible that you will refuse Lord Stormont's proposal of marriage when he comes calling tomorrow."

In stunned silence, Clarinda felt the blood leave her face. "You can't mean this."

"But I can. I've thought it over carefully." Rissa's face suddenly clouded. Tears sprang to her eyes. "Don't you understand I love him? I want more than anything in the world to be his wife. I dream of being mistress of Holly-ridge Manor. I would have the most wonderful parties and dinners and balls. I'd be the perfect hostess, much better than you because you don't care about those things. Be-sides"—Rissa's brow furrowed in an affronted frown—"I saw him first."

No you did not see him first, Clarinda wanted to say, but stopped herself. She wasn't concerned with Rissa's childish logic, but rather with the shocking demand Rissa had just made. Surely she couldn't be serious. "Rissa, might I ask how long you have known about this proof that Sara So-phia is a countess?"

Rissa thought a moment, obviously mulling over how much she should reveal. "I have known for a while," she finally answered cautiously. "Actually since Lord Wester-lynn died in our driveway."

"Ah, so he told you something?"

Another long pause. "Yes. And he gave me something."

"What?"

"Make that promise and I shall tell you."

Clarinda shut her eyes for a moment in disbelief. "But I cannot!" she cried. "Lord Stormont wants to marry me, not you. I love him, too, desperately." She took a moment to calm herself. "We know about your visit to Lady Lynbury's, claiming you were me. I think it's despicable and so does Robert. Can't you see? Even if I reject his offer, do you think he would ever want to marry you?"

"Of course I do." Rissa's tears had vanished. She was confident again. "I just need a little time, that's all. Once he knows you won't marry him, he will naturally turn to me." She smiled brightly. "What's the difference? Don't we look exactly alike?"

Clarinda felt sick inside. "Rissa, you simply cannot ask that I give up Lord Stormont. I love him. I plan to say yes when he comes calling tomorrow."

"Fine," said Rissa. A tensing of her jaw revealed her deep frustration. "Then we shall forget about Sara Sophia. She shall live in misery the rest of her life, and all because of you."

"That's not fair!" Clarinda felt the impulse to grab her sister's shoulders and shake her, a fate she well deserved, and worse. But she knew such a tactic would get her nowhere. "I need time to think," she said.

"Take all the time you want," replied Rissa. "Just make up your mind before you tell Robert you'll marry him. That would indeed be a tragedy because then I shall burn a certain paper and Sara Sophia will never, never know who she really is. I shall leave you now—give you time to think."

After Rissa left, Clarinda curled up on her bed, a compact bundle of misery. She had faced dilemmas in the past, but they paled in comparison to this horrendous decision she faced now. On the one hand, she recalled that blissful moment this morning when Stormont proposed. After all that misery, it was wonderful to think that with Stormont by her side, she could live the rest of her life happy and content, and never ask for anything more.

On the other hand . . .

Oh, Sara Sophia, how can I let you down?

If their positions were reversed, would Sara Sophia make the same sacrifice for her? The answer came loud and clear: of course she would. Sara Sophia would not think twice. She was, and always would be, a loving, caring, generous friend. No question, she deserved the same treatment in return. Clarinda groaned aloud, awash in misery. Much as she loved Lord Stormont, she would lose all honor if she did not help her friend. *I could never live with myself,* she thought dismally.

But perhaps a compromise? Yes, at least she could set a time limit, although the very thought of staying away from Stormont for any length of time was almost more than she could bear. At least there was one incontrovertible fact in her favor. Even if she stayed away from him a hundred years, Stormont would never, ever love Rissa, no matter what she tried.

At least I don't think so.

Clarinda found her sister in her bedchamber, as usual preening before her mirror. "Three months, Rissa," she said.

Tugging at a curl, Rissa addressed her sister's reflection in the mirror. "What do you mean, three months?"

"I mean I promise I'll stay completely away from Lord Stormont for three months, during which time you can flirt with him and ply your womanly charms all you please."

"A year," Rissa flung back.

"Six months. Really, Rissa, be reasonable. If you can't snare him in six months, then you can't snare him at all."

Rissa took some time to consider. "All right, then, six months." She turned to face Clarinda. "But you must not tell him any of this, agreed?"

"Agreed."

"Nor anyone."

"Of course."

"Stay right there." Rissa left the room and shortly returned with their father's Bible. "Take it and swear."

"It really is not necessary—"

"Swear!"

Sighing with resignation, Clarinda took the Bible in her hands and swore that tomorrow she would reject Robert's proposal.

"And you must stay away from him and make him think you don't like him anymore."

Clarinda felt sick again. Six months was a lifetime. In six months Robert could find someone else. But what could she do? "All right. I swear I shall stay completely away from Lord Stormont for six months, and . . . and . . ."—oh, how hard it was to get the words out!—". . . make him think I don't like him anymore."

For the first time in her life, Clarinda felt dizzy and faint. Her knees went weak and she had to sit down.

After a moment, she gathered her strength and asked, "Now will you kindly tell me the truth about Sara Sophia?"

Chapter 14

"**I** can hardly believe this."

With increasing astonishment, Clarinda read Rissa's labored translation of the letter from Louise Marie de Clarmonte. Reading it was difficult. Not only were the pages scratched and splotchy, they were covered with Rissa's childlike, near unintelligible scrawl. Nevertheless, Clarinda struggled until she had read and understood each and every word. The moving tale of a woman caught in the Reign of Terror of the French Revolution touched her deeply. "The poor woman," Clarinda whispered as she let the last of the pages drop to her lap. "How horrible that must have been, standing in that jeering crowd at the Place de la Liberté, watching all those poor souls being led to the guillotine, and then seeing your own husband . . . I cannot bear to think of it."

Rissa shrugged. "At least it's quick, having your head chopped off."

"Yes, but—" Clarinda closed her mouth. Rissa was simply too shallow to understand. "Do you still have the original letter?"

"It's here." Rissa drew several pages of parchment from the bottom of her sewing box.

Clarinda took them carefully, almost reverently, in her hands. A lump formed in her throat as she studied the graceful, perfectly formed letters in French, written all those years ago. "Just imagine how awful it must have been for her to lose her home, her husband, everything she owned, as well as her whole way of life."

"Terrible, I'm sure." Rissa frowned with impatience. "Now that I've told you, what will you do?"

"I hadn't thought." Louise Marie de Clarmonte's poignant story had kept Clarinda so engrossed she had been just barely aware of the momentous changes this letter would bring to the life of Sara Sophia. Now, as realization took hold, she was suddenly bursting with excitement. "Rissa, this is wonderful news. And the paintings? You know where they are?"

Rissa reached into her sewing box again and withdrew the two old rusted keys. "Do you remember the old gatehouse at Hollyridge, and the doors that were always locked?"

"That's where the paintings are?"

"I've seen them. I find it hard to believe they would be worth anything."

Clarinda chose to ignore her sister's ignorant remark. Rissa knew nothing of art and had never tried to learn. "It's like a fairy tale come true, isn't it?" she exclaimed. "Not only is Sara Sophia a countess, she's rich."

"I suppose now she'll be the darling of the *ton,*" Rissa remarked without enthusiasm.

"Sara Sophia won't care about the *ton.* What she'll care about is that now she can marry Lord Wentridge."

Rissa scowled. "You still haven't answered my question. How will you tell Sara Sophia? What will you do with the paintings? What of Lord Wentridge?"

In deep thought, Clarinda bit her lip. "There's so much to think about. First, Sara Sophia must be told, of course."

"And how do you propose to do that, send her a letter?"

Clarinda thought a moment. "What I would really like to do is order Timmons to ready one of the coaches immediately. Then I would journey at top speed to Rondale Hall and tell Sara Sophia to her face who she really is. Can you imagine her reaction when she hears the news? She could leave that dreadful position immediately. She could return to Hollyridge Manor—I am sure Lord Stormont would allow her to stay. She could ride Sham again. And soon Lord Wentridge would arrive from London and ask for her hand." A cry of relief broke from her lips. "I feel so excited, just thinking about it."

"You had best curb your enthusiasm," Rissa answered sourly. "In the first place, have you forgotten you're restricted to home? Mama and Papa would never allow you to take such a journey alone, especially now."

"I know." Clarinda's joy fell flat. "Do you realize we are

twenty years old, yet we cannot do as we please? At times like this I feel so restricted. I hate being treated like an inferior being. Sometimes I wish I were a man."

"How can you say such a thing?" Rissa looked genuinely bewildered. "Women truly are inferior. God made us that way. Thank goodness, we have men in our lives to guide us, or I don't know what we'd do."

"I would know," Clarinda answered ruefully, deciding to say no more. She had argued with Rissa before about a woman's place in the world, to no avail. "But you're right. We must rely on a man to help us—I should think Lord Stormont."

Rissa scowled. "Remember your promise. There's no need to go rushing off to tell Stormont. Let us wait until his visit tomorrow. Then we'll tell him the news."

Clarinda's euphoria vanished in an instant. "But of course," she replied, swallowing the despair in her throat. "Then Papa must be told."

"He returns from London tomorrow afternoon."

"I hate to wait that long."

"You have no choice."

Clarinda was suddenly struck by a startling realization. "Rissa, you've known all this since the day Lord Westerlynn died. That was months ago."

"I suppose."

"Why did you keep the letter and the key a secret?"

Rissa bristled. "I really don't have to answer that. Suffice to say, Sara Sophia was no friend of mine. Why should I go out of my way to help her?"

Clarinda was stunned. Such an act of omission was so calloused, so totally without feeling, even for her selfish sister. She stared at Rissa with reproachful eyes. "Do you realize what you've done? How could you have kept silent, knowing Sara Sophia had to leave the only home she'd ever known to go off and be a governess? You knew she and Lord Wentridge had fallen in love, and that this"— Clarinda shook the letter practically under her sister's nose—"would have made all the difference in the world."

Rissa's chin jutted defiantly. "I don't have to explain to you."

"Not to me, perhaps, but how will you explain your delay to Papa?"

For a moment, Rissa was taken aback. "I'll think of something," she replied sullenly. Her face brightened. "I shall tell Papa it was you who were with Lord Westerlynn when he died."

"No you won't." Clarinda could not conceal her scorn. "Everyone knows it was you. If you recall, you made everyone aware of how marvelously brave you were that day, rushing to Westerlynn's aid. You were *such* a heroine."

"It won't matter." A mocking smile crossed Rissa's face. "I was in such a state of shock I forgot about the letter and the keys. Papa will believe me, and you know Mama will. They believe everything I say."

Clarinda let out a ragged sigh, knowing Rissa was right. "It's pointless to argue."

"Indeed it is," Rissa answered smugly. "I almost burned the letter and threw the keys away. You should be grateful I saved them. You should be glad I have told you about Sara Sophia and just be happy for her good news."

Clarinda thought of Stormont and felt the gall rising in her throat. "Yes, but at what a price."

"You agreed to it." Rissa sniffed disdainfully. "I have nothing to fear, my dear, honorable sister. I know you. You swore on the Bible. You would rather die than go back on your word."

She's right, Clarinda thought disconsolately. She had been so excited about Sara Sophia, she had ignored her own sorrow, but now it all came flooding back. Tomorrow Robert would come calling, wanting his answer, and she, doing the hardest thing she'd ever done in her life, would have to say no.

Clarinda spent the next morning alternating between feelings of joy for Sara Sophia and despair for herself. She tried not to think of Lord Stormont, but that was impossible. The day dragged until finally, in midafternoon, Papa returned from London. Soon Clarinda, with Rissa close behind, hastened to the grand salon, where Papa and Mama were settling themselves for tea. "This is rather unexpected," Papa remarked. "It is not often I see you girls together anymore. To what do I owe this honor?" His business affairs in London must have gone well, Clarinda noted. He was smiling.

Mama remarked, "All day I have sensed something was afoot, m'lord, but neither one would tell me."

Clarinda sank to the settee and eagerly began, "I have wonderful news . . ."

She proceeded to relate the story of Sara Sophia. She had even brought the keys with her to show, as well as the original letter in French and Rissa's translation.

When she finished, Mama, clearly thunderstruck by the announcement, exclaimed, " 'Pon my soul, a countess!" She fingered the keys and glanced over the letter. "Sara Sophia is a countess," she repeated several times, as if she still could not believe such a tale.

"Not just any countess," Clarinda emphasized, "but a French countess in her own right, and wealthy."

"But we must have her back immediately," Mama said. "I shall take her under my wing. We shall do the London Season. I shall order her an entire new wardrobe, do something with her hair. You *did* say she has wealth hidden away?"

Clarinda nodded. "Some paintings—"

"I am thrilled!" Mama's joy appeared to know no bounds. "Just wait until I tell Lady Lynbury. Imagine all the gossip in London when our young French countess appears from out of nowhere." Mama's head bobbed up and down with knowing emphasis. "I always thought there was something special about that girl."

In contrast to his wife's overblown enthusiasm, Lord Capelle had retained his usual composure. "That is excellent news, Clarinda. You must be most pleased and happy for your friend."

"But first she must be told," Clarinda told him quietly. "I would like to travel to Rondale Hall myself and give her the news."

"Impossible," Mama interjected quickly. "You must not forget you are not to leave home." She addressed her husband. "Is that not right, m'lord?"

Papa cleared his throat. "Er . . . perhaps under the circumstances—?"

"Absolutely not!"

"Er . . . of course, my dear." Papa gave a weary sigh. "Very well, then. How would it be, Clarinda, if you wrote a letter to Sara Sophia instead? I shall send one of our footmen with the message, direct to Rondale Hall. Tell her it is of the utmost urgency that she return to Hollyridge Manor immediately. When she returns, you can give her the news."

At least her father had found a reasonable compromise. "That will be fine, Papa."

"I have a question," Papa said, turning thoughtfully to Rissa. "Lord Westerlynn gave the keys and letter to you on the day he died?" When Rissa nodded, a puzzled expression spread across his face. "Westerlynn died months ago. Why did you withhold this information until now?"

Rissa started to turn red. "Because . . . because . . ." She stopped and bit her lip. Mama quickly interrupted.

"The girl was in a state of shock, m'lord. She was not thinking clearly."

"Odd," remarked Papa, "she was thinking clearly enough to write this translation." He held Rissa's splotched pages up distastefully. "Messy though it may be."

Mama opened her mouth, no doubt to continue her defense of Rissa, but at that moment, Manning, the butler, entered and addressed her.

"Lord Stormont to see you, m'lady."

All else forgotten, Lady Capelle beamed and threw Rissa a quick smile. "There, what did I tell you? Have him come in, Manning."

Clarinda stood hastily. "Have him wait a moment, Manning. Mama, I have just developed a headache. I shall retire to my room."

"Nonsense," said Papa. "Lord Stormont's a fine fellow. No need to be rude. You stay put, young lady."

"Yes, Papa." Clarinda sank back on the settee in such an inner torment she wasn't sure she could endure seeing Stormont again, knowing he could not be hers.

Robert had awakened in a marvelous mood. *Clarinda shall be mine*, he kept thinking over and over again. He could not get over his marvelous luck in finding a woman who could ride a horse as well as he and was not only bright and beautiful, but a woman who disdained society's follies and foibles, as did he, and, unlike most of the young chits he knew, had no affectations.

This afternoon, when he visited Graystone Hall, he

would somehow get her alone, and she would accept his proposal. They would be married as soon as possible. Soon she would be lying in his bed, in his arms, and he, so tormented by his thoughts of her these past few weeks that he could hardly think straight, would at last make her truly his.

Stop acting like a green schoolboy, he chastised himself, but no use. For the sake of the servants, and Lucius, who was visiting, he carefully maintained his cool facade. But inside, thoughts of Clarinda were so dizzying he was not at all sure he could last to the hour when good manners decreed he could pay his visit to Graystone Hall to ask for her hand.

When they were married, what long, lingering, trailing kisses he would give her! Starting with her smooth, white forehead—sliding slowly to her soft mouth, where he would linger, caressing her lips again and again, until her arms would creep around his neck and he heard the beginnings of passion in her sigh. Then he would slide his lips to the inviting hollow of her neck. And then . . .

Damn society's rules!

Why could he not go visiting when he wanted to, which would be the crack of dawn, the way he was feeling. But he had controlled himself, quelling the maddening pulsing of desire that spiraled deep within him every time he thought of her. Now, dressed to the nines, feeling confident as a falcon in flight, he strode into the Capelles' drawing room.

"Ah, Capelle, back from London I see," he smoothly remarked to the older man, who had stood to greet him. "Lady Capelle," he acknowledged with a bow, noting the woman was smiling for a change. "Rissa, how lovely you look." He bowed again, wondering if the girl would ever stop that silly simpering. "And, Clarinda." *My God, what is wrong*? he thought as he looked into his beloved's pale, unsmiling face.

"How delightful to see you, Lord Stormont," she said, in a voice both unnatural and strained.

He would have asked her what was wrong, but Lady Capelle spoke up. "Dear Lord Stormont, do sit down and have some tea. We have the most remarkable news to tell you concerning Sara Sophia."

For the next few minutes, Robert, teacup in hand, lis-

tened to the astounding tale, told, for the most part, by
Lady Capelle, embellished here and there by Rissa. But
not a word from Clarinda, who sat, still as a stone statue,
on the settee.

"What a remarkable story," he said when they had
finished.

"Indeed," said Lord Capelle. He nodded toward the
keys, now held by Lady Capelle. "I trust you don't mind a
bit more trespassing, but I s'pose our next step would be
to see if those paintings are still there, and if their value is
as high as this Louise Marie de Clarmonte seemed to
think."

"But of course," Robert answered amiably. Rissa had
indeed trespassed, but he would ignore that. "We can go
to the gatehouse now, if you like." He had been only half
listening. Surely the revelation about Sara Sophia was wonderful. She was a gentle, bright young woman whom he
liked very much. At some other time he would have been
delighted at her good fortune. But not now. All he could
think of was, what had happened to Clarinda? He must get
her alone.

"Lord Stormont . . . ?"

Lady Capelle was talking to him, but he hadn't heard.
Really, he must get his wits together. "Umm, yes, m'lady,
why don't you and your daughters come to the gatehouse
by carriage? As you know, the tower is in a remote corner
of the estate, in an area still unkempt, but I do believe we
can get within walking distance. Lord Capelle, why not saddle Jupiter and ride back with me?"

"Splendid idea." Papa stood, eager as he always was
when anticipating a ride on his beloved stallion. "Come,
Edwina, girls, we shall see you at the gatehouse."

The paintings were there, still safe in the musty tower
room of the gatehouse, and so magnificent Robert forgot
for a moment his concern over Clarinda, so awed was he
by the smuggled treasures that lay unrolled before him. "A
Rubens," he exclaimed, "and look here, m'lord, engravings
by William Hogarth."

"All absolutely splendid," proclaimed Lord Capelle, as
awed as he. "And worth a fortune, just as the countess

said. Without doubt, Sara Sophia will live in luxury the rest of her life."

"I would never have guessed they were worth so much," said Rissa. "Even that fat, naked lady," she said with a giggle, pointing at the Rubens.

Lord save us from bird-brained women, Robert thought, pitying the poor man who would end up marrying the silly chit. As for Clarinda . . .

What was wrong with her? She had stood quietly, obviously pleased and excited when some of the canvases had been unrolled, and yet, hardly saying a word.

I must get her alone, Robert thought, *if only for a minute.*

His chance came when they all left the tower room and had to tread down the narrow, stone steps one by one. Except for himself, Clarinda was the last to go down. She was about to set her foot on the top step when he touched her shoulder.

"What is wrong?" he whispered. He hated this sort of subterfuge, but he was desperate to know.

"Nothing's wrong," she said.

"Just like a woman!" he fiercely whispered back. He gripped her arm. "Now tell me!"

She made to continue on, then thought a moment, seeming to realize he deserved an answer.

"I cannot marry you," she said with averted eyes.

He was thunderstruck. For a moment he could not speak. Finally he managed, "But yesterday I thought—"

"No!" She looked directly at him, her blue eyes full of remoteness. Holding her head proudly, she replied straight-out, "You thought wrong, sir. Now I really must go."

Clarinda pulled her arm from his grasp and without another word, hurried down the flight of stone steps to join her family. He stood watching, his innards shocked. He was too appalled to say another word.

"Light more candles, Jennings," Robert crossly demanded that night at dinner. "This room is dark as a dungeon," he muttered, glancing around at the shadowed mahogany paneled walls of the dining room. "I have half a notion to move back to Oakley House."

From Robert's right at the dinner table, a puzzled Lucius

regarded him. "You are out of sorts tonight, old fellow. Whatever is the matter with you?"

Out of sorts? Robert thought ironically. Such a description could hardly begin to describe the bleak hopelessness of the mood that enveloped him. For one thing, he had been obliged to decide whether or not to tell Lucius the stupendous news regarding Sara Sophia. He yearned to tell his friend, yet was cautious enough to realize much could still go wrong. Surreptitiously, he regarded his dinner companion. Lucius was thinner—dark circles under his eyes. Worse, his enthusiasm for life, acerbic though it had been, had fled. In his grief for Sara Sophia, Lucius had become a dull, drab shadow of his former self. Now, after the heartache he had suffered, it would be cruel to raise his hopes, only to have them dashed again. More prudent to wait, Robert decided. He would break the news to Lucius when Sara Sophia arrived safely home.

That decided, Robert's thoughts now dwelled continually, without respite, on the undeniable and dreadful fact that Clarinda had rejected him. He had been stunned by her words, partly because, he had to admit, he had never before been rejected by a woman. Never!

"Robert? Are you listening? You seem a million miles away."

"Er, sorry, Lucius. My mind was elsewhere." Robert debated whether or not to say more, but decided he would not. In fact, he vowed, he would not think of her, he would not talk of her. But then, almost as if they had a mind of their own, the words popped out. "It's Clarinda. I proposed and she rejected me."

Lucius's eyes went wide. He nearly dropped his fork. "*You?* Proposed to a woman?"

"To what else would I propose, a stump?" Robert snapped.

"Sorry, I didn't mean—"

"Of course not," Robert interrupted, instantly remorseful. "No need for me to bite your head off. It's just . . . I love her, Lucius. I thought she loved me. I was confident when I proposed she'd fall into my arms crying, yes, she'd marry me. But no! She rejected me, Lucius. I, who have never been rejected by a woman before, have been most definitely put in my place." Robert's lips twisted into a cynical smile. "A lesson in humility. Much needed, don't you think?"

"Perhaps," replied Lucius, who had listened carefully. " 'Pride goeth before a fall,' they say. That is certainly true in my case. I was a user of women, plying them with gifts and attention, then casting them aside when they no longer suited me." Lucius shook his head regretfully. "With never a thought to their feelings. Now I've learned . . ." His voice broke. He took a hasty sip of water. "I've learned the meaning of the word hurt, Robert. Never shall I hurt a woman again."

"I'm as guilty as you," Robert admitted. "I never loved any woman, until Clarinda."

"But surely you would not have proposed had you not been sure she would accept."

Robert blurted, "That's what I thought, but then there was all the excitement over Sara Sophia—"

Damme! Robert clamped his mouth shut but not soon enough.

Lucius, still holding his crystal water glass, set it slowly back on the table, then gazed at Robert with sharp, assessing eyes. "Tell me, Robert," he said, his voice thick with emotion. "Don't hold back or I shall, at the very least, use my bare hands to throttle you."

Robert told, he had no choice. All of it. The rusty keys to the old gatehouse—the paintings—the astounding letter from Louise Marie de Clarmonte, which clearly established the fact that Sara Sophia, heretofore impoverished orphan, was in reality Countess Sara Sophia Alexandrine de Clarmonte.

At the end, Robert apologized. "Sorry I didn't tell you, old man. I myself only found out this afternoon. I was going to tell you, but first—"

"No, no, it's all right," said Lucius, waving his hand to stop any further apologies. He had listened, almost without expression, to Robert's revelations. Now he shut his eyes, as if attempting to absorb the news with all his attention. A tear trickled down his cheek. "Oh, God," he finally murmured, "how could I have been so lucky? I've been given a second chance." Trembling with emotion, he put his head in hands, and Robert, touched and nearly overcome himself at the overwhelming emotion of his friend, spent the next minutes comforting him.

Lucius finally sat straight again and pulled himself together. "If you tell anyone in London . . ." he said with a warning glance.

"That Lord Wentridge, that heartless rake, actually shed a tear?" Robert asked, mockingly aghast. "Never!" He smiled at his friend. "She should be home in a day or two. Meanwhile . . ." His spirits dipped again, even farther than before because his friend's happy tidings reminded him of his own loss. "Ah, well, at least one of us has reason to celebrate tonight."

His old self again, Lucius remarked, "Knowing you, you would never have proposed, lest you were sure she had some affection for you."

"She did," Robert replied, "or so I thought. Only yesterday, I kissed her and she kissed me back with such warmth I was sure she cared for me." Robert brought his fist down so hard on the table Lucius jumped. "Dammit, she did care. But then, today, she treated me like some cur she'd like to kick aside."

"Well, then," Lucius said in his most logical voice, "did it ever occur to you that something must have happened between yesterday and today to make her change her mind?"

"I hadn't thought," Robert began, then fell into silence. "The only thing that happened was the discovery about Sara Sophia."

"So?" Lucius gazed at him significantly.

"I shall think about it," Robert said. Back in a dim corner of his brain, certain facts were beginning to fall into place.

Chapter 15

Clarinda awoke the next morning with a headache, a real one this time. As she came fully awake, the events of yesterday came crashing back, both the good and the bad. She groaned, thinking of Robert and how she had lost him. But today, she firmly told herself, she would try to concentrate on Sara Sophia's good fortune. Already a footman had been dispatched in one of the smaller coaches, carrying her letter. By tomorrow he should reach Rondale Hall. She pictured her dear friend's face when she read,

> Dearest Sara Sophia,
> Something wonderful has happened. It is a matter of the greatest urgency that you return home immediately. Bring all your possessions, for it is highly unlikely you will ever return to Rondale Hall once you have heard the news.
> My father's coach will bring you directly here, to Graystone Hall, where I shall be eagerly awaiting your return. I am looking forward to telling you of the most remarkable and fortunate events that have occurred. Trust me, you will not be disappointed.
> Most sincerely,
> Clarinda Capelle

She could hardly wait! Now, as she sat at her dressing table, staring at her pale face in the mirror, she had not one regret. If her sacrifice would bring happiness to her dearest friend in the world, then all the misery she felt, and would continue to feel, perhaps the rest of her life, was well worth it. Lord Wentridge was here, visiting Hollyridge Manor. That meant the lovers would soon be united. Just picturing their joyous reunion made Clarinda's heart swell.

But thinking about reunited lovers soon brought her back to that dismal scene yesterday in the gatehouse when she had been compelled to reject Robert's proposal. How stunned he had looked. He was a man who brimmed with self-confidence and no doubt had never given a thought to the possibility she might say no. And why should he? What right-minded woman would reject a man as bright—witty—charming as Robert, Lord Stormont? Let alone, she thought wryly, a man with his vast wealth and high title.

How she wished she could take back her words of refusal to his marriage proposal. Her mind searched for ways to reunite with him somehow, but no use. Whether Rissa captured him or not, six months was a lifetime. Considering the cold way she'd treated him, he would never come back. She swallowed the sob that rose in her throat and admonished herself, *Don't think of him.* If she allowed herself to dwell on the loss of the only man she had ever truly loved, she might not even wish to survive. But that was foolish, even though she knew she would never get over her love for him. Despite her resolve, her spirits plunged as she envisioned a desolate future. She had felt the same when Jeffrey died, but for different reasons. Then, she had been a giddy young girl infatuated with a book of poems and a handsome uniform. But with Robert, she loved the man himself. How could she not help but mourn his loss?

But if I'm brave enough, and strong enough, I can get over this. Surely I can create a reasonable, happy life for myself.

She heard a quick knock on the door. Estelle entered, asking, "M'lady, what will you and Lady Rissa wear today?"

Clarinda succumbed to the tide of rebellion that rose within her. "I shall not be dressing like my twin anymore. Ever!" She thought of her gold necklace lying on her bosom and pulled the chain over her head. "Nor shall I be wearing this any more, either." Disdainfully she dropped the necklace on her dressing table.

Distressed, Estelle protested, "But, madam, what will her ladyship and his lordship say?"

"They can send me off to North Wales for all I care. The way I feel today, I would be glad to go."

"But won't Miss Sara Sophia be coming back soon,

m'lady? Surely you would weesh to be here when she arrives."

Amazing, how quickly servants discovered every single happening in their employers' lives. Nothing was sacred. Resigned, Clarinda replied, "You're right about Sara Sophia. Of course I should be here, and I shall be. I really must stop moping about." She thought of Robert and sighed.

"Oh, m'lady, I am so sorry." In a gesture totally uncharacteristic of her, Estelle, who had always been the perfect lady's maid, stepped out of her impersonal role and patted Clarinda's shoulder. Her brown eyes filled with sympathy. "It ees hard, I know, what weeth Lady Rissa"—she paused and shook her head—"but I say too much."

She knows about Robert, thought Clarinda, touched by Estelle's sympathy. "There's nothing to be done, I'm afraid, but don't worry, I shall survive."

Estelle picked up a brush and started brushing Clarinda's hair. "There are other men in the world," she said.

Looking straight ahead, Clarinda addressed Estelle's image in the mirror. "Not for me there aren't. I shall never marry."

"Oh, madam, no!"

"No man could ever replace him, so why should I even try to find someone else? Besides, are men everything? Surely, a woman could live happily with other interests in her life."

Estelle regarded her shrewdly. "Like what?"

"Well, like horses. There's Donegal—Dublin—Sham—Jupiter. My love of horses will keep me alive." In the mirror she saw Estelle smother a smile. "You think not?" she demanded.

"Someone as beautiful as you should not remain single. *Mon Dieu,* what a waste if you do!"

Perhaps Estelle was right. Clarinda thought of all the spinsters she knew and felt dismayed. Most were forced to live a second-class existence, dependent upon the charity of their relatives. They were treated like servants, or even worse. But surely that would not happen to her. "Rest assured, Estelle, even if I never marry, I shall not turn into a dried up, embittered old ape leader." She glanced about her spacious bedchamber. "This will always be my home.

Papa will always make me feel welcome, and when he dies, Alexander will." An old resentment flared. As a woman, she would not inherit a farthing. So unfair! But today it hardly mattered. Nothing mattered except the joy she would soon experience for Sara Sophia.

"That is all very well and good, m'lady," Estelle was saying, "but aside from the horses, what will you do with your life?"

Clarinda thought a moment and tilted her chin defiantly. "I shall spend my days riding horses, of course, and doing good works like taking care of the sick and carrying food baskets to the poor."

It didn't take Estelle's amused sniff to tell her how ludicrous that sounded. Yet what was she to do? She had lost Robert. Never would she risk her heart again.

It was still morning. Clarinda's headache was worse than ever. Estelle had helped her dress and fixed her hair, but now she was lying on her bed, a cold compress on her forehead. Manning knocked. She called to him to come in.

"A visitor to see you, Lady Clarinda."

Wincing from her headache, Clarinda swung her legs to the floor and regarded the elderly, dignified butler with surprise. "Me? Not her ladyship?"

"You, m'lady."

She glanced at the Ormolu clock on her mantel. "But it's only ten o'clock."

"I am aware of that, m'lady. It is Lord Stormont. Given the time of day, I had no idea what to do with him, so I put him in the music room." Only a slight twitch of his nostril indicated Manning's low opinion of any guest who would dare to call before early afternoon.

What on earth could he want? Concealing her agitation, Clarinda said coolly, "Tell Lord Stormont I shall be down directly."

When Manning had gone, Clarinda hastened to her mirror. She turned this way and that, assessing her appearance in her simple, sky blue crepe gown. She looked presentable enough, she supposed, not that it mattered.

She started down the stairs, caught herself descending much too fast, and slowed herself to a more dignified pace. Entering the music room, she found Stormont, an unreadable expression on his face, leaning casually, arms folded, against the piano.

"Good morning, m'lord," she said, offering a slight curtsy.

He did not immediately respond, but looked her up and down. "No?" he asked, slightly cocking his head.

She frowned in puzzlement. "What do you—?" Suddenly it came to her. He meant her answer yesterday.

"No?" he asked again.

"That is correct, sir, I said no."

"I have come to ask why."

This was going to be so hard! She searched frantically for a reply that wouldn't be a lie. "No is no. That's all I have to say." *What a stupid answer.*

Though Stormont's stance was still casual, she perceived from his hardened expression he was deeply affected. "That's hardly a sufficient answer from a girl who was in my arms but two days ago," he said bluntly. "Odd. If memory serves correctly, she said she loved me."

Out of sheer misery and frustration, Clarinda's heart started pounding. This was getting worse and worse. She forced a laugh. It sounded so fake she stopped abruptly. "Well, you know how we silly young girls are," she managed. "Always flirting. Mercy me, you should not believe a word we say."

With a snort, Stormont strode to the double doors of the music room and shut them tight. He turned back, regarding her with an expression of unmitigated disgust. "Don't be ridiculous. I would strongly advise you not to use any sort of empty-headed belle pose on me. In the first place, you're not fooling me. In the second, I deserve a better answer."

What more could she say? She felt a wild desire to escape the room, but his dark, smoldering eyes held her to the spot. She spread her palms. "I simply will not marry you. Is that not clear enough?"

"Damme, there's something wrong here," he said, his face slowly becoming a glowering mask of rage.

In all her sheltered life, Clarinda had never before witnessed the anger of an enraged male. She was seeing it now. Not that she felt physically threatened—his fist was not clenched, he had not yelled. Nonetheless, she felt the power of his suppressed fury and it made her tremble.

"I . . . I have nothing more to say," she answered in a small voice. With what dignity she could summon, she continued, "So if you do not mind, I shall take my leave."

She looked toward the doors, but got no farther. Stormont was on her in a flash, wrapping her in his arms, pulling her to him so roughly she involuntarily gasped. "So take your leave," he said in a voice thick with anger, "but first I shall give you a final farewell."

Before she could resist, he crushed his mouth to hers in a long, hard kiss of such fierce intensity she could hardly breathe and her knees went weak from the shock of it. She tried to push him away, but the assertive demand of his lips soon sent a hunger pulsing through her. Loath though she was to respond, her arms crept around his neck of their own volition, and she found herself returning his kiss with eager abandon.

Suddenly he broke off the kiss. He did not set her free, though, but instead swiftly cupped the back of her head with one strong hand. Roughly entwining his fingers in her hair, he pulled her head back, and in a voice hoarse with emotion, demanded, "Say you don't love me. Say it!"

"I . . ." She stared into the glowering face hovering over her, too overcome to speak.

"Say it!" He gripped her shoulders. "Say it!" he demanded again, his harsh words accompanied by one swift, furious shake.

"I . . . don't . . . oh, I cannot!" She could stand no more of this. "Let me go," she demanded, striking her fists against his chest.

Visibly trembling from the intensity of his rage, Stormont released her and backed a few steps away. She felt dizzy. Gripping the edge of the piano, she watched as he stood silent, staring at her. He was drawing in ragged little breaths, his chest heaving up and down. Gradually they subsided. Finally he appeared back in control. "You will forgive me," he said in a deadly calm voice that only on the edges held the trace of a rasp. "This won't happen again."

"I trust not," she replied, hating the stiff formality in her voice.

His fury ebbed. For a long time he looked at her, his expression filling with such tenderness she had to restrain herself from hurtling back into his arms. "We would have been good together, you and I," he finally said, his voice filled with regret.

Her own regrets assailed her as she slowly shook her head. "Perhaps. But it's over."

He asked, "It's Rissa, isn't it?"

"I don't know what you mean."

"Yes you do. I don't know how, or why, but somehow it's Rissa who's come between us."

For a moment she closed her eyes. "I have nothing more to say." She had to get out of here. Half blind with tears, she stumbled to the double doors.

He followed her. She could tell his anger had returned when he grabbed the knobs and flung the doors wide. "Leave, then. I've had enough of your dissembling."

She forced herself to step away from his tense, hard body. "Then it's good-bye."

"No, it is not good-bye." A gleam of determination lit his eyes. "If you think you're rid of me, you had better think again."

"But I told you—"

"I want you, Clarinda, far more than I have ever wanted any woman in my life. " He offered her a sudden, arresting smile. "And I intend to have you."

"You can't have everything you want."

"I can't? We shall see about that."

"Manning will see you out."

Turning blindly, she stumbled once, caught herself, and with her head held high, walked with stiff dignity across the grand entryway and ascended the stairs.

Robert stared after her. Good God, what had he done? No woman had ever treated him in such a fashion. Never had he felt so humiliated, so deflated. Worse, he, in his complete frustration, had lost control of himself and made his beautiful Clarinda cry. *You fool!* he told himself.

"Why, Lord Stormont, what a delight to see you, and so early too!"

Good God, here came the twin down the stairs—the last person in the world he wanted to see.

Or was she?

Rissa had reached the bottom of the staircase and was beaming at him. "How rude of Clarinda to leave you standing here. Won't you come into the drawing room? It's early, but I shall order tea."

Stormont smiled smoothly, betraying nothing. "Would you step into the music room, Lady Rissa? I want to talk to you."

Chapter 16

Within himself, Robert fought a battle of restraint as he followed Rissa into the music room and with great deliberation shut the doors. It would not do to rebuke her, much as he would derive a certain satisfaction from telling her exactly what he thought. To achieve his purpose, he must exercise the utmost self-control.

Rissa had not ceased her chattering. Now, as they stood facing each other, she was pointing to a sampler she had embroidered, framed and hanging on the wall. "Clarinda was never much good at needlework," she babbled. "You will never find one of *her* samplers on display, whereas mine . . ."

Robert felt a small rush of compassion. A twin jealous of her twin was much to be pitied. How sad for her. She would not be history's first envious twin, he supposed. No doubt, all her life Rissa had felt inferior to her sister, and no wonder. In nearly every way, the poor girl *was* inferior.

". . . and I excell in watercolors too," Rissa was saying, "which is yet another womanly skill my sister has no interest in." Rissa smiled up at him, eyes bright with eager anticipation. "So what did you have to say to me, m'lord? Was it, perhaps, a question?"

What in blazes? Does the chit think I am going to propose?

Pity forgotten, Robert hastened to set her straight. "I have no questions for you, Lady Rissa," he said pleasantly but firmly. "I decided it was time to get you aside and tell you of my feelings for your sister."

"My sister?" Rissa's face had already started to cloud. "And what might those feelings be?"

"I am deeply in love with Clarinda," he said, taking pains

not to sound as if he relished his words. "I felt you should know that."

In a low, ominously calm voice Rissa asked, "Has she consented to marry you?"

"I have proposed, but, alas, she has told me no." He gave her a withering stare. "She hasn't given me a reason, but, quite frankly, I suspect you are to blame. How, exactly, I don't know, although I am aware of some of the other mischief you have caused." He paused, mainly for effect, and continued in his most commanding manner. "Let this be an end to it. There will be no more nasty little plots aimed at discrediting your sister. If another one occurs, you will have me to answer to. Agreed?"

With a shocked expression on her face, Rissa backed a step away, pressed her hand to her mouth, and wordlessly stared at him. A blush of anger crept over her cheeks. "You led me on," she finally exclaimed, her voice shrilly indignant.

"I did no such thing."

"You did! You sought me out. You showered me with attention. Naturally, I was led to believe—"

"I apologize if I gave that impression. Trust me, I was merely being polite."

Rissa came close to wailing as she protested, "But I was expecting you to propose! How could you love her instead of me? Don't we look exactly alike? What do you see in her? I am the one who excels at needlework and watercolors and all the womanly arts, while all she does is ride horses."

"You would never understand," Robert said, suppressing his urge to smile. "I have no wish to wound you, but I shall be perfectly candid. I do not love you. I shall never love you. Most assuredly, I shall never marry you, even if, God forbid, Clarinda were to depart this earth this very day."

Rissa's mouth dropped open. She appeared too stunned to speak until finally, in a shaking voice, she managed, "This is Clarinda's doing, isn't it? She put you up to this."

Robert gazed at her intently. After a time he muttered, "Hopeless," strode to the door and turned. "Heed well what I said. I regret the indelicacy of my remarks, but bear in mind you have only yourself to blame. Have I made myself clear?"

A Chinese porcelain vase stood on a small table. Rissa picked it up and flung it at him. Robert dodged and it missed, shattering against the wall into a thousand pieces.

"Apparently I have," Robert dryly remarked, and left the music room without another word.

Clarinda's fault! This is all Clarinda's fault, Rissa thought as she sped up the wide staircase and headed for Clarinda's bedchamber. She would confront her perfidious sister this instant! Estelle was in the upstairs hallway. Seeing Rissa, she raised a finger to her lips and whispered, "Shh! Lady Clarinda ees suffering from a dreadful headache. I gave her a spoonful of Kendal Black Drops and now she ees asleep and should sleep for hours. Eet would be best not to disturb her."

Rissa snapped, "Oh, very well," and with an indignant toss of her head, marched to her own room and slammed the door. She stumbled to the bed, where she flung herself facedown, gripped the coverlet, and began to sob. *I do not love you,* he had said. *I shall never love you.* Oh! She wished she were dead! And wouldn't they be sorry if she were? Perhaps she should really do away with herself. She could—what?—slash her wrists? Yes, that should do it. Imagine the grief that would ensue when they found her poor, lifeless body. Clarinda would never get over the loss of her beloved twin. Mama and Papa would be overcome with sorrow. And Stormont . . .

Her sobs subsided as she pictured the arrogant, holier-than-thou Lord Stormont, weeping inconsolably over her casket. What a supremely satisfying thought. How stricken with guilt and remorse he would be! His life would be ruined, of course. Doubtless he would never marry, and would spend the rest of his days in bitter, lonely repentance, cursing the day he had said those dreadful things which, in truth, he didn't really mean.

It seemed a fine plan, except . . .

There was just one problem with her plan—she'd be dead.

Well, there was no fun in that, Rissa thought as she wiped her eyes. No suicide, then, but somehow, someway, she must get her revenge. Never had she been so humili-

ated! She cringed with embarrassment, just thinking of
Stormont's stone cold eyes when he told her . . .

Ah, she could not bear to think of those awful moments
in the music room.

Could she impersonate Clarinda again? Hmm . . . she
would have to think about it. What could Clarinda do that
would be so terrible, so unforgivable, that she would be
packed off immediately to North Wales, never to return?

"Alexander, are you feeling better?"

The little boy, who was just recovering from his latest
bout with illness, was dressed warmly against the chill of
the day and sat on the carpet in front of the burning fireplace of his bedchamber, playing with his marbles. "I'm not
sick anymore," he proclaimed with a pout. "It's not fair,
Rissa. Mama says I mustn't go outside today. I have to stay
right here, in my bed chamber." He kicked at his marbles.
"I wanted to ride Captain."

Laughing, she knelt beside him. "I'm Clarinda, not
Rissa," she said. "For once you guessed wrong."

Alexander looked surprised. "But I always know which
one of you is which, and you're Rissa."

"But you're wrong this time," she said and laughed
again. "Just look"—she fingered the gold necklace that
hung from her neck—"here's my necklace with the 'C' to
prove it." She glanced down at the well-worn gray riding
gown. "Besides, would our Rissa wear this old thing?"

"I guess not," Alexander said, frowning.

"Come on," she said, "I've come to take you riding."

"But Mama said—"

"She changed her mind. You could ask her, but she and
Papa are riding out this afternoon, clear to Cousin Clara's
house, I understand. They are staying overnight and won't
be back until tomorrow."

Alexander sprang to his feet. He looked out the window
at the dark, chill, cloudy day. "We had best go quick, before it starts to rain." His cheeks were pink with fever. He
was caught by a coughing spell that bent him nearly double.

"Stop that!" she said, laughing. "We'll have no more of
that coughing now. Do you want to ruin our ride?"

At the stables, Morris looked aghast. "*Jupiter?* But, Miss
Clarinda, his lordship never—"

"I said Jupiter. Papa asked me to ride him. For the exercise. And get Captain for Alexander."

Morris gazed at the sky. "Those are mighty dark clouds, m'lady. Looks like rain, and it be cold today. Are you sure—?"

"Saddle them, Morris, and be quick."

Minutes later, she was practically frozen with fear atop Jupiter. It had taken all her courage to mount the snortish, skittish animal, but with Morris's help she had managed. And quite nicely, she congratulated herself.

Looking gravely concerned, Morris watched as she and Alexander rode out of the cobbled courtyard and turned their horses toward the river path. "Be sure to find me when you get back, m'lady," he called, "Jupiter will need his rubdown, and Captain, too."

"Of course!" she called back over her shoulder. *Rubdown indeed.* Jupiter tossed his head back, whinnying his delight at being out of his stall. Damnation! If she could just manage to hang on to the back of this cursed animal, all would go well, exactly as she planned.

A raindrop splashed her forehead. She gazed tenderly at her little brother as he rode beside her. "A little rain won't hurt us!" she called gaily. "We shall go for a nice, long ride. Won't this be fun?"

Rained poured, thunder clapped, lightning lit the late afternoon sky as, hours later, they came back from their ride. Alexander, drenched and shivering, had long since ceased to speak, but simply hung on to the saddle, his face pale and drawn.

Morris was nowhere to be seen as they brought their horses to a halt in front of the stables. *Now how am I supposed to get off this wretched horse?* she wondered. It stood seventeen hands. Just jump off, she supposed. She jumped and landed, splat! into a puddle. *Odious beast.*

Less than an hour into the ride, Rissa had decided maybe this wasn't such a great idea after all. She was freezing cold, as was Alexander. The rain had started coming down in buckets, and that was before they got lost. It had taken her forever to find the right path back, all the while, Alexander coughing and hacking, and whining about how he wanted to go home.

She could hardly wait to get back to her cosy bedchamber, to the warmth of her fireplace. Picking herself up from the puddle, she saw Alexander slide from his horse, moving ever so slowly, as if he were stiff from the cold. "Come, we shall run to the house," she called.

"No!" Alexander shouted back, his thin voice barely audible over the sound of the storm. "First we must take care of the horses."

"Morris will see to that. Come along."

"No! We cannot let the horses stay out."

Little brat. "All right then, we shall get them inside."

They led Jupiter and Captain, dripping wet, shivering, and still with their saddles on, into the stables and put them in their stalls. "There, that's enough," she said. "Let's be off."

Looking at her little brother, she began to worry. He was white as a ghost and shivering violently. "But, Clarinda," he protested through chattering teeth, "you know we must take their saddles off and rub them down."

"That's Morris's job."

"But he's not here." Alexander looked desperate. "Can't you see Jupiter's cold and shaking, and so's Captain. We must rub them down, Clarinda. Papa will kill us if we don't."

"Papa won't be back till morning," she told him. She'd had no idea Alexander would look so awful. She must get him into the house and get him warm. "We are going to the house this instant," she told her brother firmly, "then I shall go find Morris and he can take care of the horses."

Rissa's remorse grew as they hurried through the driving rain toward the main portico. She hadn't thought that Alexander might have a relapse. She hadn't thought it would rain, or that they would lose their way. At least Mama and Papa weren't home. There, indeed, was a blessing. All she needed to do was get Alexander to his room and into dry clothes, get her own dry clothes, and then sneak into Clarinda's room and put the necklace and riding gown back.

But this is going to work, she assured herself. She pictured the scene next morning, when Papa discovered Clarinda had gone riding in the rain, not only taking along his precious little son, but riding Jupiter, his sacred, sacrosanct, stupid horse. He would be absolutely livid. Clarinda could deny it all she pleased, but how could she prove she hadn't done it? Especially when Alexander said it was Clarinda who took him for the ride, and Morris said Clarinda was the one who had ordered him to saddle Jupiter.

Perfect! Her little scheme wasn't so bad after all.

They reached the front entryway and ran up the steps. At the top, she heard the sounds of hooves and jangling harness. It sounded like . . . oh, no! It sounded like a coach. Rissa stared, paralyzed. Mama and Papa must have cut short their visit to Cousin Clara's. They were coming home.

In the front entryway, water dripped from Rissa's skirt and puddled on the marble floor as she cowered before her mother. Never, in all her twenty years had she seen Mama so angry. "But, Mama, you don't understand," she said, trembling, tears running down her face."

"I understand well enough," Mama shrieked, her features contorted with anger. "How dare you take Alexander for a ride when I forbade him to go out? The boy is sick! You know how fragile he is. If something should happen to my one and only son . . . !" Mama took in a deep breath, attempting to get control of herself. In a slightly less frenetic voice, she continued, "This is the last straw, Clarinda. I shall tell Papa he should pack you off to North Wales immediately, this very moment."

Papa, who had carried Alexander up to his bedchamber, came hurrying back down. "The nanny has him," he said to Mama. "Perhaps it's not too serious. Some hot soup, a poultice of verbena on his chest, he'll be fine."

Mama glared at him. "You must send her off to Grandfather Montague's this instant."

Yes, but not now! Rissa screamed silently. Not until she'd had a chance to switch the necklace back and become Rissa again. She waited, her heart in her mouth, for Papa's response.

"Let's not be too hasty, Edwina. Doubtless Clarinda didn't realize it was going to rain—"

"That's not the point," Mama declared. "Lord knows, the girl's been given enough chances. Now I want her out of my sight."

"Let us calm ourselves," Papa said in a reasonable tone. "No need to fly into the boughs and do something rash."

Manning appeared from the back of the house, followed by Morris. He addressed Papa. "The groom would like a word with you, m'lord."

Soggy hat in hand, Morris stepped forward. "M'lord, uh . . . uh . . ."

"Well, speak up, man," Papa said gently.

Morris gathered his courage. "I be no teller of tales, sir, but this is about Jupiter and I thought you ought ter know."

Papa's benign expression vanished. "What about Jupiter?"

"Well, m'lord, she"—he inclined his head toward Rissa—"took Jupiter out on that ride and when she brought him back, she just left him, sir, not rubbin' him down. Him and Captain. The horse was shiverin' when I found him in his stall, sir, as was Captain."

"Are they all right now?"

"Well, I've got me boys rubbin' 'em down now, but you know how horses is, sir, especially when they be in weather like this and then they ain't rubbed down proper."

"I do indeed," Papa said with on-the-surface calmness, but Rissa could almost see his gritted teeth. He shot Rissa a glance that was so flat, hard, and passionless it made her blood run cold. "Thank you, Morris. You may go now. And when you get back to the stables, tell Timmons not to unharness the horses, but to bring the coach back around."

Papa watched the servants leave. Then he turned to Rissa, glowering with rage. "You dared ride my horse, Clarinda?"

"I didn't think you would mind. Papa, please—"

"And you failed to give Jupiter a rubdown?"

"Well, but you see, I thought Morris—"

"God's blood!" yelled Papa, erupting like a volcano. "Nobody mistreats my horse, even you, Clarinda. You're no daughter of mine and you're going to North Wales. Now! This instant!"

"Oh, Papa, no!" Rissa cried. Sheer, black fright swept over her. This wasn't the way she had planned things at all. Her heart pounding wildly, she flung herself at Papa's feet and gripped the hem of his coat. "Please, Papa, don't send me away! I am not Clarinda, I am—" Reality dawned, but too late. How on earth could she explain?

"Not Clarinda?" Papa asked. He bent, ripped her necklace off, and examined the gold filigreed "C." "Not Clarinda, eh?" he said, shaking the necklace under her nose. "Then pray tell me, why are you wearing this 'C'?"

"I can explain."

"Then explain," said Papa. "But be quick. You're leaving as soon as Timmons brings the coach round."

"But I'm cold, and my clothes are wet." -

"Your brother was cold, too, and Jupiter and Captain, but did you care? No!" A new surge of rage seemed to strike him. Blindly he strode across the marble floor and struck his fist hard against the paneled wall. "I want you out of my sight!"

Dear God, he couldn't mean this. Desperation seized her as she begged, "Please, Papa, I really am Rissa, the good twin. You cannot send me away."

Mama spoke up. "Indeed, if we thought you were Rissa, we might let you stay, but you're not. Rissa would not dream of acting in this fashion. This is a continuation of your abysmal behavior, Clarinda."

Papa stepped back, folded his arms, and glared down at her. "I shall ask again. If you are truly Rissa, what were you doing with Clarinda's necklace around your neck?"

"I . . ." Oh, how could she explain? "It . . . it was a joke, Papa. I was playing a joke on Clarinda, but I guess it was not a very good one, and I'm very, very sorry."

Papa looked beyond her, to where Estelle, who had no doubt been on the landing listening to every word, was coming down the stairs. "Come here, Estelle," he said. "You've always been able to tell the twins apart. Tell me which twin this is." He looked down at the cowering girl. "On your feet!"

Rissa's heart lifted as she arose, knees shaking, and looked, silently pleading, into the lady maid's eyes. Estelle would set Papa straight. She could indeed tell her and Clarinda apart.

"Of course, m'lord, I shall be happy to tell you weech is weech," said Estelle. Rissa stood shaking as Estelle examined her carefully, taking her time, her gaze sweeping over her from head to toe.

Suddenly something in Estelle's expression—was it that little quirk at the corner of her mouth?—caused Rissa to be seized by a fearful, desperate feeling. *Perhaps I should have been a little nicer to Estelle.* She remembered the many

times she had teased Clarinda for saying please and thank
you to a mere lady's maid. Clarinda never snapped at Estelle, and, to Rissa's disgust, had always treated the lady's
maid almost like an equal. Servants were made to be yelled
at, everyone knew. But still, perhaps she could have been
a little nicer.

There was a strange, vengeful gleam in Estelle's eye, as
if she were remembering Rissa's past behavior. With great
deliberation, she finally spoke.

"What have you done now, Clarinda?"

When Clarinda awoke from her long nap, she had the
eerie feeling something was wrong. She was not sure what,
exactly, it was just that the house didn't sound right. There
were not the usual noises of servants bustling about, just
utter stillness, until . . . *is that someone yelling?* Hurriedly
Clarinda flung off her coverlet and slipped off the bed,
noticing with relief that her headache was gone. She slipped
into her dress, smoothed her hair, and decided to go downstairs to find out what was the matter.

Passing Alexander's room, she saw the door was open.
Hearing the boy coughing, she peeked inside. Alexander
lay in bed, his face flushed with fever, his nanny hovering
close by. Clarinda hurried to his bed.

"Oh, dear, you look sick, Alexander."

He gave her a wan smile. "Not so very. I was riding
Captain and it started to rain . . ."

Her little brother proceeded to relate the events of the
day, ending with, "She told me she was you, Clarinda, but
I knew she wasn't, even if she did have your necklace on.
I knew!"

"But why would she say she was me?"

Alexander shrugged. "I don't know, but Mama and Papa
are really mad at Rissa, only they think she's you, and the
coach is all hitched and Papa's going to send her off to
Grandfather Montague's."

"This very moment?" Clarinda asked, appalled. When
Alexander nodded, she whirled around and hurried to the
stairs.

Halfway down, at the curve of the staircase, Clarinda
halted. Below was a sight she had never thought she'd see:
Estelle smirking, Mama bristling, Papa shaking with rage.

And Rissa! Her clothes were soggy and her hair straggling in a totally unfamiliar state of disarray. How strange to see the favored twin quaking before her parents, and in tears.

When Rissa saw Clarinda standing on the stairs she drew a sharp breath. "Clarinda!" she called. "Please, please come down here and tell them who you are."

Clarinda continued down the staircase, saying nothing, her mind in a whirl. Since childhood, she had suffered from the envy of her twin. Rissa had done so many dreadful things to her, she couldn't remember them all. She most definitely remembered Jeffrey, though, and how Rissa had deliberately stolen him away. A blessing in disguise, she thought wryly, but she hadn't thought so at the time. There were so many things, not only from when they were children, but recently. She'd had to take the blame when Cranmer kissed her. She'd suffered the consequences from Rissa's impersonation of her at Lady Lynbury's. And then there was the business of Rissa's hiding the letter to Sara Sophia, and the heartbreaking promise she'd been compelled to make in order to save Sara Sophia.

And now this. Once again, Rissa had impersonated her, apparently with only one thought in mind: to get her into trouble. Serious trouble this time, judging from the absolutely furious expression on her father's usually composed face. She didn't know how, exactly, but apparently at long last Rissa had been caught in her tangle of lies and was about to be sent off to North Wales. How fitting!

And why did I allow her to do this to me? Clarinda thought back to all the times she had been a victim of this silly, foolish girl. She had been wrong to remain silent, thinking no one would believe her, nothing could be done. But she would not stay silent anymore. *Rissa will never hurt me again.*

With newfound courage, Clarinda reached the bottom of the stairs and looked at her sister, her mind churning with memories, a long-overdue realization, and a plan.

"What do you want me to say, Clarinda?" she asked.

Chapter 17

Upon hearing Clarinda's affirmation that she was Rissa, Papa pointed dramatically toward the door. "Out!" he ordered Rissa.

The sound of hooves and jangling harness announced Timmons's arrival with the coach at the front portico. Now truly alarmed, Rissa cried, "No, Papa, no, she's wrong! I am not Clarinda, I am Rissa."

"Out!" Papa bellowed again.

Rissa's defiant expression faded, replaced by sheer horror. "But I have no clothes, and I'm all wet, and I'm hungry."

Papa addressed Estelle. "Go pack her valise, quickly. Just a few things should suffice. Where she's going, she'll have no need for fancy gowns."

Rissa, her eyes wide with panic, turned to Clarinda. "Please, please, tell them who I am!"

"I have no idea what you mean," Clarinda answered with an insolent, Rissa-like toss of her head.

"Yes, you do. Please help me," Rissa wailed. "I'll do anything. I don't want to get sent off to Grandfather Montague's."

"Anything? Such as releasing me from my promise?"

"Yes. yes, anything! I release you from your promise. Now tell them!"

A world of pain and frustration lifted from Clarinda's shoulders. Her ploy had worked. Rissa didn't know, probably would never know, that she would never have gone through with such an underhanded deception, deserved though it might be. With a deeply relieved sigh, she addressed her parents. "I had a reason for saying I was Rissa, but I'm not, I am Clarinda. Rissa has done wrong, but I know you won't send her away." With an ironic smile, she added, "She's the good twin."

Clarinda waited for her parents to acknowledge her admission of the truth, but to her surprise, an expression of deep suspicion crossed Mama's face. "I don't believe you," she exclaimed. "Can't you see, m'lord? Our dear Rissa loves her sister so much she wants to shoulder the blame. You must not let her."

"I am not in the least deceived," Papa agreed. He pointed again, glaring at Rissa. "To the coach! Your sister can tell all the lies she wants, but I know you're Clarinda. The necklace proves it. Nothing has changed."

Clarinda cried, "Papa, you're wrong—"

"Silence! Not another word," Papa roared.

"But, Papa—" Rissa begged.

"Out of my sight! Be gone!"

Shocked into silence, Rissa slunk from the entryway, shoulders slumped in defeat, and into the waiting coach. Soon Estelle, attempting to look solemn but not succeeding very well, brought the hastily packed valise.

Soon after, Clarinda stared, astounded, as the coach and four rolled down the driveway, carrying "the bad twin" to the farthest reaches of North Wales.

A pall hung over dinner that evening. At least Papa was in a slightly better mood, Clarinda noted, after he had assured himself that Jupiter had suffered no ill effects from Rissa's neglect. Mama, too, was calmer. Alexander was comfortable and appeared no worse for his ride in the rain.

So far, Clarinda had said nothing. Better to wait until everyone had recovered from their shock over that dreadful scene in the entryway. As far as everyone still knew, she was Rissa.

Papa had remained silent until, over his claret, he looked at Clarinda and asked, "What was that business about releasing you from your promise?"

"It's a long story, Papa."

"Well, tell it."

"I would be happy to, only . . ." Her parents would be absolutely horrified when they heard the truth, but they would have to hear it, and soon. She supposed now was as good a time as any. "Papa, I really am Clarinda. I tried to tell you, but you wouldn't listen. It was Rissa you sent away."

Clarinda braced herself, waiting for her father's astonished reaction, but instead, Papa offered her a forgiving smile. "You think I don't know my own daughters?" he asked quietly. "I know very well whom I banished to Wales."

There was a startling clatter as Mama dropped her spoon to her plate. Horrified, she asked, "You mean it was Rissa you sent away?"

"Yes, my dear, it was Rissa."

"And you knew it?" By now, Mama's face was beginning to resemble a thundercloud.

"I knew it," Papa replied flatly. "For some time I've had my suspicions. It seemed unnatural to me that while Rissa was continually a peerless paragon of virtue, Clarinda appeared to be evil personified. Tonight it all came clear. Clarinda has been the victim of Rissa's duplicitous behavior for years. I recognized the ring of truth in her voice when she told us she'd had a reason for saying she was Rissa, but she was not, she was Clarinda. I believed her, if for no other reason than her eyes did not contain that hint of deviousness that gleams deep in Rissa's eyes." Papa paused for a wry smile. "Stormont is a wise man. From the start, he could tell the twins apart. Now, so can I."

"Well, I never!" Mama was obviously working herself up to a fine rage, but to Clarinda's surprise, Papa cut her off.

"You can stop right there, Edwina. Rissa is spoiled, self-centered, and shallow, thanks, in part, to us because we spoiled the girl from the day she was born. I should have acted upon my suspicions long before now. I let it go because"—he gave a self-deprecating shrug—"I knew you would defend her, and I lacked the fortitude to discipline her as she deserved. Today changed all that. Seeing Clarinda acting as bravely as she did helped me make up my mind." He glared at his wife and pointed his fork at her. "I shall entertain no more discussion on the subject of Rissa. If she behaves herself, learns to respect others, develops even a modicum of humility, I might allow her back in due time. Meanwhile, madam, I shall not entertain one more word on the subject of Rissa. Is that clear?"

Mama looked dumbstruck. At another time, Clarinda

might have felt a certain satisfaction in seeing her parents' belated recognition of the truth. But not today. Too many distressing things had happened.

Papa said, "You were going to tell me about that promise."

Clarinda pulled her thoughts together and told her father the whole story of Stormont's proposal and why she had rejected him.

Papa listened with growing astonishment. "Rissa actually made you swear on the Bible?"

"That I would reject Lord Stormont," Clarinda confirmed, "and so I did. I hurt him badly. It was terrible."

Papa sat for a time, drumming his fingers. At last he said, "I shall send a note to Stormont asking him to stop by tomorrow. It would appear it's time for me to buy back your horse."

A cry of relief broke from Clarinda's lips. "Oh, Papa, can you afford—?"

"It's not a matter of whether I can afford it or not," Papa said with a thoughtful smile, "it's a matter of setting things right."

Chapter 18

This morning was full of surprises, thought Robert as he approached the music room at Graystone Hall. First, Lord Capelle, without explanation, had bought back Donegal at the full price Robert had paid, and had insisted upon adding ten guineas more. Actually, Robert would have preferred to keep the fine Irish hunter, but he had always made it a point to accommodate friends and good neighbors, such as Capelle.

Another surprise: Rissa was not anywhere about, and if the servants' rumors were true, good God! What a boon for Clarinda if that devious chit had really been sent off to Wales.

Then he had been more than surprised, he had been astonished, when, at the end of his conversation with Lord Capelle, the kindly man had said, "Oh, by the way, there's someone in the music room who wants to see you."

As Robert opened the double doors and stepped inside, he wondered if it was Clarinda who would be waiting. If so, he could not imagine what she wanted. Hadn't his heart been bruised and trampled upon enough? There was no point in his subjecting himself to further torment. If, indeed it was she, he would quickly depart.

He took a quick, sharp breath. It *was* Clarinda, sitting at the piano, toying with the keys. She looked lovelier than he had ever seen her with her golden hair piled atop her head, her throat warm and shapely over the low-cut bodice of her blue gown. She stood when she saw him, a smile lighting her face. "Robert," she said softly, and came around the piano to stand in front of him.

"Clarinda," he said, placing a chill around her name. She moved a step closer. "No, don't," he said, and backed a step away.

She began, "But I want—"

"What could you possibly want?" he asked coldly. *Haven't I been hurt enough?* he wanted to add, but pride prevented him. "I am a firm believer in putting disappointment behind me, so if you're trying to assuage my feelings—"

"May I change my no to yes?" she asked, looking up at him with those blue, compelling eyes.

He was momentarily speechless. "What the deuce do you mean?"

"I mean I want to marry you." She moved closer. "If it's not too late? If you haven't found someone else in the meantime?"

"You know I haven't." His mouth quirked into a rueful smile and he asked, none too politely, "Just what has changed your mind?"

She reached and gently placed one of her soft, white hands high on his sleeve. He stared at her delicate wrist as her fingers slowly traced a path down his arm with a feathery touch. Then she reached and did the same with her other hand, so that instead of his being able to think straight, his heart started hammering.

"I should be happy to tell you what changed my mind," she said, sliding her hands around his neck, "but I'm wondering, could you kiss me first?"

In his last reasoning moment before passion overpowered him, he asked, "You do have a good explanation?"

"Oh, a very good one," she said as her warm fingers caressed the back of his neck, causing instant heat to radiate from the core of his being. Then she pulled his head down to where she, on tiptoe, could press her warm lips to his. He was immediately hers, of course, amused at himself as the last of his resistance fled—as if there had been much to begin with!—and he swept her into his arms. He pulled his lips from hers long enough to ask, "Was it Rissa?"

"Mmm," she said in reply, which probably meant, yes, it was indeed Rissa who had caused whatever the problem was. Right now, though, as he surrendered to his aching, burning need to possess his beloved Clarinda, it mattered not one whit.

Epilogue

"Here they come!"

Lady Clarinda Stormont's joyous laughter filled the air as she stood at the front portico of Hollyridge Manor. "It's going to be wonderful, seeing Sara Sophia again," she remarked to Robert as the coach-and-four, doors adorned with the elaborate Wentridge coat of arms, came rolling up the driveway.

Robert curved his arm affectionately around her shoulders. "It's been a while since I've seen Lucius," he commented with a smile. "The old boy never visits London anymore. Hard to believe he was one of the most notorious rakes in town. Now they've forgotten his name at White's, let alone all his favorite taverns."

"What a pity," said Clarinda, casting her husband a teasing glance. "Now the poor man is buried in the countryside with a wife he adores, and two fine sons. Such a fate!"

"He's a fortunate man," said Robert, turning serious. "As am I."

"Sara Sophia is fortunate too." Clarinda looked up at Robert, her adoring husband, who for the past five years had been her heart's passion, companion, steadfast support. She flashed a radiant smile. "And I'm the most fortunate one of all."

She glanced fondly down at Phillip, her two-year-old son, who played at her feet, and at Elizabeth and Catherine, her four-year-old twins. At the moment they were behaving like little ladies, but that would not last long.

Lady Sara Sophia Wentridge peered eagerly from the window as the coach rolled to a stop at the front portico.

"Almost there, Lucius," she said to her husband who sat across from her. "I am so looking forward to seeing Robert and Clarinda and the children." She reached to take the small bundle Lucius had been holding. "Here, let me have the baby. He's drooling on your coat." She peered out the window again. "There they are, waiting to greet us. How handsome they look! There's little Phillip, and, oh, my stars! There're the twins. They are so adorable with those blond curls and blue eyes. So exactly alike!"

"But I'd wager dressed totally unalike," Lucius noted with a chuckle.

"They will never dress the same," Sara Sophia said. "Not as long as Clarinda has anything to say about it."

"Which reminds me, my sweet countess, how is her twin?"

"Rissa? From what I hear, she's doing passably well, although, frankly, I do not believe those two years she spent in North Wales changed her one whit. She's the same old Rissa, self-centered as ever, yet different, too. She seems to have lost much of that bubbly charm she had when she was younger."

"Unlike Clarinda."

"Indeed, Clarinda hasn't changed. But poor Rissa . . . Though I hate to say it, the last time I saw her she reminded me of her sour-faced mother."

"Married one of the Suftons, did she not?"

"Yes, and he keeps her buried in the country while he spends his time in London, leading quite the life of debauchery, from what I understand."

"Didn't know he was the type."

"He wasn't." *Not until he married Rissa*, Sara Sophia thought but didn't say, loath as she was to vilify anyone, even Rissa.

The coach rolled to a stop. Sara Sophia flung open the door, jumped down, and practically fell into the arms of her dearest friend. "What a joy to see you again!"

Clarinda made no attempt to hold back her tears. Silently she hugged Sara Sophia tight.

Lucius ascended. After a warm greeting, Robert remarked, "Come, Lucius, you must see my thoroughbreds. I've had more success with them here than I ever could have at Oakley House."

As the two strolled away, Clarinda felt a torrent of memories come flooding back. Over a lump in her throat, she said, "Forgive me, I was just thinking of the old days and those horrid times we went through."

"I think of them often," Sara Sophia replied. "I like to remind myself of that awful time I spent as a governess, just so I'll appreciate how lucky I am now."

A thoughtful smile curved Clarinda's mouth. "Remember when my parents sold Donegal? And I thought I'd have to marry Larimore? And I was sure my father didn't love me anymore?"

"Of course."

"And all the trouble with Rissa? I thought I'd never be happy again, but now . . ."

Gazing about her, Clarinda took in the beauty of Hollyridge Manor and the magnificent horses grazing in the green fields beyond. Graystone House lay but a mile away. Often she went riding with her father, he on Jupiter, she on her beloved Donegal. She caught sight of Robert's wide-shouldered, long, lean form, as he strode with Lucius toward the stables. She thought of how proud he was of her—their children—his expanding stable of thoroughbreds and her heart swelled with love and pride.

"Isn't life wonderful, Sara Sophia?"